GUARDIAN:
THE WITCHES OF PIONEER VALE
BOOK 2

DAVID COMBS

ALSO BY DAVID COMBS

Thieves' Honor

THE WITCHES OF PIONEER VALE SERIES

Ascension

IN LOVING MEMORY

Zachary Keen

&

Joel Przekurat

Brothers-in-Law

Brothers In Our Hearts

ANGELICA BRIGHTON CONCEPT ART
BY DAVID COMBS

ACKNOWLEDGMENTS

This is a work of fiction. Any similarities to real places, people, or events are unintentional, coincidental, and accidental. In short, this all came from the depths of my imagination.

There are forms of address used within this story that may seem insensitive to Native American culture. The usage was meant solely for the purpose of authenticity for the time period in which they occur and in no way is a reflection of my personal views of Native American culture in general or the Nipmuc people in particular.

Dave Combs

Cover art by oliviaprodesign

Alistair Carmichael

Anne-Marie Carmichael
b.1643

Jeremiah Carmichael
b.1640

The Firstborn

The Inheritors

Aiden Carmichael b. 1661

Thomas Carmichael b.1668

Kenton Carmichael b.1690

Abigail (Carmichael) Hunter

Phoebe Hunter b. 1711

Devlin Hunter b.1712

Levi Hunter b.1736

Barnaby Hunter b.1747

Kelvin Hunter b. 1778

Grace (Hunter) Cooke
b.1784

Kathryn Cooke b. 1811

Renee (Cooke) Wright
b.1813

Brooke Wright b.1845

Jacob Wright b.1850

May Wright b. 1880

Faye (Wright) McCowen
b.1885

Jennifer McCowen b. 1912

Michael McCowen b.1918

Mitchell McCowen b.1941

Gwendolyn (McCowen) Brighton
b.1943

Christopher Brighton
b.1961

William Brighton b.1971

Angelica Brighton b.2001

Jamie Brighton b.2007

Carmichael Family Tree

CHAPTER 1
FIRST DO NO HARM – PRESENT DAY

"You failed me tonight," growled the swirling darkness.

The shadows created by the billowing sulfurous smoke drew in upon themselves and took shape. A massive wolf on hind legs materialized out of the gloom and howled at the pale moon above. His muzzle dripped blood and decaying flesh fell away from the yellowed bone. Vermin crawled through his greasy black fur. Tattered trousers and a ragged cloak adorned the monstrous beast's powerful frame. He towered over the crouching human who trembled on the ground before him.

"Lord Shade, the young witch was more powerful than I anticipated," said Aiden Carmichael. "Her strength was unlike any Firstborn we have faced before. She is gifted even among the ranks of the Guardians." He raised his head, black fire swirling in the depths of his eyes. Dust and broken glass fell from his chestnut hair with the movement. His robes were riddled with scorches, and his skin was covered in the zig-zag scars of electrical burns. His left arm hung oddly askew, dangling from the man's twisted and disjointed shoulder.

"Just like your mother," Shade spat in disgust. The demonic wolf paced back and forth as if sizing up the wall of a cage holding him at bay. "You are fortunate that our new adversary came after you alone. Had she and that bitch who whelped you combined their might, you would have been destroyed, and my plans undone. Perhaps I should find a new servant who lacks the blood ties that hinder you. " Shade lunged at his servant with animalistic ferocity, his jaws snapping before the man's face and spraying him with saliva that sizzled on Aiden's skin.

"Do not underestimate my resolve or my contempt for my mother," said the man as he defiantly met the beast's smoldering red eyes. "I will open the gateway, just as I have promised. My power in their realm grows."

"And yet you had to flee back to me. Running like a cur with its tail between his legs." Contempt dripped from Shade's words.

"You mock me despite what we have achieved tonight," snarled Aiden. "We are already bolstered by the fear of the bystanders who saw tonight's battle. They know how close they came to death and even now tremble at the thought. The barrier weakens through my work, Lord Shade," he sneered. "Another not-so-gentle push is all that we require for it to collapse entirely. You shall soon have an entire world to feast upon and I shall have dominion over those peasants in your name."

"Their terror is not enough," roared Shade as he kicked his apprentice in the ribs. Aiden slid across the ground, grimacing as his wounded arm grated in the socket. With his clawed fist, Shade grabbed the front of the man's tattered robe and lifted him from the swirling smoke floor. "The Guardians must fall. Punish them directly. Hunt down someone close to their hearts. As retribution for my imprisonment, I want to hear their screams right before I rip your mother's heart from her chest." The beast cast a glance at Aiden's arm swaying limply at his side and wrenched it back into place with a sickening pop. Aiden's shriek echoed through the hellish wasteland as Shade threw him back to the ground. The Father of Nightmares fell into a crouch beside his apprentice and growled a single command.

"Make them suffer."

*   *   *

Another ambulance siren wailed in the receiving bay of Pioneer Vale General's Emergency Room. The paramedics looked as rough as some of the teens that had been wheeled in throughout the night. The usual smell of antiseptic was tainted with the scents of gasoline and smoke that clung to the clothes of the dozens of patients brought in after the accident at the high school. The lights in the waiting room flickered as the generators, brought to use by the surges from broken and disrupted power lines, struggled to keep up. The worst was over but it had been an exhausting night for the field teams. For the hospital staff, the night was only just beginning.

Ben Hibble stared at himself in the men's room mirror. He didn't care much for the face that stared back at him. Too much gray was creeping into his dirty blond hair. The bags under his eyes made his baby blues seem sunken into his head. He didn't remember the last time he had shaved but the stubble wasn't too overwhelming yet. He snorted as the ruckus from the waiting room invaded his little bastion of solitude. He picked up the stethoscope lying on the counter and draped it around his shoulders. He didn't need this crap at the beginning of his shift.

He opened the door and was taken aback at the size of the crowd. The doctor threaded his way through the congested lobby, pushing past frantic parents trying to get in to see their children who had been brought in earlier. He was already short-staffed tonight because of the football game and the crazy inflow of people squeezing into the ER was pushing his crew to the limits. He finally made it over to the nurse's station and half-heartedly waved at the woman who rushed over to him.

"We've got quite a mess in here tonight, Doc," said Rebecca Harmon. The head nurse dumped an armload of charts onto the countertop beside him. Some of the pins were missing from the tight bun she wore her hair in and she brushed some errant strands behind her ear. Dark circles under her

3

eyes told Ben that she had volunteered well past the end of her regular shift to help out. "We need to start turning out whoever we can right away. There aren't many serious injuries here. Just a lot of bruises and scrapes. It's just dumb luck that these kids aren't more banged up than they are."

"And hello to you too, Nurse Harmon," Ben said with a smirk as he took a patient's chart from the top of the stack. "Dumb luck happens to be my specialty."

"Really? How many years of med school did that take?"

"Not enough apparently." He frowned as he skimmed through the nurse's notes. "Did we ever find out what happened over there tonight?"

"Most of these kids are telling the same story. They were riding along on their way back from the State Championship game and got hit by a lightning strike. The bus rolled over and all the passengers got tossed around. Local news seems to think a gas main exploded somewhere along the way. The school's chemistry lab was blown up. Tore out the entire front wall of the building. A lot of bystanders are saying that there was a burst of fire that lit up the sky for several seconds and then went out."

"That doesn't make any sense. Would a gas line just shut itself off like that? Fire off in two specific points instead of blowing along the entire line?"

Rebecca stared at him with an arched eyebrow. "I don't know, Doc. I must've been out the day they covered public utility maintenance in nursing school."

"Right, sorry. Not our pay grade to figure it out. Let's take care of what we know how to do. Get Tess and Bobby to start sending home the bumps and bruises. Why don't we clear this place out and try to give ourselves some breathing room in case we get any everyday emergencies rolling in? Who do we have that needs a little extra TLC?"

"The patient in exam room three is in bad shape. She doesn't appear any more banged up than the others, but I had to sedate her. Big time. Poor thing was traumatized by what she saw apparently. Her parents have already been taken back and are waiting with her." She pulled a clipboard from the stack and handed it to him.

"Ok," said Ben as he took a quick sip from his coffee mug and flipped through the paperwork. "I'll go check on her. Call upstairs and give them a heads up that we might need some images done." He scowled again as he read the name.

"Something wrong, Ben?" asked Rebecca.

"These folks. They are the ones that keep trying to get me to attend church with them. They brought me this amazing casserole right after I first moved to town. Truly kind-hearted people, and now they are here for this. No good deed goes unpunished, I guess."

"Doesn't mean good deed doers should stop."

"Hmmm. Jury's out on that one, Nurse Harmon. In my family, those who kept on turning the other cheek only ended up with sore cheeks and bruised feelings once the arguing stopped. Anyway, I better get down there and talk to them." Ben slipped past a couple of football players who were high fiving each other over their accounts of flying through the air in an oversized soda can. He headed down to the third curtain in the ward and slipped inside. His heart sank as he recognized the man and woman who stood hand in hand beside the bed.

"Hello, Jim. Hello, Paula," he said as he shook hands with each of them. "I am so sorry to see you here tonight, but I assure you we will give …"

"What happened out there tonight, Ben?" interrupted Jim. The man wrung a faded John Deere baseball cap in his callused hands. "A lot of these other kids are ready to go home, but my daughter was raving like she

5

needs to go up to the psych ward. Becky had to knock her out, for Pete's sake. Biggest damn needle I ever saw too. Looked like enough juice to knock out a plow horse."

"Jim, this was a particularly traumatic accident and these things can affect people differently. We are just taking a few extra precautions to ensure that your girl didn't take a head injury or anything that might have caused such an extreme reaction as she had. She got shaken up pretty badly, same as all of these kids, but maybe she just got a bit more rattled than the rest."

"She was carrying on about a dead girl throwing lightning at a giant wolf," said Paula. "That sounds like more than just a bump on the head, Doctor."

"Well, we're hearing all sorts of hard to believe things about what happened at the school tonight. Lightning strikes, gas mains blowing up. Even the police reports aren't exactly sure what to make of it all. Either way, it appears to me that your girl ended up with a front-row seat to whatever hit the bus, and with all that rolling around, her brain may have just added some details that weren't actually there. Has she had any other recent stressful events?"

"Yeah, she's been through a hell of a lot lately. Dealing with a big personal loss," said Jim. "Shoot me straight, Doc. Do you think she's cracking up? That she has lost her mind?"

Ben scratched his head and sighed. "Nope, I'm not saying that at all, Jim. Whatever events she has been going through probably just forced its way into some delusional images as a result of the accident. I'll have a better answer for you folks once we run a few tests. What I can tell you is that it is my job to make sure that your daughter is healthy, and I promise you that's exactly what I intend to do. I will keep her safe. We're going to send her upstairs, take a few pictures, and make sure that there is nothing else going on. As soon as we are all satisfied that she is going to be alright you can take her home."

The young woman on the bed groaned and started to stir.

"What the hell?" said Ben. The girl thrashed about. Her feet kicked out and knocked over the blood pressure stand beside her bed. Her lips quivered, and a thin mewling rose in volume the more agitated she became.

"Rebecca! Need you in here," Hibble yelled. Ben tried to hold her wrists as Nurse Harmon rushed in. "Did you chart that sedative dose correctly? There's no way she should be struggling like this."

"I drew it up myself, Doctor," she replied. The nurse tried to grab the patient's ankles, but the thrashing was more than she could hold. The girl broke loose from Hibble's grip and a flailing fist hammered his nose, adding a resounding crunch to the rising din.

"Prep another dose and find some restraints," Ben ordered as blood flowed down his chin and onto his scrubs. He dove right back in, pinning down the girl's forearms although she fought like a demon.

The young woman's mouth opened in a silent scream and arched her back as the doctor tried to push her down flat onto the exam table. The girl fought back, however, and with incredible strength, she hurled Hibble away from her. Ben crashed into the charting computer and tumbled to the floor. He shook his head to steady the spinning room while sparks showered over him. Jim held his wife in his arms as they watched their daughter writhe and twist before them.

Clarissa Brenner sat up as her eyes snapped wide open and the soft whine in her throat rose into a terror-stricken wail. The entire emergency department cowered as her single cry echoed through the hallways.

"ANGELICA!"

*   *   *

7

Kimberly Brighton struggled to open her eyes as a wash of heat rolled over her body. The taste of dirt and ash filled her mouth, and smoke thick with the stench of burned flesh choked her. She pushed herself away from the grass, unsure how she had ended up on the front yard of the farm. Embers scorched the soles of her bare feet, and she jumped from one foot to the other. The hot wind clutched at the thin nightgown she wore and whipped her brown hair around her face. She looked over her shoulder and gasped as she watched blue-black flames roll across the fields of their land.

Corn stalks waved like torches held by an angry mob in the rows. Dead livestock littered the yard. The horse carcasses were scored with bloody rips along their sides, and their chickens recognizable only by patches of bloody feathers that littered the mangled coop. It was the sight of the farmhouse that nearly drove her back to her knees.

The proud home, the bones of which had stood for generations, was blasted apart. Splintered wood and broken glass littered the yard. All that remained was the front corner of the porch on its river stone foundation and the charred frame of the front door.

"What on earth happened here?" she whispered in breathless horror. She shambled up the steps, clutching tightly to the post that she always leaned against when she waited for her children to get home from school each day. The paint peeled away in the blistering heat, yet she found some measure of strength as she rested her forehead against the rough grain of the wood. She swallowed hard and refused to let the tears welling up in her eyes escape. The destruction weighed upon her heart already full of sorrow.

A low growl rumbled from the darkness beyond the ruins of the house. Lightning flashed, sending spots dancing before her eyes, but she caught the shadow of a massive shape that lurked within the cloak of night there. She snatched up a jagged piece of wood that had once been part of the walls of her home and held it leveled before her like a spear.

The growl became a dark chuckle that rode the thunder around her. "You'll need far more than a pointed stick against the likes of me, sweetling," purred a voice in her ear. Kimberly spun around, but there was only the flicker of the fire from the burning fields behind her.

"What is this?" she shouted. "Where are you?"

"To your first question, normally this would be little more than a bad dream for you, my dear. Tonight, however, we'll call it more akin to a premonition of promised vengeance." The rumble of a predator's snarl shook her body. The hairs on the back of her neck stood as the air felt charged with sinister energy. "Someone close to your heart will pay for indignities caused to me, and this is but a taste of what I will inflict. As to your second question, turn around."

Kimberly spun again, but this time a massive cloaked figure towered over her. Its face, or was that a muzzle, was lost within the shadows of the dark hood. Red embers burned within the depths of the cowl and the smell of spoiled meat filled the air as the creature's hot breath blew upon her. A mighty fur-covered arm that ended in black clawed fingers grabbed her by the throat and lifted her effortlessly from the ground. The beast's other hand slid the piece of wood from her grasp, and with a squeeze snapped the long spar into a wickedly pointed stake. She kicked the beast in the stomach, but her blow had little impact. She pulled at the monstrous hand but couldn't break the mighty grip that held her aloft.

"Your fate has been sealed by your daughter, and I will show her the terrible price that such obstinance extracts."

"My ... daughter...is...dead," Kimberly croaked. Her vision blurred as the creature drew her in closer. The ragged hood fell away, and Shade's snarling rotten face leaned closer.

"Not yet," purred the demonic wolf as a predatory smile creased his maw, "but soon enough." Kimberly watched his black tongue slip past his fangs and felt the rough caress on her cheek. She tried to scream as the demon's venom seared her skin in its wake, but she couldn't draw her breath. She struggled, but she was a rag doll, weakly flailing as he chuckled in her ear. The sliver of wood in his hand drew back, disappearing from her view and then the heavily muscled arm pumped forward sharply. Kimberly felt an explosion of agony rip through her stomach. The creature opened his hand from her neck and she fell hard on the ground, the pain in her abdomen rolling through her in waves. Without a word, the demon moved by her, melting away into the greasy black smoke.

"This is just a bad dream," she said. She saw the faces of Will and Jamie swim into focus then fade away. As the darkness descended, she saw streaks of blue-white light flashing through the inky clouds all around.

"Stay with me, mom," said the soft echo of a voice that she hadn't heard in weeks, and Kimberly wept. She struggled to reach out, but her pain grew worse and the lightning faded.

She needed to hear that speaker one last time.

Her daughter.

Angelica.

This was only a bad dream.

* * *

A man in green scrubs came in quietly and handed Ben a folder. He shot a nervous sideways glance at the scowling girl, and then slipped back out as fast as he could. Hibble lowered the ice pack pressed against his swollen nose and flipped the report open, skimming through the pages it held.

"It wasn't a dream, mom. I know what I saw," said Clarissa. The young woman had been moved out of the ER and into a private room after she had calmed down. "Angelica was fighting with some guy on the school lawn."

"A werewolf, Clarissa? You think you saw her throwing lightning bolts at a werewolf?" Paula squeezed her daughter's hand, but the girl pulled away.

"I never said he was a werewolf. The guy had this shimmery fog ghosted around him that looked like this shadowy wolf thing. He had this weird black fire that was...wrestling with Angelica's lightning."

"You probably just saw smoke lingering from that gas line explosion," said her dad. "And what you thought was Angelica was probably just a sparking power cable. They were down all over the lawn."

"Dad, Angelica Brighton has been my best friend since Kindergarten. I would know her even if I was blindfolded and had cotton stuffed in my ears. It was her. She was wrapped up in lightning and was throwing it from her hands."

"Clarissa," said her mother, "baby you rolled over and over in that bus crash. I am sure you think that's what you saw but..."

"This is not because of a bump to my head," Clarissa shouted. She threw the cup of water in her hand across the room showering the wall and counter with the spray. "Please, believe me. The only reason any of us that were on that bus are alive is because Angelica Brighton saved us somehow. We were about to blow up. I saw the fire racing across the spilled gasoline toward the wreckage. She somehow sucked the entire blast away from us and shot it straight into the air. It wasn't a damn gas main exploding."

"Well, the good news is that your images all came back clean. No brain injury evident here," said Ben. "So, nope, it's not because of a bump to your head. I concur with your diagnosis, madam." He smiled but realized that his levity was lost in this room as the teenager glared at him from the bed with her arms crossed over her chest.

"So glad you agree, Doc," the girl said.

"Clarissa, trauma like what you went through tonight can show itself in all different kinds of ways. I understand that you have had a rough time since Angelica disappeared a few weeks ago, and I have seen in the papers how hard you have organized the ongoing search efforts. Your mind might be idolizing her as a way to help you cope with such a deep loss."

"He's right, honey," said Jim. "It may be time for you to accept the worst about Angelica. We all hope that she is going to turn up any day now, but at some point, we may have to face that she may not ever come home. If she was at the school tonight, then why didn't she stick around?"

"Because she was hurt and somebody took her away," said his daughter. "I was dazed but I saw her fall to the ground after the bus blew up. There was a purple light that hovered near her for a moment and then she was gone. I'm not crazy. I'm telling you that my oldest, dearest friend is somehow involved in all the strange things that happened tonight,"

Hubble cleared his throat. "Your devotion to your friend is truly an inspiration, but try to think clearly. Does it make sense that she showed up all of a sudden throwing lightning from her hands like she is that..., what's that local urban legend you guys have? I didn't grow up around here." He looked over at her parents.

"The Witch of Pioneer Vale," answered Paula.

"Right. Do you believe that your missing friend has been out learning magic over the last couple of weeks while she has been gone?"

Clarissa met Ben's eyes with an intensity that sent a chill down the doctor's spine. Hibble had never seen such cold determination in anyone.

"That will be the first thing I ask when I find her."

CHAPTER 2
RUDE AWAKENING - PRESENT DAY

The wind whipped Angelica's long brown ponytail out behind her as she raced down the forest trails that surrounded Whisperwind, the mystical cottage that was home to the most recent few of Pioneer Vale's Guardians. Birds sang an encouraging song, pushing her harder as she leaped over logs and ducked under the ancient leafy branches. She burst into the clearing where the polished midnight-black marble slab of the Widow Stone welcomed her with a sense of peace as it gleamed beneath the noonday sun.

She plopped down on a tree stump, her eyes closed as she drew in slow cleansing breaths. The fragrance of the wildflowers that dotted the grove and the buzz of honeybees flitting between petals filled her senses. The gentle thrum at the back of her mind soothed her as mystical energy poured into her body, refreshing her muscles and lighting up every nerve with the tingle of the magic that was hers to command. She sighed and smiled to herself, as she rose and turned toward the trail that would take her back to the cottage.

A cloud rolled across the sun, sending a sudden chill through the clearing. The song of the woods ended abruptly as if someone had flipped a switch. The sweet perfume in the air took on a sickly smell, tainted by an underlying scent of decay. A dull thud hit her stomach, twisting at her insides as an ache rose from deep within. Angelica gritted her teeth against the pain and clenched her fist. A nimbus of blue-white lightning crackled up her forearm as a low rumble filled the sky.

"Come out and play," she called as she stood tall in front of the fallen monolith. "I'm ready whenever you are."

A tall figure wrapped in a ragged black cloak stepped forth from the shadowy edge of the far tree line. The hood was pulled high over its face losing the newcomer's features in the cowl but the cold red gleam of the eyes within told the young woman that the Father of Nightmares stood before her. The black claws at the end of the demon's feet dug furrows into the earth as Shade padded closer.

"You shouldn't be out all alone, Guardian. You never know what lurks in these wilds," he growled.

"Nothing I can't handle," Angelica retorted. Her guts roiled as she stepped forward, discomfort rising to shrieking agony as she closed the gap between them. Her vision blurred until all she saw was the rotten muzzle peeking out from the hood, and Shade's lurid smile gracing his toothy maw.

"So certain, are you? Do you think that because you sent my apprentice running that you may now contend with me? I think you will find your skills still lacking, Firstborn," he said with a sneer.

"I guess we're about to find out," Angelica replied. She snapped her open palm forward and hurled forth a blinding rope of electricity that rattled the trees surrounding the clearing. Shade raised his arm, wreathed in a shield of blackish fire that caught her bolt, and swirled it away to nothing. Undaunted, the girl let the raw magic funnel through her in a white-hot torrent of power that battered away at the demon, but to no avail.

Shade snapped his free hand into a fist, and the air shimmered with a gray rippling curtain of force. Angelica felt the strange wave pass over her, and the Whisper of the Guardian, singing so strongly before in the back of her mind, faltered, then faded, as did the flow of her magic. Her lightning fizzled out, going from a raging inferno to a scattering of sparks in a heartbeat. The pain in her stomach doubled her over and the floodgates of her mind burst open.

Angelica's mind surged with images of the school bus exploding, the column of fire that she had channeled into the heavens, and the flashing claws that had ripped through her abdomen in her fight with Aiden on the school's front lawn. She gasped as a blossom of blood spread across the front of her shirt. Her knees buckled and she staggered against a tree trunk.

Shade dropped to all fours and howled into the sky. Dark energy flowed into his body as his muscles rippled and popped under his hide, his frame growing ever stronger until he was the size of a bear. His wicked grin became a slavering snarl as he crouched lower, poised to spring forward. "How fast can you run, little rabbit? Tell me, do you think that you can make the door of the witch's den before I catch you? I'll even give you a head start."

Angelica gritted her teeth, biting through the waves of pain, and bolted for the trail behind her that led back to Whisperwind. The hammering thud of massive paws tearing up the ground filled the air behind her. Her heart pounded in her chest as she pushed herself to her limits.

Through the tree canopy, she saw the cozy cottage ahead, smoke rising in lazy puffs from the chimney. Butterflies flitted above the herb garden. The white paint of the picket fence looked fresh enough to still be wet. The thatch on the roof looked like it had been newly mowed from the fields. Before her, the sanctuary was the picture of serenity.

Behind her, death gave chase.

Shade's growl, closer this time, shook the ground and the agony in her stomach knifed through her once more. With the lunge of one mighty paw, the demonic wolf swept her unsteady feet and she fell into a roll across the uneven ground skinning her knees and shins in the loose white gravel path that led to the front door. Shade slid past her, barring the way between her and the cottage, and Angelica scrambled backward as he slowly turned to face her. He stood tall, the sun lost as he loomed over her, his eyes alight with hellfire. His claws tore furrows in the trail and the vibrant foliage withered in his wake. Shade's fangs glistened as his mouth opened wide, and he lunged.

Angelica raised her arms in front of her face right before the force of his impact slammed her head against the hard-packed dirt and his weight crushed the wind from her lungs. She couldn't find the breath to scream as his claws ripped flesh from her shoulders. Shade's roar deafened her, and blood ran from her ears. Angelica stared into the throat of her doom when his jaws opened and his breath blew hot against her face. He reared back, his wicked talons splayed out above his head. As she waited for the blow to fall, a murmuring whisper pushed back into her mind, and a blue-white spark flickered at her fingertips.

"Go to hell, wolf. This is not my end," she croaked as her fist filled with her own white flames.

Shade roared to the heavens as his claws, limned in a gray-black fire swiped down toward her face.

*   *   *

Angelica shrieked as she bolted upright in her bed. Her breath came in shallow gasps as four lances of pain ripped across the torn muscles of her belly. She rolled over and tumbled to the floor with a thud, the landing sending a jolt through her elbow. Her limbs flailed as she thrashed around, kicking at the suffocating stranglehold of her sweat-soaked sheets that entangled her. A chill swept through the room, raising goose bumps on her bare skin. She shivered, which only caused her to writhe once more as she held her arms across the bloody bandages that were her only covering. Her head thudded like a drum, pounding to the beat of her pulse. The flickering violet candle flames cast their frolicking shadows across the room and did nothing to ease her unsteady vision.

The scarred walls around her and the lingering acrid smell of lightning in the air told her that she was back in her ravaged room at Whisperwind still fresh from her encounter with the Elder Guardian. Devastation reigned in the wake of the encounter. Scorch marks marred the paint and splintered furniture littered the room. Only her bed seemed to have escaped the raw might that the powerful being had unleashed. Strangely untouched, Angelica saw a faint ripple of energy wash back and forth along the mattress and frame. She grabbed the corner of the nightstand to pull herself back up, but her arms were like rubber and her elbow buckled. Her hand slipped and she crashed back to the singed carpet.

The bedroom door swung open, and Anne-Marie rushed into the room. The normally crisp lines were absent in the simple skirt and blouse that her mentor and 10th great grandmother wore. The wrinkled clothing had clearly been slept in, and the 17th-century farmwife's green eyes were dull and red-rimmed with dark circles underneath. Errant strands of her coppery mane flew wildly around her head. Angelica hugged the woman back when she dropped to the floor and cradled her head against her chest.

"Lay still, child," Anne-Marie said. "You'll tear those gouges wide open again, and I've only just managed to get them closed."

"We're in danger," Angelica said as she squirmed in the embrace. She clutched her teacher's arm, seeing her wince as her fingernails dug in with a strength born of fear. She looked wide-eyed into Anne-Marie's face, her voice a quivering whisper. "Shade is in the grove."

"Hush, my dear. He is still locked away in his own realm." Lavender fire flared around her arms and she effortlessly lifted the young woman from the floor and placed her back among the pillows. She brushed Angelica's matted hair away from her sweaty brow. "The old cur merely

17

took your weakness as an opportunity to send you a new nightmare. We are safe for now." Anne-Marie gently kissed the top of her head and then held her hand over Angelica's wound. Her brow furrowed and a flash of lavender fire enveloped her hand. Wispy flames flickered down and tickled her stomach, but the pain eased under the healing warmth. She saw the tears welling in Anne-Marie's eyes, but the woman managed a weak grin for her. Then with a deft twist of her fingers, the flames winked out.

Angelica drew a deep breath and sank into the down pillows behind her. She smiled back and nodded her thanks. "So which of my screw-ups came closest to taking me out? Facing Aiden alone or running an entire bus explosion through my guts?"

"I would venture that all of your misdeeds were in contention." The older woman lowered her head into her hands and her shoulders quaked. "I thought I had lost you," she said with her muffled voice. Angelica reached out and squeezed her hand, which Anne-Marie kissed and held to her cheek. "I have spent the last three days pouring all the healing magic I could muster, and using every bit of herb lore I could think of to try to mend the damage done to you. I didn't think that your fever was ever going to break. Even the thinnest of your clothes spiked your temperature to a point that should have killed you. You bled through one shirt after another anyway, so I felt it more prudent to just leave you undressed. I truly had no idea if you would make it or not."

"Yeah, felt a little touch-and-go there myself," said Angelica. Anne-Marie grabbed a t-shirt thrown across the foot of the bed and helped her pull it on over her head. "Thanks for making my bed. Guess you didn't get a chance to tidy up the rest of the place?" she said as she waved at the shambles of her room.

"I'm sure the burn marks on the walls come with a remarkable story, and you simply must share it with me one day," Anne-Marie said with a toss of her hair and a raised eyebrow. "We'll save that until you are feeling better. I'd rather you were fully recovered before I lose my formidable temper with you."

"Let's just say that the Elder Guardian can speak louder than a Whisper. Why did you bring me here instead of the lab? Wouldn't that have been closer to your herbs and medicines?"

"As it happens, whatever occurred in this room before you ignored my counsel and rushed off left an incredible residual magic aura. There is immense energy here that has held you together far more effectively than my powers could influence."

"Is that why my bed is glimmering like a mirage?"

Anne-Marie nodded. "And likely played a part in why you are still alive. You were raked by the Nightmare Hand, a particularly nasty enchantment of Shade's invention. I've never heard an account of anyone surviving such an attack. I can only assume that was because Aiden hadn't reached his full power yet."

"Well, I don't intend to give him another shot. I had him hurt and on the run. We need to track him down and finish him off." Beads of sweat ran down her forehead as she struggled to lift herself from the sheets. She gritted her teeth as she pushed herself to a sitting position as Anne-Marie propped another pillow behind her back.

"You are in no condition to charge headlong into yet another ill-advised fight." The redhead rolled her fingers through twists and turns that left tongues of lavender fire trailing after her hands. A hole ripped open in midair beside Angelica's bed and Anne-Marie's arms disappeared up to the elbows as she reached deeply into it. When she leaned back, she held a wooden tray with two steaming bowls upon it. She smiled as she set the tray down on the scorched nightstand. She offered Angelica the first bowl with one hand while her other played with the glittering amethyst pendant that hung on a gossamer silver chain around her neck.

Angelica looked skeptically at the thick yellow liquid. Chunks of orange and green floated in it. "I know you can work miracles with the stuff in your garden, but is this really necessary?"

Another flash of violet flame brought a spoon into Anne-Marie's hand and she dipped it into the bowl. Before she could protest, the Guardian stuck the spoon in Angelica's mouth.

"That tastes like chicken soup," she said as her eyes widened in surprise as Anne-Marie ladled another spoonful.

"That's because it is. I could concoct dozens of mystical remedies to help you along, but right now you need to regain your strength. For that, I suggest something a little more worldly, and chicken soup remains the best of them all. Just pray I don't mix up the bowls," Anne-Marie said with a wicked grin. "The other is a healing poultice and I assure you that the taste would be far less pleasant. Pull your shirt up enough for me to see your injuries."

"So how bad was the fight at the school?" Angelica asked as she tugged the shirt back up over her belly. She then slurped more soup from the spoon as Anne-Marie gently peeled back the soiled dressings on her stomach. The older woman frowned as the bloody fabric pulled at the healing skin beneath. Angelica tried not to look down, but her heart sank as she saw the way her teacher pursed her lips.

Anne-Marie shook her head and reached for the second bowl. She scooped the gooey brown salve onto the end of a wooden stick and gently applied it to the wounds. Angelica gritted her teeth as the cold salve touched the torn flesh. She felt as though a thousand needles poked into the raw muscle. Anne-Marie nodded her head and put the stick back in the bowl.

"No one was killed if that's why you are asking. The media is ablaze right now with theories about the multitude of unanswerable questions. How did the bus flip? What blew apart the Chemistry Lab?" She took a dramatic pause and glared at Angelica. "Who was the young woman throwing lightning at a giant shadowy wolf figure?"

"Come on, now. Someone reported that? They had to sound insane, right?"

"It might have blown over if there had been only a single person calling in such a claim." The older woman wrapped fresh bandages around Angelica. She sighed. "You were seen by dozens, Angelica. Not only by the passengers of the bus but by curious neighbors peeking through their windows to see what all of the commotion was from. Lightning and thunder on the front lawn, cars exploding, and a column of fire that blazed into the heavens. I have no doubt that your antics will be the showcase of the internet soon."

Angelica bristled under Anne-Marie's condescending stare and her anger burst through her restraint. "Good. Maybe the fight will go viral and we can get some help. The world has a right to know about the danger it is in. There is literally a monster on our doorstep and the only one trying to actively stop him is me. You sure as hell haven't done a damn thing to help me hunt Aiden down!"

"You still don't understand the importance of our anonymity, do you?" Anne-Marie said softly as a wistful smile found her lips. "With your spectacle at the school, what reaction do you think the common folk will feel? Adoration? Gratitude?"

"I saved everyone on that bus."

"And do you think that's what will be the subject of hushed whispers? Talk around the cafes and water coolers? I have been through this before, child. Save a thousand and you will be remembered only for the one you couldn't. All of those people will be peeking out of their living room windows, watching for monsters creeping along their streets. Searching the skies for flying broomsticks. Clutching whatever weapons they own ready to attack anything that rattles their doorknobs. They have become so terrified that the town will not sleep, and Shade will feed on that."

"And here come the torches and pitchforks," said Angelica as she rolled her eyes. "Why do you still believe the people would turn on us if they know the truth?"

"Because I have lived it!" Anne-Marie hurled the bowl in her hands against the wall, smashing the crockery to bits.

Angelica shielded her eyes as Anne-Marie spun away from her bedside. The wash of heat from the lavender flames that engulfed the other woman's body blew aside the wreckage in her path as her anger took form. Her grandmother stormed over to the window and stood like a phoenix ablaze, staring out into the calming forest beyond. At last, she unclenched her fists and the fires flickered away. Anne-Marie lowered her head and shook her coppery mane slowly.

"I have been in the hands of a frightened mob, with my life on the line because the town feared what I might be capable of. Uncertainty breeds terror and that favors our enemy. He draws strength from it. You must remember one basic truth. Our lives are all that prevents Shade from fully entering this world and you have nearly died once already, child. Shade would love nothing more than for the folk of the town to discover that we truly are the witches of local legend and carry out an Old Salem Barbecue."

"Not everyone is like that. We just need to find the right people. You know as well as I do that there are those who would fight beside us if they only knew what was at stake."

"Yes, there are good and just folk who would stand with us now, just as there were in ages past," Anne-Marie said with a nod. "Are you prepared to watch those brave friends die in droves as foul magic tears the skin from their bones? We would have to step to their defense or watch them fall when our focus should be on our own fight."

"So your plan is to sit and hide until your son makes his next move."

"My plan is to do as the Guardians have done for millennia, child. We protect from the shadows. We watch over those who cannot perceive the threats around them. When the world has no knowledge of our existence, they can't fear us. The last thing we want is for the townsfolk actively looking for the Witches of Pioneer Vale." She bent forward and kissed Angelica on the forehead, then gathered up her serving tray and the pieces of the broken bowl.

"So even when we try to do the right thing, Shade keeps getting stronger."

"So it would seem, but that doesn't mean we stop doing what is right."

Angelica pulled the edge of the blanket back up onto the bed and hugged it tightly against her body as images of her nightmare still danced through her mind. "The dream Shade sent to me. Does that mean I am going to face him by myself someday?"

"Only over my dead body, dear," Anne-Marie said with a wink as she pulled the door closed behind her.

*　　*　　*

As soon as the door closed, Angelica's composure collapsed under the grip of excruciating pain. Her stomach felt as though knives twisted their way deeper into her flesh. Sweat broke on her forehead as she gritted her teeth. Her vision blurred as she fell against the pillows, but within the haze, she saw ropes of ambient magic twining throughout her room. Instead of the usual wispy tendrils that fueled her power, thick cables of energy pulsed around her, clearly left behind by her encounter with the Elder Guardian.

She clenched her fist to steady her trembling fingers and then plunged her hand deep inside the nearest one.

Her body bucked from the incredible energy that charged her senses, unlike anything she had met with since becoming a Guardian. Every fiber of her body sang and she struggled to hold in check the unbridled forces that blasted through her core. The devastation around her bedroom stood testament to what might happen if such power ran unchecked. The teasing ecstasy of the Elder's might called to her as before, but she held it at bay and directed the magic to her injury.

Her inner eye spotted the infection right away. Black venom coursed through her belly like a writhing serpent, barely contained by a gossamer cage of Anne-Marie's own fire that she had brought to bear while the girl remained unconscious. It punched against the barrier but was knocked aside with each effort to breach the ward. Angelica's mind drifted long enough to see the fundamental difference that set her and her mentor apart. Anne-Marie sought ways to contain and imprison Shade's foul workings.

Angelica chose to fight them head-on.

The energy at her command took on the crackle of her own signature lightning and tore through Anne-Marie's barrier, replacing it with her own might. At her will, Angelica's cage constricted and grabbed Aiden's poison like a choking hand throttling a snake. She imagined the squeals of fear as the sickness tried to slip away, but the power she wielded wouldn't allow it. With the hint of a snarl on her lips, she fired a cleansing blast of magic that burned into the viscous poison. The coil of darkness thrashed and snapped, seeking an escape, but the young witch left none to be found. When the last drop boiled away, her pain subsided and her breath came to her without anguish for the first time since she regained consciousness. Though still sore and tender, she knew that her wounds would heal with time. She fell back onto the sweat-soaked sheets and released the magic from her hand.

As she closed herself off and drifted away into a healing sleep, she felt a comforting presence and sensed eyes alight with lightning and flame watching over her.

CHAPTER 3
A WOLF IN SHEEP'S CLOTHING

Ben shivered as he opened his eyes but all was pitch black. He rubbed his hands together to get some feeling into his numb fingers. He fumbled for the lamp at his bedside, but he jammed his fingers into frigid stone.

"What the hell?" he swore softly as he shook his hand. He realized that he was wearing jeans and a flannel shirt rather than the scrubs that he had passed out in after stumbling into his apartment from his shift. He patted his pockets and dug out his lighter. With a clumsy flick, the meager flame revealed that he was not in his own home any longer.

Leering skulls grinned all around him from barrows in a worked stone tomb. Scorched bones littered the floor around his boots. The hairs on his neck shot up as a low menacing growl rumbled from beyond the edge of his meager light. The sound reverberated throughout the chamber making its true location impossible for Hibble to determine which direction it came from.

"Ahh, the deserter comes before me," purred a gravelly voice from the edges of the shifting shadows. "Those of your particular stripe often do."

Ben cried out as a stabbing pain lanced through his head and memories of his life before Pioneer Vale were wrenched from recesses he thought were long sealed. He ground the heel of his hand into his temple and squinted at the shapes moving in the dark. "What is this?" he snarled through gritted teeth.

"This is the final stop for you, doctor. No more running away. The time has come for you to either take a stand against the tiresome oppression of your past or cower before your antagonists and pay your dues." A snarling chuckle brought Ben's attention to the side, where two red eyes burning like dying coals gleamed in the dancing shadows. A murky shape pressed forward. Fangs in a slavering maw glinted in the orange flame that his lighter shed.

"I don't understand. You can't change my past."

"No, but I can shape your future. The world hurtles toward a day of reckoning." The growl softened into what Ben could only think of as a savage playfulness. "Wouldn't you like to be on the winning side for once in your life? Spit back in the faces of those who belittled you, preyed upon your guilt?"

"I accepted everything I deserved. I just try now not to spend too much time thinking about it. I have made mistakes, but I won't punish others for my own lack of honor."

The ground beneath his feet shook, and dust fell from the ceiling as a bloodcurdling roar shattered the air. Hibble fell back, his hands over his ears against the deafening echoes, and bumped into a stone table. He reached out to steady himself and found the surface was warm, wet, and sticky. He had spent enough time in the ER to know the feeling of fresh blood.

Torches along the wall burst into flames, throwing aside the hidden veil over the grisly altar. Before him, a rolling mist of midnight black grew darker still as it twisted into the shape of a massive wolf. The creature towered over the doctor, the exposed sinews in its decaying muzzle popping the wicked jaws snapped shut. The beast looked into the air above Ben's head, drawing the man's attention upwards. A massive statue of the very monster before him glared down from the cobwebs above. The stonework was so realistic that Ben could swear that it bent its head to follow him.

"Then here shall you fall," growled the beast as it paced back and forth before him. A pinpoint of crimson light appeared in the air between them and slowly elongated into a wicked-looking knife that pulsed with a dull glow. It twirled lazily in the air and then stopped, the point aimed directly at him.

The wolf snapped his fingers and Ben watched the blade flash across the chamber, slamming into his stomach before he could react. Fire ripped through his stomach but even his shriek couldn't drown out the sinister laughter of the demon as it drew closer.

*　　*　　*

The bar was dimly lit, and a haze of cigarette smoke hung in the air. The jukebox in the corner warbled out the same three songs over and over. The gouged pool table in the middle of the room stood level only because of a chunk of wood that propped it up. The dartboard on the wall hung askew and had so many holes that a dart wouldn't even hold fast anymore. The floor was stained and sticky from years of spilled drinks.

Ben took a drag from his cigarette and blew out a cloud, contributing to the surrounding fog. Why the hell was his life such a wreck? One of his ancestors must have messed with a mummy's tomb or something. His nose ached from where Jim Brenner's girl had slugged him. He still had goose bumps from that damn nightmare, and it had dredged up more than a few ghosts from his past that he had thought conquered. Now he found himself returned to the local watering hole even though he had already sat on this same stool earlier tonight. He lifted his beer to his lips when someone bumped his elbow and he sloshed foam all over his shirt.

"And there's that unbreakable Hibble luck," he muttered.

"My sincerest apologies," said a skinny man in jeans and a denim jacket. "This place is rather crowded tonight, and there isn't a lot of seating, to begin with. If you wouldn't mind the company, I would be happy to buy you another round."

"Help yourself," said Ben as he soaked up the spill with a handful of napkins emblazoned with a deer's head. "I'm not much in the way of good company though, friend. Had a rough week."

"Ahh, then maybe you wouldn't mind sharing some information with a traveler then?" The man waved to the girl behind the bar and pointed at the nearly empty bottle in Ben's hand.

"Don't know that you'll get your money's worth, pal. I didn't grow up around here, but hell, you want to buy me one, I'll take you up on it. Name's Ben Hibble."

"Aiden Carmichael," the newcomer said as he sat down on the barstool and placed a twenty on the bar. The waitress placed two fresh drinks in front of them. "Thank you, Ashley. Please keep them coming whenever we run dry." He took a sip from the bottleneck and smacked his lips. "So tell me, are you just passing through town too?"

He shook his head then took a pull from the fresh drink placed before him. "Nope. I'm stuck in this hole for the time being. Came down from New York about a year and a half ago. Needed a change of scenery. Personal stuff that I ...needed to leave behind me."

"Uh- oh. Let me guess. Girl trouble?" Ben didn't respond but raised his beer into the air before taking another sip. "Yes, I have a certain measure of that going on right now myself," Aiden said with a frown.

"So what's your story?" he asked. "You from around these parts? Isn't Carmichael the name of that farm outside of town? Relatives of yours?"

"Distantly, on my mother's side. I grew up nearby, but I've been gone for a very long time and have only recently returned."

"Oh, been away at school?"

"Not exactly, although my time away has certainly proven educational. No, my return was, for lack of a better term...delayed."

"Uh-oh. Let me guess," Ben said with a grin. "Family matters?"

A snarl flashed across Aiden's face that caused him to jump and nearly spill his drink again. The stranger's hand lashed out with lightning-fast speed and steadied the bottle before it fell. "That is putting it mildly, but you are surprisingly on point." He cleared his throat and glanced around the bar. "This place is so different from the way I remember it from my childhood. There used to be antlers and pelts adorning every bit of the walls. It has not fared well over the years."

"You hang out in a lot of bars when you were a kid? Damn, I thought my parents needed work. Someone told me that this used to be a nice restaurant, but it changed ownership awhile back. Hell, that had to have been before you were even born though."

"I'm a bit older than I look," Aiden said. "We had some good times here when I was a child before I was branded the black sheep."

"Family can be tough to deal with. My mom used to tell me that we've had one generation after another trying to escape the crap that the previous generation left behind. I always thought that she was joking, but after my circumstances in the city, I couldn't take all of her scoldings for me to 'do the right thing' and 'live up to your responsibilities'. It got old fast, and so I packed up my stuff and ended up here. Keeping the tradition alive, I guess."

"Anything in particular about Pioneer Vale that drew you here?" asked Aiden.

"Coincidence, I guess. I bounced from town to town looking for a new job and there was nothing. I was almost to the point where I thought I'd have to start eating the laces of my shoes when the opening at Pioneer Vale General popped up. I applied and was hired almost immediately. I don't think the admins even bothered to check my references."

"Lucky break for you," Aiden said. "I don't think highly of coincidence. Maybe your destiny called you here."

"The strangest bit was how much this place felt like home as soon as I settled in. I don't know. There was a familiarity that fell over me. Like for the first time in my life, I belonged somewhere."

"Sounds to me as though you are here for a reason." He raised his drink and clinked the bottleneck against Ben's.

"Fate, coincidence, whatever you want to call it. I am still waiting for the family curse to strike. Things just don't pan out for the Hibble family. Bad luck. Being in the wrong place at the wrong time. It's like misfortune goes out of its way to find us. Like this kid the other night at the hospital. I'm just trying to do my job, make sure nobody is seriously hurt. Doing no harm, like I vowed in med school. This girl flips out, and while I'm trying to get her settled down she hauls off and breaks my nose."

"What was she carrying on about?" asked Aiden.

"Crazy stuff. She was raving about seeing a friend of hers throwing lightning and fighting a werewolf or something. If her scans hadn't come back clean, I'd have thought it was just the ranting of a head injury."

"That sounds like quite a story," Aiden purred as he pushed a fresh beer toward him. "Please, tell me all about her."

*   *   *

With the snap of her fingers, Anne-Marie shot forth streaks of lavender flame to light the candles around the Holding Chamber. Shards of shattered crystal, still scattered across the floor where they had fallen during

Angelica's furious assault, glinted in the flare. Shadows that had remained undisturbed since that night scurried to the dark corners of the room. As she crossed the threshold Anne-Marie felt the familiar tingle of magic that always accompanied her passage into a pocket realm of her own creation.

The woman clapped her hands above her head and brought her clenched fists down sharply to her sides, wrapping herself in a shroud of whirling purple fire that burned away her everyday skirts and blouse and changed them into the more fitting trousers, corset, and ruffled top that was her signature Guardian's outfit. The amethyst pendant at her throat flashed with its own brilliance. Her polished black boots crunched across the dusty floor as Anne-Marie approached the empty pedestal.

She closed her eyes and felt the rush of power as the magic of the Guardians, the Whisper of the Elder, flowed through her body. She placed her hands on the marble and felt an ancient sinister energy lash out at her. She knew all too well that the smashed gemstone was far more than just a prison for her fugitive son. The crystal was a droplet of the Adversary's own blood, spilled during a titanic battle eons ago. It was a focus of malevolent magic and it was this hated stone that had given birth to her own enemy. Lavender flame engulfed her once more as she visualized every sliver, every mote of the broken crystal lifting from the floor and returning back to its former place. When she opened her eyes, the sickly yellow gem hovered in the air, the cracks throughout its surface held together through her own force of will.

"I know you can hear me, Shade," she called out. Her voice crackled with power that shook the very mortar from the walls. "You cannot hide from me, wolf."

A swirling shadow passed across the face of the crystal as if smoke from the darkest pits crept out from behind the facets. A shape formed, split by the cracks riddled throughout the gem, twisting and stretching until it finally became the hideous visage of the Father of Nightmares.

"Hello, sweetling," purred the whispery voice. Shade's usual gravelly tone now carried the tinkling of broken glass to her ear. "Come to beg for mercy as your final days rush ever closer?"

"You should be more concerned about your own miserable hide, you cur."

"And what have I to fear, witch?" snarled her enemy. "Your latest Firstborn? The girl is an unruly pup, full of bark, but she will cower to one good swat across her nose, I think."

"Angelica may still have much to learn, but I am the one you need to fear." Her eyes blazed as she met the demon's fractured glare. "You will not take another of my children."

Shade's rolling laughter was cruel and wicked. "Then maybe you should stop sending them to me," he said. "Perhaps we need to place one of those 'Do not feed the animals' signs above the door of your miserable little hovel. It might serve as a poignant reminder of what I have done to all of your whelps."

"Things are different this time, demon. Angelica is not some frightened child, unsteady in her resolve. She is my equal in ferocity, and second only in her hatred toward you."

"Pray that she resists my invitations. A whisper of power promised has served me against your line before, my dear."

"Aiden was never a true Guardian of the Vale. He possesses only as much power as you grant him. Angelica is an open pipeline to the oldest of magics and trains every day to perfect her prowess. My son is no match for her."

"Do you not find it disheartening that you cannot hope to save them both? Will you kill your own son if you must in order to save her? I find it delightful to know that ultimately your hands will drip with the blood of your family once more."

Anne-Marie crossed her arms over her chest and frowned. "You seek to unnerve me with my fears that you know so well, old foe. So long as I draw breath you remain shackled. One day, I shall send you back to the hellfires that spawned you. I grow weary of your threats, demon. Search your own nightmares for me."

The shadows in the crystal boiled, a black pulse of energy rippled through the room, staggering Anne-Marie as Shade threw back his head and roared. Dizzying visions of mangled children screamed as horrible phantoms ran them down with flashing claws. "When you and the little bitch are destroyed, I shall take savage pleasure in spilling every last drop of Carmichael blood that remains in your world. Every son and daughter that can trace their lineage back to you shall see my face just before their assuredly gruesome end."

"I will burn the hide from your black bones first, monster," Anne-Marie screamed back at him. The fires in the room blazed to the ceiling, scorching the stone. The dark shapes fell away as her fury burned away the deep places in the room. "You have already stolen enough of those dear to me because of your hateful schemes, and you will not threaten another."

The darkness within the crystal swirled, wispy under the Guardian's rage but then resumed Shade's shape. He butted his head against the prison with enough force that the gem swayed as it hung above the pedestal. The lines of the shadow grew crisper, more defined, and Shade's chuckle rang in her ears once more.

"Your wards falter, and soon I will see you flushed from your den and your life taken for my pleasure."

"I have stood against you for centuries, and will not fall so easily."

"You sense it the same as I do, witch. Our ongoing dance draws to an end. This will be the final turn. You shall not contain me much longer."

"Given that we are both immortal, I suspect that we shall continue circling one another for some time to come."

"You are long-lived," Shade growled, "but you are not deathless. There is a difference and one that I look forward to clarifying for you soon enough."

"Prepare for our final battle then, monster. I will be ready." The purple flames winked out around the floating gem and it fell to the ground with the tinkling crash of a thousand fragments falling away from one another. Anne-Marie spun on her heel and left the room, the warmth of Whisperwind returning to her the moment she crossed the threshold once more.

As she leaned against the stone wall of the great spiral stair in the extra-dimensional space of her home, Anne-Marie felt one final intrusion into her mind.

"Marshall your forces, witch, for I assure you that I gather my own."

*   *   *

Ben staggered out of the bar, his arm draped around Aiden's shoulder, although the doctor felt that the other man was doing most of the walking. He giggled as the world spun around him. He knew he was in for one hell of a hangover tomorrow, but he had actually enjoyed his new friend's company. The nightmare that had taken him to the bar in the first place seemed childish and distant now.

"How come you aren't stumbling as bad as me? You matched me drink for drink in there," he asked, trying not to trip over his own feet.

"Just one more of my considerable talents, Doctor," Aiden replied as he steadied Ben down the stoop to the gravel and weed-strewn parking lot. "I know a few other tricks that will ... blow you away."

"Got anything to wipe out 35 years of bad luck?"

"What if I told you that it isn't a rabbit's foot that you need, but retribution?"

Ben laughed and gave the other man a halfhearted punch in the arm. "I'd say you better work on your sales pitch. You got someone for me to blame for a lifetime of screw-ups?"

"You've been tormented since the day you were born," said Aiden as he leaned in close. Ben caught a whiff of rotten eggs and smoke as the man spoke to him. "What if there was someone you could punish for the misfortune your family has known? Make them pay for all that you have suffered. Stand tall above those who brought you such pain, and take back the life that you deserve. Maybe even erase your own guilt."

Ben felt like he was blacking out, and could only hear Aiden's whispery purr in his ear. The man's voice was soothing, and the doctor's mind swirled with images from his past. Words that might never have been spoken. Fists that might never have clenched. Tears that need not have fallen.

"Yeah," he said softly. "There are a lot of things I'd like to forget. What's the catch? You asking me to sell my soul, because I doubt mine is much of a prize?"

Aiden stiffened but then chuckled. "I may know a guy, but his terms are murder."

"He'd still catch the crappier end of the deal," Ben mumbled with a hiccup. "Let's get going. I need to get out of here."

"Of course. You mentioned yours is a blue pickup truck?" asked Aiden. Ben felt an icy tingle pass through his body Aiden effortlessly helped him navigate through the sea of parked cars in the lot.

"Yep. I got keys someplace," Ben said as he patted down his pockets.

"I don't think we need them just yet. We appear to have company to attend to first."

Ben swung his head around and saw two beefy men near his truck. One leaned against the mirror while the other sat on the hood, bouncing his foot against one of the headlights. Empty beer bottles littered the ground between them, and the scorch marks of several cigarette butts marred the paint where they had been extinguished.

"Damn Roughnecks," Ben muttered. He saw Aiden's eyebrow raise up, and he shook his head. "That's what the locals call them. Drifters who roll into town, make a few quick bucks by helping out with handyman and odd jobs on the nearby farms for a couple of days, and then vanish."

"Modern-day mercenaries," said Aiden with a gleam in his eye. His chuckle sent a shiver down the doctor's spine.

"Hey, guys. Do you mind getting off my truck? You're playing hell on the wax job." Ben hoped his words sounded bolder than his knocking knees would imply, but then again if the two men understood a single word that slurred from his mouth, it would be something magical.

"We'll move when we're finished," said one of the men. "Unless you two twigs think you can speed us along." The workman crossed his thick arms over his barrel chest. His friend took a stray bottle cap and deliberately dragged it across the door, gouging a deep furrow in the paint. Hibble freed himself from Aiden and drew his arm back, fist clenched.

"You son of a ..." Ben started to say when, for the second time this week, a fist smashed into his nose. He had a moment to reflect, as blood ran down his chin, that this one hurt a hell of a lot more than the punch from the Brenner girl in the ER the other night. "Joke's on you, Jack. Already had my nose broken once this week." His legs became jelly and he stumbled backward, falling fast until Aiden caught him. His drinking companion leaned him against the nearby trash dumpster.

37

"Stay here and do not come out," Aiden said. His voice was a low growl, cold and icy, and Ben saw the strangest flash of fire pass through his friend's eyes. Too much booze, he thought as he slumped to the ground. Not a good way to enter a bar fight. He fought to stay awake, shaking his head to clear the cobwebs. He tried to push himself from the concrete, but his arms wouldn't obey him and he collapsed. He saw Aiden's blurry outline disappear behind another car as he stepped boldly toward the other two men. The moon overhead passed behind a cloud, and the lights in the parking lot dimmed. The lengthening shadows crawled forward across the pavement, the darkness dragging forward with grasping fingers. He watched the long silhouettes of the two men as they raised their fists and approached, but then Ben's bleary eyes snapped wide open when Aiden's shadow crossed theirs.

The hulking shape of a man-shaped beast with a wolf's head lunged forward. Ben's heart lurched in his chest as the images from his nightmare clawed their way back through the alcohol-induced haze. A piercing howl from the nearby hills outside of town shattered the night. The doctor's teeth chattered but it had nothing to do with the cool night air.

Ben crawled away from the fight, scrambling to get himself behind the dumpster. He heard a deep snarl, and a wet tearing noise that his medical knowledge knew all too well was ripping flesh. A shrill scream echoed against the block wall of the bar. Something slammed against the other side of the dumpster hard enough to scrape the heavy metal container across the concrete and launch the doctor into the bushes beyond. A spray of blood splashed across the ground. Boots crunched in the gravel and a strange light flared from the other side of the bin. The temperature plunged suddenly and Ben saw frost in his frantic panting for breath. Something large was dropped into the trash container and the lid crashed down with a bang. The strange light vanished, and the street lamps around the parking lot came back up. The world spun madly around him and he squeezed his eyes shut as tightly as he could. Soft steps like padded feet stopped beside him and a cold hand gently shook him. He slowly opened his eyes to see Aiden kneeling beside him.

"I told you I knew a few tricks," the man said with a grin. His teeth seemed sharper, his smirk almost predatorial. "Come, my friend. Let's get you home." He hauled Hibble to his feet and pulled him back into the light.

"What the hell just happened?" Ben grabbed Aiden's shirt and shoved the man away from him. "Where did those guys go?"

"Men of that sort are nothing more than bullies. Once I showed them that I wasn't such an easy mark they, ...how should I put this? Lost their stomachs for the sport." His eyes flashed mischief and he giggled. "Anyway, one of them dropped this in their hasty retreat. Consider it spoils of war or at least compensation for damages to your truck." He handed Ben a steel flask, wrapped in black leather, and adorned with a large purple gemstone.

"I don't know if I want this. It's beautiful, but.... Why don't you keep it?" The doctor ran his thumb over the stone, marveling at the inner fire that danced within. He felt his racing heart slow as he touched the gem.

Aiden shook his head. "Doesn't really suit me. Never cared much for amethysts. Keep it, or throw it away. It's your choice. However, you sir, are in no condition to drive yourself home so let me get your keys from you. On this score, I will not be swayed." Ben handed over the keys to his truck, and Aiden opened the passenger door. Food wrappers from the local burger joint fell to the asphalt.

"Sorry. I eat on the go a lot," said Ben.

"Not to worry. Let me throw this in with the rest of the trash and we can get out of here," Aiden said as he picked up the fast-food bag, and crumpled it up. He walked over to the dumpster and paused with a glance over his shoulder at Ben. A feral grin flashed across his face as he opened the lid just enough so that he could toss in the garbage.

Ben was spared from seeing the grisly contents that the local garbage men would find the next morning.

Aiden climbed behind the wheel of Ben's truck and fired up the engine. "All done. Time to get you to your apartment without further incident."

Ben's head lolled back and forth. His nose hurt, his stomach churned, and his only relief was that he didn't have to work tomorrow. He glanced over at Aiden who whistled to himself as he pulled the truck into the main street, and sped along the road.

"Look at you being such a mother hen," Ben said and then burst into drunken laughter. "I bet your mama is so proud of you."

Aiden slammed the brakes and the truck screeched to a grinding halt.

Ben catapulted forward and rebounded off the dashboard. His arms barely prevented his nose from getting crunched once more. He looked over as Aiden threw the gear shift into park, and grabbed the front of his shirt.

"You are deep in your cups tonight and as we have only just met, I can't expect you to know a thing about my relationship with that woman."

"Whoa," said Ben. He raised his hands up. "Damn, I'm sorry. I didn't mean to hit a nerve."

Aiden's lips pulled back in a snarl then he sat back, shaking his head and smiling again, as he put the truck into gear once more.

"Of course you didn't. My apologies, Benjamin. She simply tends to be a sore subject for me." He shot a sideways glance over to his passenger then pointed his finger as he spoke. "I have only a single thing to say about my mother...."

CHAPTER 4
COURTING DANGER - 1671

"Anne-Marie Carmichael is a witch!" Parson Corbin Reynolds slammed his fist down upon the podium before him. The preacher knew from the oohs and ahhs that erupted around the room that his fire and brimstone delivery had enraptured the crowd, just as he held them in thrall during his weekly sermons. Folks from all around Pioneer Vale had assembled to hear more about the charges leveled against Anne-Marie. He swept his pointed finger across the wide-eyed assemblage and his voice dropped to a deep rumble. "It is well known that she is skilled in herb lore and no doubt is a practitioner of alchemy. The manufacturing of nefarious potions is but one of her implements with which she pollutes and corrupts the good people of this town!"

Reynolds paced before his audience before coming to a stop at the stand where Anne-Marie stood. The preacher paused as he studied the woman. Despite the manacles clapped around her wrists, and the filthy clothes that she had worn since the night of her incarceration two days ago, she held her head up high. Her fiery red hair flowed free around her shoulders in a tangled mass of crimson curls. Her face was streaked with grime from her cell, and his observant eyes spotted the sodden hem of her dress where she must have tried to wipe her face clean before being led down the street to the council chamber. He met her eyes, and to her credit, she never flinched under his cold stare. Corbin turned away first and cleared his throat as he approached the front of the room.

The platform at the end of the long chamber held a grand table where the five townspeople drawn by lots listened to him present his case. Dorothea Brenner tapped her finger against her close shaved scalp and rolled her eyes.

"A point that you have been droning on about for the better part of the afternoon, Parson Reynolds," said the mistress of the Hirsute Huntsman tavern. "You'll need a bit more than her skill with herbs, however, to prove your accusation as far as I am concerned. If she's a witch for knowing how to use a few leafy greens then what does that say of me? Any man who has ever dined in my husband's taproom could level the same charge against me based on what all I have growing in my own yard."

"We do not speak simply of the craft of seasoning meat pies, Goody Brenner," retorted Corbin.

"Do you call what I craft simple, Parson? You might get tossed into the stockade yourself if any of my customers were to hear such words."

"This woman uses her knowledge to create plague and sickness."

Dorothea scoffed. "Were you not one of many in this room that Anne-Marie cared for two winters past when that abysmal fever tore through our ranks? Each morning she rode to town through the snow to aid the sick. What was she doing? Checking on the handiness of her latest curse?"

"She uses her arts to cloud the judgment of men. To corrupt the virtuous of our town!"

"I think we all know that there is already more corruption than we want and less virtue than we need in Pioneer Vale without her meddling, thank ye very much," said the feisty woman.

"Her wicked arts can change a man in unnatural ways."

"Then perhaps instead of this tribunal wasting its time watching you fumble about in your clumsy attempt to provide any evidence of real substance, we should instead take a census of the town," said Dorothea. "I dare say that we have a few less men and a few more toads among us these days. Which may I set to your name, Parson?" Raucous laughter filled the hall, and Reynolds felt the heat rise up in his cheeks as Anne-Marie's longtime friend belittled his argument against the accused woman.

Gideon Carter, the town carpenter who had been chosen as the head of the council, pounded his gavel onto the table. "Enough of this," he bellowed. "Parson Reynolds, we do not seek to make a mockery of your charges, but I must in fairness agree with Goody Brenner in this. You have given us little to consider as proof of the accusations leveled against Anne-Marie Carmichael. Have you anything more conclusive to bring forward?"

Corbin looked over at Anne-Marie and was shocked to see pity in her eyes as she stared back at him. She lowered her head, and he felt the crushing weight of guilt wash over him. Reynolds spun away from her only to face the shadowy corner of the hall where Preston Mathers watched him conduct the proceedings with a steely gaze and mocking grin. Corbin felt the moneylender's icy stare pierce his soul as the despicable man chewed on the end of his clay pipe. The parson closed his eyes, hoping that he appeared to seek guidance from above, as he slowly leaned against the podium. He sighed and braced himself, gathering his resolve before he looked into the crowd once more.

But then he saw her.

His beloved Madeline sat in the gallery watching him with an adoring smile on her lips. Her breathlessness appeared no less than those who sat near her, but Corbin knew there was something different to his lover's reaction. The flush that adorned her cheeks was less likely from the day's excitement and due instead from his child that he had burdened her with in his moment of weakness. Reynolds' heart raced as she batted her long lashes at him. His mind wandered to his perpetual daydream of taking her hand, leaving Pioneer Vale, and starting his life anew without his lifelong shame of deception that followed him still. One moment of honor and selflessness was all it would take and he could free the accused and condemn the true evil of the town.

Yet he sighed and clenched his fists for he knew that he lacked the courage to do what was right. A shadow fell across the room as if the sun hid behind a passing cloud, and Reynolds shivered.

"Parson," said Carter. "Are you alright, sir?" Corbin laughed softly at himself and straightened his shoulders as he faced the head table. A broad smile found his face and he held his hands out wide.

"Good folk of the council, I confess that I am somewhat unprepared for today's gathering. I do have an ongoing investigation that will undoubtedly lend credibility to these terrible charges, but...." His mind raced for an excuse, and then he grasped at an idea. "There is a Witch's Sabbath coming along with the next full moon. It is then that I intend to gather the conclusive proof you require that Anne-Marie Carmichael is the very fiend just as I have set forth." Corbin's nails dug into his palms helping him hold the iron of his stance while he silently hoped that no one would see beyond the load of excrement that he had just concocted.

The members of the council conferred in hushed tones for a few moments before Gideon pounded his gavel once more.

"It is the unanimous decision of this fellowship that Anne-Marie Carmichael shall be held in custody until the full moon. If at that time, Parson Reynolds cannot produce any further evidence of the charges that he has placed before us, then this matter shall be concluded and Goody Carmichael released. So sayeth us all." He pounded the gavel and the assembled folk began to talk amongst themselves.

Reynolds watched as Anne-Marie stepped from her podium and walked past the two burly townsmen who waited to escort her back to the stockade. She stopped in front of him, and gently touched his cheek, drawing his eyes back to her when he tried to look away.

"You don't have to do this, Corbin," she said softly. "I know this charade is not of your own making." He followed her eyes as they darted off to the side. Mathers stood with his arms crossed and his foot tapping as he watched them.

"I …." He felt hot tears well up in his eyes as her compassionate stare ripped away the curtain of his resolve. He smiled sadly and shook his head. "I have a duty to protect the innocent from wickedness. Please, return her to the stockade," he said with a wave to the two men who stood nearby.

"Off with ye, witch," snapped one of the guards as he roughly grabbed her arm. Reynolds' resounding slap rocked the man's head back as he stepped between the guard and Anne-Marie.

"With some respect, oaf," the clergyman shouted, drawing all eyes to himself. Corbin straightened his waistcoat and cleared his throat. "Her day of reckoning will come, but her sentence is not yours to pass."

Anne-Marie nodded her head to Reynolds and then glared at her escort. The musket held by one of the men shook. He swallowed hard as his partner rubbed his cheek and then motioned her toward the door. With head held high, the woman led the guards away for the short walk back to the stockade in which she had been staying.

"Well, that was a clever way to buy yourself some time," said Preston Mathers. Corbin whirled around to face the pudgy moneylender who had put him up to this whole thing. "Witch's Sabbath on the full moon? Masterful stroke as long as nobody questions why a sorceress of such incredible power hasn't blasted apart the cell that she has been kept in. Fortunately, I doubt any of these superstitious simpletons would have so errant a thought. At the very least, it keeps her right where I want her a little longer."

"I thought you wanted this resolved quickly," said Reynolds with a snarl. "Wasn't her execution all part of your diabolical plan?"

Preston chuckled and the smoke from his pipe swirled around his head, almost coalescing into the shape of horns before it blew away. "Her eventual execution," Mathers said, stressing the second word, "will be under far different circumstances. I still have need of her and these ragtag peasants appear in little hurry to decide her fate."

"What game are you playing at, Preston?"

"The Carmichaels cheated me out of some extremely valuable land holdings,…."

"Cheated you?" Corbin deadpanned. "By paying off the debt that they owed?"

"...Which I intend to recoup," Preston continued with a glare. "I have set plans in motion that will allow me to claim far more than I had originally hoped, although now the price will be paid in blood."

"I want no further part of your schemes, Mathers. I may be many things but I am not a murderer. I will not have the blood of an innocent on my hands."

"Corbin, you shall be whatsoever I require you to become. Would you have me break my silence of our arrangement? Have you so easily forsaken the reputation of your paramour?"

"You have cornered me into a Devil's Bargain."

"And it is a bargain to which I still hold up my end in good faith, Parson," Mathers said with a wicked grin.

"You are a despicable excuse for a man, Mathers. I pray that I will be at hand whenever your final reckoning comes due. Swear to me again that you will hold my secret, and I shall continue with this farce against Anne-Marie."

"Your secret remains safe with me. Despite what misgivings you think I am possessed of, I am a man of my word.

"And on my word, the Carmichaels will soon pay dearly for their interference."

*　　*　　*

The common room was dimly lit by sparse candles. The music of the place was the clink of coins on the wooden tables as rough-looking men rolled dice, arm-wrestled, and played cards. Villainous laughter over bawdy jokes drowned out hushed whispers of lewd negotiations between the coarse rogues and indecent women in the shadowy corners. Every now and again, one of the men would wave or raise a glass to the private table at the back of the room, sighing in relief when the solitary figure there would nod back in silent acknowledgment.

The seated man's cold gray eyes kept watch over his men. A clay mug sat untouched, the sour ale in it too warm now to drink. He wore a dingy white shirt that had once been finer linen, but sometimes the dirt and blood from so many battles just couldn't get washed away. His hair was honey-gold in color, from his mother's side or so he had once been told, and he kept it short for practical reasons. An enemy couldn't grab what wasn't there, and his aim wouldn't be fouled by an errant strand. His beard too was little more than stubble and had his reputation not carried the weight that it did, one might jest that a little milk and a hungry cat could remove it from his cheeks. There was a deadly calm about him, his lean frame and wiry muscle ready to explode into action at the first hint of trouble.

Tonight, he expected nothing less.

As if on cue, the door to the notorious little tavern swung open, and a hulking shape ducked low to enter the squat doorway, the man's face lost in the darkness of the ceiling's low hanging beams.

One of his men stationed beside the door jumped from his table and blocked the newcomer's path with an upraised hand. The laughter and rowdy antics died away quickly as the brothers-in-arms waited to see if they might find some new sport.

"Private party, friend. Do yerself a favor and drop us whatever coin you have on you then be on yer way," said the bouncer as he poked the giant man in the chest. "Otherwise, somebody might get hurt." The room roared with mocking laughter, but the man seated in the corner, leaned forward in anticipation.

The shadow snarled, and the man's hand struck like a coiled serpent, grasping the bouncer's wrist with crushing force. His other hand shot out in a balled fist that sent teeth and blood spraying across the floor. The other ruffians fell over themselves, spilling their drinks and falling from their chairs. Only a few kept their wits enough to fumble for weapons, and even then their nerve was shaken as the man moved into the light.

The intruder fell into a fighting crouch, full of savage confidence and ready to tear out the throat of the next man who dared to threaten him. The flash of his white teeth stood in stark contrast to the angry purple scar that ran behind the black cloth over his missing eye. His hand hovered above the bone hilt of the knife at his belt, a clear message that gave pause to the battle-hardened cutthroats that he needed no other weapon.

"Stand down," called the deep commanding voice of the man at the back table. "This fellow is my guest here tonight and we have business to discuss. As you were." Weapons were sheathed as hushed whispers and mumbled gripes replaced the laughter from earlier. The commander of the group nodded to his guest and waved his hand toward the empty seat at his table.

"You certainly know how to make an entrance, Master Erickson, or may I call you 'Patch'?"

"You may call me whatever you like, so long as your men understand who they answer to."

"They will follow my orders to the letter, sir, as I will follow yours so long as I like the heft of your coin purse. I am Cyrus Forrester, Captain of Forrester's Reavers, at your service, sir." He smiled. "May I offer you a drink?"

"This isn't a social call, Captain. I hope that your men will prove more capable than your door warden for the tasks I need you to perform. I can't say that I have been impressed by what I have seen so far. Your fee seems a little steep for this bunch of rabble."

Forrester's eyes narrowed and he leaned back in his chair, pointing his finger at Patch's face. "My company's reputation is well deserved and we are more than a match for whatever you would hire us for."

"Is that your trigger finger, Captain?" said Erickson coldly. "If so, then your most prudent course of action is to remove it from my face. Now." He tossed a leather bag onto the table that landed with a heavy clunk and the telltale rattle of coins within.

Cyrus kept his eyes on the brute before him, but lowered his hand and untied the drawstring. He gasped at the cascade of coins that spilled from it. With trembling fingers, he picked one up and bit into the edge, the give of the metal between his teeth assuring him that he wasn't dreaming.

"Those coins are pure gold," he said breathlessly. "I haven't seen so much in one place since we were hijacking the Spanish trade routes."

"Let me be crystal clear where we stand, Captain. I demand the professionalism that your distinctive reputation has suggested you possess.

50

When I give instructions, I expect them carried out without question. Do this and that bag of gold will be but a drop in the bucket of what you will receive. Do we have an understanding?"

"What if I give the order to make sure that you don't get out of here alive? What I have here would set my boys up for quite some time. Do you think you could make the door, Patch?" Forrester put a mocking lilt on the nickname. Erickson leaned forward and grinned.

"How many men are you willing to lose to find out, Captain? I was told that you are a better businessman than that." The two men stared at one another, neither flinching until at last, the cold steel of Erickson's gaze sent a shiver down his spine as no living man had ever done before. Cyrus slapped his knee and started laughing.

"My apologies, Master Erickson. Yes, we have an understanding. Forrester's Reavers await your first commands. What would you have us do, sir?" He picked up the mug on the table and took a swig.

The corner of Patch's lips turned up in the barest hint of a smile. "The first thing is to spend a little of that gold on getting your men cleaned up. Bathed and groomed. I need soldiers, not highwaymen.

"Your time for getting dirty will come soon enough."

*   *   *

Anne-Marie heard the outer door open and threw off the thin blanket that had been on the straw pallet. She ached all over as she might as well have slept on the bare stone floor. It would likely have been more comfortable.

"Good morning, Dorothea," she said, grateful that her friend made sure that she ate well during her stay. She tensed up however when she realized that the shadow that crossed the floor before her was much wider than the slip of a woman could have made.

"I beg your pardon, Goody Carmichael," said Preston Mathers, "but it appears you were expecting someone else." He held a covered serving platter and lifted the lid enough for the wonderful smell to reach her. The moneylender set the tray on the room's table and sat down with his fingers steepled over it.

"Where's Dorothea? If you have hurt my friend in any way, Mathers, I'll…,"

"You'll do nothing," Preston snarled. Then his face softened and he smiled wickedly. "Unless that is, you have actually developed the abilities that have landed you here, to begin with. You have no cause for concern, however. My ill will is reserved solely for you and your husband. Magistrate Lucas merely relieved Dorothea of your meal and advised her to go back to her establishment."

"So what are you doing here, pig? If you think that I am intimidated by you, then you are sorely mistaken. I thought it was rather clear to the whole town that your trial is nothing but a farce. You don't have a shred of evidence to convince anyone of your accusations. They will be forced to set me free and once they do, I will bring the whole town against you when I show them what you've been up to in those hills." The heat of her magic rose with her flaring temper and flames crackled to life at her fingertips. Anne-Marie snuffed them quickly, forcing the conduit of magical energy shut, thankful that the heavy door barred Mathers' view.

"My dear," Preston said as he leaned back in the jailer's wooden chair, "I have no concern for either your trial or the verdict. Did you think that it was ever my intention to allow you a fair testimony? Rather, I have come to have a word with you, witch," Preston said. His lips curled into a sneer on the last word. "You and I both know that you have some information that a certain…predator of our mutual acquaintance requires. I have been sent to make you an offer."

"Shade doesn't want to negotiate. He wants me dead."

"Indeed, he does. And yet still I am tasked with ensuring that the outcome falls within certain guidelines. You should be grateful that, for the time being at least, the beast finds your presence necessary." Preston's eyes narrowed again. "There are those that stand close by you that are not afforded the same courtesy. Tragic accidents can call forth one's day of reckoning so unexpectedly."

"Again, you threaten my friends and family. You and the wolf have a lot to learn about offering someone a tender mercy."

Preston chuckled as he took the spoon from the tray and scooped a large bite of the hearty porridge into his mouth. He sucked in and blew out air as the food burned his tongue. He grabbed a glass of water and gulped it down. "Oh, my that is tasty, I must say. Did you know that I once offered Dorothea a position in my home as my personal cook? Her brutish oaf of a husband refused my generosity in her stead. Ah, but my mind wanders. Where were we?"

"I was hoping to see you choke to death on the next bite you took."

"Ah, sweet lady, your wily charms are lost upon me." His sarcastic grin turned to a scowl. "You do mistake our terms, however, my dear. The tender mercy I dangle before you on Lord Shade's behalf is not for you personally, as your demise is assured. Rather he proposes to minimize the atrocities he will commit for your continued insolence. To put not too fine a point on it, should you refuse to give him the information he seeks, our friend will garishly illustrate for you exactly how far his dark reach extends. The bloodbath that he promises shall be upon your hands, and the implications will be such that the whole town shall hold you responsible. No tribunal will protect you from becoming the very monster that you are already accused of being. Your friends will be lost to you, and any of your surviving family shall be driven from that accursed farm. 'Anne-Marie

Carmichael, the Witch of Pioneer Vale' has an ominous ring to it, wouldn't you say?"

"You don't even know why he wants me and yet you follow him without question. He is a monster that feeds on fear, but you believe that he wouldn't turn upon you? Shade would rip out your throat without a second thought if it furthered his own ends. Has he shared with you what victory brings him? You can't possibly understand the cost of whatever prize he has dangled before you."

"I know not what the beast wants, and frankly I don't care. When he calls upon me again, I shall drag you back to his dark shrine and rip from you the information that he needs. And I do so hope your obstinacy allows me the chance to take those instructions literally. For my cooperation, I have been promised wealth beyond my wildest dreams. I will be the lord and master of the economies of every settlement up and down the coast of this growing land. Ultimately, I shall one day be the Governor of what will become a nation to overshadow all others. Lord Shade has shown me this."

"You will lord over a world of ashes. Shade will destroy everything and leave behind a wasteland of death. If you believe that his plans will end with your rule, then you are more of a fool than I ever imagined, Preston."

"And yet, who among us sits behind bars with their life hanging in the balance?" Preston hauled his girth from the seat and scooped up the key to the cell door. He sauntered over with that same wicked smile on his face. He slid the slender key into the door's heavy iron padlock and then snapped it with a fierce tug. The broken metal rattled into the mechanism's inner workings.

"Since you have time to sit and ponder, allow me to pose this question. How many lives are you willing to give up before I deliver you to my dark ally? Who among your circle shall be the first sacrifice to your stubbornness?" He chuckled darkly and tossed the remains of the key over his shoulder. He waggled his fingers in a mocking wave before slamming the door behind him with an ominous boom.

CHAPTER 5
HUNTING THE HUNTER - 1671

A soft breeze rustled the fallen leaves in the clearing, but the mine entrance was otherwise deathly still. No birds chirped from the nearby trees. No squirrels frolicked in the gnarled and bare branches that canopied the worksite. Tools lay scattered across the ground near the cold smelter. It was as if something sinister leeched forth from the black scar in the mountainous bones that towered overhead, and drained the vitality from the woods. Like a lurking beast, the craggy opening waited for someone to fall unsuspectingly into its maw

Marcus Brenner gripped his musket a little tighter as he watched the place from the nearby bushes. Anne-Marie's directions had been easy enough to follow and the skilled woodsman had found both her tracks and those of the wagon that Preston's men had driven back and forth to the site. He shuddered as his sharp eyes studied the cheerless place, so unlike the forest that the man had hunted and fished in for the past decade. His keen hunter's senses were alive and on edge as he waited for some malevolent creature to reveal itself.

"Pull up your skirts, Brenner," the man muttered to himself as he stepped into the clearing. He made his way to the tunnel opening, peering into the gloom that fell away into the belly of the mountain. He found a lantern sitting on a crate nearby and with a practiced flick of flint and steel he felt comforted in the soft glow that the feeble light brought to the tunnel before him. He slung his musket over his shoulder and drew forth his favored pistol. The weapon, a gift from the town given in thanks for his providing food during harsher times, gleamed in the scant sunlight but soothed the brawny man's spirit in this unwelcoming place. He squeezed the grip a little tighter as he raised the lantern above his head with his other hand and plunged into the shadowy entrance.

Marcus cautiously rounded every twist and turn as he crept through the tunnel, on guard for any surprises. The air grew colder with each step he took, and his breath soon showed up in drifting puffs. He could feel his beard crisping up with frost around the edges of his mouth and nose. He sniffed the air and caught the faint tang of gunpowder and smoke, lending support to Anne-Marie's tale of escape from the clutches of Preston's thugs, caught and killed by an exploded powder keg.

His way was unmet by any threats though and the huntsman soon found the narrow shaft widening into a vast cavern. The wall across from the tunnel mouth glinted in the lantern light and Brenner's jaw dropped open as his eyes adjusted to the murky expanse. He let out a low whistle when he saw the glimmer of unmined gold that climbed in jagged veins up to the shadows of the ceiling.

"Bugger me," he whispered. "The girl wasn't wrong about this place." He took a step closer when a soft scritching noise to one side drew his attention. He whirled with his pistol at the ready but sighed when he saw the flicking tail of a rat darting behind a fallen worktable. Marcus shook his head and laughed softly as he walked over to look for the little scavenger. He stopped suddenly when he saw the rodent perched on the boot of a body lying face down on the dusty floor. Marcus rolled the corpse over and jumped back as the lifeless eyes of Hollister Adams stared past him into space. He kicked Adams' foot, but there was no reaction.

"What were you expecting, you dolt?" the hunter chided himself. The rat chattered at him and then scampered a short distance away beyond his light. Marcus followed a few steps behind until his lantern revealed the corpse of the hulking Landry Cross. Even in death, the brutish man looked intimidating. The pointed end of a broken pickaxe pierced deep into the man's barrel chest, but the wicked grin that creased his burned face made it seem as though he had defied the injury that made his end.

"Always wondered if I could have taken you in a tussle, Cross. Guess we'll never know." The rats had already done some work on both men as some of the more tender bits of their faces had been chewed away. Marcus shook his head and rose back to his feet. He felt something bump against his boot and saw the rodent staring up at him, washing his face with tiny paws.

"Something else you want me to see, little fellow?" Marcus asked. To his surprise, the rat turned and dashed past the edge of the lantern's glow, came back as if to see if he followed, and then disappeared again. He found his unlikely guide sitting on a small pile of gold nuggets, haphazardly spilled from an overturned bucket, but the creature cowered unexpectedly as Marcus neared. With a frantic squeak, the rat bolted away from the hunter and vanished.

The hairs on Marcus' neck stood up as a foul wind carried a mournful howl to his side. He spun around but all that he saw was a shadowy recess at the back corner of the cavern. Slowly, the huntsman approached, acutely aware that the light from his lantern did little to pierce the inky veil of darkness as it did in the rest of the chamber. This was the place that had given Anne-Marie such a fright. It was here where he would find the proof he needed to clear her name. Marcus swallowed hard and scowled. With the weight of the pistol in his hand bolstering his courage, he plunged into the tunnel.

The darkness drew him deeper into the bowels of the mountain. Hissing whispers taunted him from the edges of the lamplight as he made his way down the tunnel. The rictus grins of long-dead skulls interred in the walls jeered at him as he passed by. The scrape of a shuffling footstep echoed off the worked stone walls ahead. Marcus closed his eyes and took a deep breath to steady himself. Soft wails moaned in his ears and icy breaths of air lingered along his arms like the caress of ethereal fingers. He gritted his teeth, and snapped his eyes open, ready to face whatever horror might have shambled up to greet him, but the tunnel ahead remained empty.

"Tricks of the wind," he muttered. Brenner shook his head and pressed on.

The air grew warmer as the chamber opened up. The dim lantern light fell upon the empty barrows carved in the worked stone walls, and the crunch beneath his boots dispelled the mystery of where the formerly interred had gone. He had spent enough nights around hunting trip cook fires to recognize the smell of burnt bone that lingered in the air and flakes of ash drifted in the currents captured by the lantern's beam. The floor was littered with charred debris, the leftover remains of some unseen conflagration. When he knelt down, Marcus was surprised to still see glowing coals and feel warmth coming from them.

Not only were these flames recently set, but it had burned hotter than any bonfire. His brow furrowed as he set down the lantern and scratched his beard. The explosion that had finished off Cross and Adams would not have thrown debris all the way into this room. There were too many twists in the passage and it certainly shouldn't still be as warm as the remains of last night's campfire. Marcus made a note to mention that to Anne-Marie when he got back to town.

A deep echoing chuckle shook the room sending cascades of dust from the ceiling and walls. Smoldering torches sprang to life one by one as a sudden terrible breeze swirled up the embers. The woodsman shielded his eyes as the glare dazzled his vision, although the shadows were still thick outside the small spheres of light. Images at the edge of his sight still loomed and twisted beyond his splayed fingers. He lowered his hand and gasped as he saw the platform ahead.

A stone altar on a raised dais presided over the cavern floor. Dark stains ran unevenly down the sides, and he could taste the metallic hint of blood in the air. Troughs etched into the edges of the granite were thick with clotted gore and sticky wisps of matted hair from past sacrifices. Marcus covered his mouth and nose with his free hand as the stench rose from the sacrificial table. He felt the heat of bile in the back of his throat as the thought of this terrible place so near the peaceful town turned his stomach.

A low growl from above his head snatched him out of his reverie, and Marcus' eyes darted up. The shrine's ceiling was lost in the darkness until two hellish red sparks began to kindle from within the shadows. The darkness melted away as their intensity grew, burning through the gloom. Even more horrifying than the bloody altar was the revelation of a great stone carving of a fierce wolf with a rotting muzzle towering over him.

With a deafening crack the great head twisted, reared back, and let loose a bloodcurdling howl. Marcus was thrown to the ground, his pistol launched from his hand, as he curled up in a ball trying to muffle the horrible wail. The baying faded off although the echoes bounced around the chamber. The great statue bent forward and breathed forth a smoky cloud upon the altar. The cloud twisted and rolled, and slowly began to take the shape of a gigantic wolf perched upon the stone. Powerful muscles wrapped around insubstantial bones, snapping and popping until at last a beast bearing that same frightfully decayed muzzle with dull embers in its eye sockets crouched before him.

"What the devil are you?" Marcus asked in a hushed whisper. He frantically searched for his pistol, but it was lost among the remains along the floor.

"Devil indeed, Huntsman," said the haunting creature before him, although the man heard the words echo in his mind instead of his ears. *"For those who find me in this place, I am either Master or Nightmare. Given that I know you have been sent here by that fire-haired witch, imagine which I shall be to you."*

Marcus scrambled away from the dais as the demonic wolf leaped down to the floor. Although it landed on solid paws, wisps of smoke curled up from the impact, as if the beast were not entirely solid. The huntsman knew from the way that the wolf paced slowly back and forth, those hellish red eyes never wavering from him, that he was being sized up as prey. He got off the floor and planted his feet, braced, and ready to fight.

"Come on then," growled Marcus. "You aren't the first wolf that has stalked me, you fiend, although I guess I'll have to figure out how to nail your smoky pelt to my wall." He considered unslinging his musket that was still across his back but knew the creature before him could pounce well before he could take aim. He drew a long knife from the sheath on his hip and brandished it.

The demon snarled and tried to rise on its hind legs. Forelimbs thickened into arms, paws lengthened and split into fingers, but then the torches around the shrine flickered, the beast yelped and collapsed back into the wolf shape.

"Not so bold when your prey isn't running from you, I see," said Marcus with a savage grin. He rocked lightly on the balls of his feet, relieved that his supernatural foe might not prove as formidable as he feared. He lunged forward, stabbing ahead, but the shadows broke apart and his blade whistled harmlessly through the smoke. From the corner of his eye, he saw the shape reform. With a snap of its jaws, all too substantial fangs buried into the woodsman's thick calf. Marcus dropped the hilt of his knife down hard on the beast's head, this time making a solid hit that staggered the creature before it once again turned to smoke and blew away.

"So if you can hit me, I can hit back. Good to know," said Marcus as he backed toward the tunnel that led up and out of this hellish place. He turned his eyes back and forth, wary to not get blindsided by the monster again. His hunter's instinct served him well when he saw the flame of a nearby torch waver as if a breeze passed across it.

Marcus tucked his shoulder and turned a solid sneak attack into merely a glancing blow that drove him to one knee. The inky smoke of the wolf skidded across the stone, but it whirled around and leaped back at him. Fast as the beast was, Brenner's blade flashed faster still, slicing across the wolf's muzzle and splattering the floor with a rotten chunk of meat. Marcus was back on his feet as the wolf retreated to stand before the dais, directly below the massive statue overhead. The smoke twisted upon itself again and rose once more into the fearsome man-shaped demon, but when it turned to face him, the beast held its ground as if unable to approach.

"How long shall you run free, Huntsman? Shall all that you hold dear fare as well? The witch cannot safeguard you forever and one day the blood of your line shall feed my darkness." Marcus said not a word, but spat into the chamber, snatched up the lantern, and ignored the mocking laughter that echoed behind him as he limped back up the tunnel to the entry cavern.

He burst into the main chamber of the mine, stumbling and falling once more as his wounded leg gave out on him. He lay there gasping for air, silently cursing the loss of his pistol. He managed to get his musket from across his shoulders and pulled himself to his feet, leaning heavily on the barrel of his weapon. He had to get back to town and warn everyone about the danger that lurked here and find a way to stop the horror that dwelt below.

"But who do I tell?" he asked himself. Marcus had once literally wrestled with a grizzly bear, but he didn't have the first clue how to fight monsters. A dark thought raced quickly through his mind. What if Corbin Reynolds' accusation was true? How deeply was Anne-Marie mixed up in all of this? The creature clearly saw her as an adversary.

Was the town about to execute the only person who could stand against the demon?

The hunter gritted his teeth and limped toward the tunnel across the cavern that would lead him out of the mine. Witch or not, Marcus refused to believe that his dear friend had any part in the evil that he had seen here. He paused half a moment.

Mathers on the other hand was a different tale.

All of the evidence against Preston clicked into place as he looked around. The mining operation alone was enough to underscore how Mathers had played dirty against the Carmichaels, and only a fool would think that the despicable man was not in league with the beast in the shrine. Certainly more likely than Anne-Marie was.

He pressed on toward the tunnel mouth again when the scratching noise from beyond the worktable caught his attention once more. The brown rat raced forward, sitting up in front of Marcus, looking expectantly at him.

"Out of the way, mouse," he said to the rodent. "I've got people to warn of this place. You should leave too if you know what's good for you." The rat merely twitched his nose and sat in place. Marcus started to step past when cold fingers latched suddenly to his wrist, ripping the musket from his grasp.

Marcus whirled around to see the gray lifeless face of Hollister Adams grinning at him. Landry Cross stepped into the circle of lantern light brandishing the remaining handle of the broken pickaxe still buried in his chest.

"Ready for that tussle, now?" purred the whispery voice of the demon from the shrine below. Marcus threw a solid punch to Adams' jaw, but the corpse shrugged it off with barely a stagger. The Huntsman drew his knife once again and made a backhand slash across Hollister's reaching hand, lopping three fingers from the dead man. No blood ran from the wound and again, the attack seemed to have no effect.

Landry swung the ax handle into Marcus's ribs, but the thick muscles from decades of hard work let Brenner absorb the blow with merely a grunt. He grabbed the wood and grappled with the brute, but slid a step back as Cross pushed forward. Landry had been one of the mightiest men in the Vale when he was alive, yet Marcus suspected that the wolf's magic had boosted the strength of his attacker's arms well above anything that the man could have brought to bear in life.

Adams' icy arm closed around his neck from behind and Marcus felt the sharp pain as the corpse bit into the bare flesh of his neck. He snapped his head to the side, dislodging Hollister's teeth, but he knew that holding Cross at bay with the weight of the other man on his back would soon prove too much.

Marcus released the ax handle and rolled forward suddenly, dipping his shoulder and pitching Hollister into Landry as the larger man lumbered forward. Adams managed to grab a handful of the hunter's bushy beard and ripped it out by the roots. He roared in pain and stumbled sideways as the two dead men tumbled into a heap on the stone floor. The huntsman saw his musket lying nearby and lunged for it, the smooth wood of the stock in his hand filling him with renewed hope. He raised the gun to his shoulder drawing a bead on Landry's rising form. Brenner sighted in right between the shambling corpse's eyes as his finger tightened on the trigger.

A brown blur raced across the floor, and tiny teeth sank into the open wound on Marcus' calf. The hunter howled as the rat darted between his feet, tripping him up and spoiling his aim. Marcus kicked the rodent across the floor, regained his footing, but Landry and Hollister had already closed the distance and reached toward him again. Adams grabbed the barrel again, his teeth snapping as he tried to get close enough to bite once more. The hunter kept the musket between them, but as Cross raised his weapon high above his head, Marcus knew that he was in trouble.

With a mighty shove, he drove Hollister back and away from him. Marcus swung the musket around at Cross, prayed his aim was true and squeezed the trigger. The boom of the black powder echoed around the chamber as the lead ball exploded Landry's head like a melon on the Brenner's practice range. The big man dropped the handle, fell to his knees, and tumbled to the floor.

Marcus faced off against Hollister as the remaining corpse shambled slowly back toward him. He swung the musket at Adams' knees like an ax chopping into a tree, but the musket's stock broke off with the impact. Adams grabbed Marcus' shoulder, and his filthy fingernails raked down the woodsman's cheek. The weight of the smaller man's body fell forward onto him, and his wounded leg simply couldn't take any more. Marcus roared as he fell under the press of the ghoul, struggling as cold hands clutched at his throat with unnatural strength. His battle cry was choked off and the dead man's snarl drowned out the fading echoes that bounced along the walls of the cavern.

Nearby, the little brown rat resumed his perch on the pile of gold nuggets once more, the shadow cast on the floor by the flickering lantern light resembling something more akin to a wolf than a rodent. With the hint of a predator's smile and its eyes now glowing with a dull red light, he washed his face with tiny paws.

CHAPTER 6
AFFAIRS OF THE HEART - 1671

The town square bustled with people frantically milling about. Horses neighed and bucked, aimlessly wandering free among the gathering crowd. Blood stained the cobblestone pavers in the street and the air reeked of filth. All around, the men of the border patrol lay battered and weary, injured, or dying. The company had collapsed where they stood, barely limping home after a battle that they were clearly ill-equipped to handle.

The women of the town acted quickly. They steered the walking wounded to nearby benches, or at least get them to sprawl out in the grass beside the road. Baskets full of bandages and thread for stitching were dropped beside the injured, and taken up by wives and mothers. A few men staggered around, their blank stares revisiting the unseen horrors they had faced on the field, while others wore the more physical scars of the fight. All bore cuts and scrapes, others waved bandaged stumps in the air, and some gasped their last breath as the chaos reigned in the plaza.

Corbin scratched his chin as he looked around helplessly. Rough hands grabbed his shoulders and spun him around. A man from his congregation, wasn't he a woodworker, stared at him with his mouth hanging slack. The patrolman's face was stark white from horror except for the blood that had sprayed across his cheeks like some macabre war paint.

"It was the local tribesmen. They came from nowhere," the man said, barely able to find his voice. His eyes slowly focused on Reynolds and his fingers dug into the preacher's arm. "The woods exploded with them, screeching and yelling. They fell upon us so quickly we hadn't the chance to fight back. If they come to town, we are all doomed."

Corbin pushed the man away and dashed through the crowd. When he glanced back, the dazed man had returned to his listless meandering. A feeble hand grabbed the leg of Reynolds' trousers as he tried to skirt through the crowd, tripping him up and he landed hard on his knees. He cried out as he looked down into the mangled face of another townsman. Half of the man's jaw had been sliced away leaving raw bone and bloody sinew open to the air. Corbin gagged as he kicked his leg free, fighting all the while to keep his breakfast from boiling up into the street. The preacher was at a loss as he stared for he knew that this was yet another man whom he might have known were it not for the horrific injury.

"Please, Parson," rasped the dying man as he reached his trembling fingers toward Reynolds. Corbin could barely make out the words through the busted lips and cloven tongue. "Can you please shrieve a poor sinner so that I can leave this world with a clean soul?"

Reynolds nodded and haltingly took the man's hand, wincing as the man's warm blood squeezed out from their grip. "Of course, my brother. Close your eyes and think only of the waiting wings of the angels who come to carry you home." Corbin mouthed a quick prayer, the words rolling from his lips by rote, and without sincerity. His eyes searched the crowd for Madeline, wondering if her own husband was in this mad throng and was she at his side even now. His attention was drawn back to the task at hand when he felt the man's fingers slacken in his own. A peaceful smile had found its way to what remained of the man's lips.

"At least one of us gets out of this easily," Corbin muttered. He jerked the man's jacket from beneath his head and wiped the gore from his hands before tossing it over the corpse's face. He hustled through the crowd, steering clear of anyone who didn't already have someone attending them. Time and again, he heard wails of "war party" and "ambush" amidst the wails of the wounded. The men around him were volunteers, not soldiers, and their inexperience had cost them dearly.

A thicker trail of blood at his feet drew his eyes to a wagon where the worst of the wounded, those mercifully unconscious from injuries, were loaded to be taken to sickbeds. His heart skipped when he saw Madeline standing near the cart. She struggled to look over the heads of the people that helped settle the patrolmen into the cargo bed. She tried to push past one burly townsman, but he held her back to let the others do their work. Corbin edged closer, hoping to catch her eye.

"Alright you lads," bellowed the cart driver. "Let's get these men out of the street and into an infirmary where they can get patched up properly." A whip cracked in the air, and the horses pulled the cart down the street. Reynolds lipped up behind her and grabbed Madeline by the elbow.

The young woman jumped when he touched her, and her hand rose back as she spun about. She dropped it when she saw him, although her eyes darted furtively about the gathered people.

"Was Horace on that wagon?" Corbin whispered. "Did he survive? What even happened?"

"I have heard both whispers and wails, but nothing of certainty," she said softly. "The common gossip seems that the patrol was attacked without warning and never even got to mount a defense. A few brave men, mainly those that were just driven away, managed to rally and drive off the attack."

"It would seem that none escaped unscathed. How fares your husband?"

Madeline scowled at him. "Do you ask for his sake, or for your own?"

"I wish nothing ill upon him, but the sad state of widowhood would release us from certain circumstances that we skulk in."

"Hush," she admonished. "Are you such a fool that you would discuss this in the streets? Go pretend as though you actually care for these men as many won't see tomorrow's light. I shall find some moment later to come to you." She rushed off, taking some bandages from a basket that another woman carried to the square, and Corbin watched her rush to lend aid to those she could help.

He looked around at the sea of entreating hands that reached out to him, begging him for any comfort or relief he could provide. While others around him knelt down to offer solace, Corbin Reynolds turned his back and hurried away, losing himself among the back alleys and out of sight.

*   *   *

Reynolds sat in his reading chair lost in the shadows cast by a solitary flickering candle. The amber liquor in the glass held loosely in his fingers caught the light as it sloshed and cast an eerie shape across the floor. Torchlight from the town square bled through his small window, but the shouts and cries of the injured and the aggrieved had finally subsided. The silhouette of a hooded figure made its way furtively to his stoop. Pausing just a moment to look over its shoulder, the shadow stepped to the door and rapped lightly. Corbin sprang from his chair and threw open the door.

"Are you going to let me in," said a hushed voice. The figure stood like the Reaper himself, motionless in judgment and hidden away beneath the cowl. The head slowly raised and the preacher realized he had been holding his breath when he saw Madeline's face melt away the darkness.

Reynolds ushered her in, slamming the door and throwing the bolt behind her. His lover threw back her hood and untied the string of the cloak that she had hidden under. Dark circles were under her red-rimmed eyes, and a smear of blood reddened her cheek where she had wiped away her tears with stained hands. The preacher stepped in to take her in his arms, but she slapped him across the face.

"Where the hell were you tonight?" she demanded. "So many of those men lay dying, their wives and children in need of a guiding soul, and you were nowhere to be found!"

"What could my empty words have done?" he shouted back. He rubbed his stinging cheek, then snatched up his glass and drained it in a gulp.

"These people look up to you, Corbin. Any words of comfort from you might have soothed what these men went through. These are our neighbors and so many now face looming hardships with their husbands and fathers dead or maimed."

"I am a fraud, Madeline, and you above all should know that." He turned around and ran his fingers through his hair.

"But you don't have to be," she said from behind him. Her arms wrapped around his waist and gently squeezed. "You have made mistakes, Corbin, but you are a good man at heart. A loving soul."

"Let's see what your Horace has to say about my loving soul," he spat. He broke free from her grip and stormed to the far side of the room. "I watched a man die in the streets today and felt nothing. No remorse. No concern for whomever the poor bloke left behind. I don't even know who the blazes it was, although I have no doubt he sat with his family in my church each week. I searched the crowd for you. Don't you see, Madeline? You are the only person in this world that I have ever given a damn about besides myself. I saw you out there tending and ministering to those folks, the same people that I should have been there for, but do you know what was on my mind?"

"Tell me."

"I wondered only if your husband had survived the assault. If he died, then I could openly court you, and we would have no need to hide our indiscretion from anybody. Your honor wouldn't be threatened, and I could...." He paused.

"You could what, Corbin?" She held his hands but he would not look her in the eye.

"I could find the courage to set free another who suffers because I am a coward and a fool." He kissed her fingers and hung his head. "So, how fares your husband?"

"He lives, and is expected to recover in time."

"Of course, he will," Reynolds said with a snort. "And so we are back to our original plan. How could it be otherwise for one of my fortunes?" He looked at her and cursed himself as he saw how his words struck her. She lowered her head, her bottom lip trembling in the same way it had that first day in the church when she had stolen his heart.

"When the attack began, Horace pulled his men back and tried to form up a line. He ordered them to open fire, and they held the attackers back for a short while. There were so many Indians, however, that they couldn't stop the charge, and the line was breached. He led his men to the wagon where the powder and supplies were stored, but soon the fighting got too close and gunfire was no longer an option. A savage leaped upon the wagon waving a torch and howling like a mad beast. Horace threw himself at the man and wrestled him down to the wagon bed. Everyone in Pioneer Vale remarks about Horace's strength, and he snapped the brute's neck with his bare hands."

"Well, isn't he quite the hero?" Corbin said drily. Madeline ignored the jibe.

"The torch that the attacker carried rolled across the wagon and set a cask of lamp oil aflame. Horace yelled for his men to get clear and he tried to put out the fire with a horse blanket that the cart driver had left behind. He didn't know it at the time, but in his heroism, he found himself astride a keg of black powder. It exploded beneath him and…. Oh, Corbin, we are undone!" She put her face in her hands and shook as sobs wracked her frame.

"I don't understand? He survived. Simply seduce him when he is recovered. Our lie can still carry us forward."

"He is unmanned! The burns were so severe that he is no longer able to father a child!" An uneasy silence fell between the two lovers. "When I begin to show, our secret will be visible for all to see. I will be branded an adulteress and most likely driven out of town."

"Run away with me then." The words leaped from Corbin's lips before he could even consider the implications. "We can leave straight away. Take whatever we can carry and start a new life. Together and far away from Pioneer Vale."

She stepped close to him and reached up, cupping his face in her hands, and kissed him gently on the lips. "My love, where would we go that we would not be discovered eventually? And even though there is little love between Horace and me, he is still my husband. How can I leave his side after he has taken such a grievous injury in the courageous defense of our town?"

"And what if he throws you into the streets once he learns the truth? Do you think his sense of duty will save you when he discovers your faithlessness?" He bit his tongue as he saw the hurt behind her eyes, and the tears struggling to stay contained.

"Our faithlessness, Corbin," she softly amended. "You are as culpable in our situation as I am."

Reynolds' mind swirled with the spiral he had found himself in since Mathers had discovered their tryst. The pressing guilt of how he had now accused an innocent woman at Preston's behest weighed every bit as heavily on his soul as having turned poor Horace Pritchard into a cuckold.

"I am even more a villain in this than you know, Madeline. I beg you to forgive me, although I do not deserve it."

"I have to go, Corbin. Someone will soon notice that I have disappeared." She looked into his eyes, and her lips trembled as if something else lingered there that needed to be said. She instead wrapped her cloak around herself once more, then turned and dashed out the door into the night.

Corbin spun on his heel and kicked the small table beside his chair. The candle that sat upon it sailed off and rolled across the floor, guttering out in the Parson's display of rage as the room plunged into darkness.

*   *   *

"Of the dozen men who were on the patrol," said Albert Jansen, the town surgeon, "only four of them have survived and none will regain their full capacities." The doctor was exhausted and sat heavily in the chair before Preston's massive desk. Mathers sat with his fingers steepled, lost in thought. He gave a quick nod to Patch who stood nearby, and the man poured a shot of brandy and handed it to their guest. Jansen raised the glass to both men and threw it back.

"It would seem that the Vale needs to take some measures to make sure that we are properly defended from the local tribe. Whatever the reasons behind this unwarranted threat, were they to fall upon us unaware, we might be wiped out to the last man," said Preston.

"Our people are farmers and craftsmen. We have no standing militia. I think that a few of the older folk may have served in their youth such as that old farmer, Abel Harmon, and myself included, but for most, those days are long past. We would have to train our younger men to fight."

"Or seek aid from outside of the town," offered Mathers.

"We can't just invite hired thugs to overrun the town despite our fears. The council of selectmen would have to vote on such a proposal."

"A council upon which both you and Magistrate Lucas are members in good standing, yes? Surely, the two of you could impress upon the other members the urgent need for such precautions?"

The surgeon stared a moment across the desk at the twisted grin on Preston's face. "You have something in mind already, don't you?"

"My good man, I ALWAYS have irons in the fire. More importantly, I have the resources to bring such a contingent to the town's aid. Should the measure pass, of course."

Erickson stepped forward and refilled the snifter in Jansen's hand. He capped the decanter and set it on the corner of Preston's desk. He crossed his arms across his broad chest and towered over the doctor, his one good eye unwavering as he silently stood over him.

"You should work on your subtlety, Preston. If I make this play for you, can I safely assume that I am released from our... understanding about certain past matters?"

"I will consider your favor repaid in full, Doctor," said Mathers as he pulled himself from his chair. "Gain the council's support for my offer. Share with them the details of those that you have attended this day and impress upon them that these same horrific ends could befall every man, woman, and child unless we take steps to protect our settlement."

"I will breathe easier once I am free from your service, sir," said Jansen as he reluctantly shook Preston's proffered hand. He turned away and walked toward the door of the study, but paused with his hand on the doorknob. "I hope whoever you have in mind is worth the money, Preston. The injuries I saw on our men were precise and deadly. Not at all what I would expect from a group of savages." He nodded his head and left.

"Is there anyone in this town that you don't have dirt on?" said Patch. He took the glass from the desk and drained the doctor's untouched refill.

"The good doctor doesn't appreciate the economy of secrets. The little malpractice incident that I swept under the rug for him would likely never have amounted to anything. The information and leverage he has given us tonight are far more valuable."

"Such a well-timed disaster," Patch said with the corner of his lip curling up in an uncharacteristic display of emotion. "What preparations do you want me to make?"

"At first light tomorrow, ride out to our colleague's camp and tell him that all is proceeding as discussed.

"We will soon have our war, and all that I have been promised will be mine."

CHAPTER 7
SETTING THE BAIT – PRESENT DAY

Angelica awoke from her nap, sore and tender, but breathing easier. She peeled away the stubborn bandages that stuck fast to the still open gouges beneath. The rips in her belly would still need tending for some time to come, but at least the raw and scabbed tears were no longer life-threatening. She gritted her teeth and replaced the wraps as torn muscles screamed at her. She sighed and pulled a loose t-shirt over her head and stumbled out of her bedroom and down the stairs at the end of the hallway.

Whisperwind's sitting room was rustic but comfortable. She plopped into the soft cushions of the chair she had come to think of as her own and looked across the low coffee table at her mentor. Anne-Marie sipped a cup of tea on the edge of her favorite chaise and watched the antique television that rested in the armoire in the corner of the room. A wisp of lavender fire lazily danced between the crooked rabbit ears that waved drunkenly in the air.

"Too much TV will rot your brain, you know," she said as she absently rubbed her stomach. Her smile faded as she saw the picture on the screen. Construction crews cleared the debris from the lawn of Pioneer Vale High. The scars of Angelica's battle with Aiden stood out like garish wounds on the peaceful town's landscape. A hazy smoke still lingered in the air as men and women in utility vests milled about the rubble. A reporter droned on in front of gathered townspeople watching the scene.

She noted that one cluster of bystanders that waved to the camera were decked out in all sorts of witch hats and brandished brooms in their hands.

"Well, at least they haven't taken up their pitchforks yet," said Anne-Marie, with a roll of her eyes. "Although I'm sure that is only a matter of time now."

"They are still reporting from the school? " Angelica asked. Her mentor nodded. "What are they saying?"

"Nothing new. Everything is all speculation." Anne-Marie turned a hard stare over to her. "They have figured out that the school explosion from the chemistry lab was separate from whatever flipped the bus, though."

"Story's nearly a week old now. This town needs to move on."

"Oh, they have. Two more mutilated corpses turned up in a dumpster behind a local bar."

"Aiden struck again so soon?" Angelica felt sick as the grisly images from another newscast flitted through her mind. "It's as if he wanted them looking for a serial killer. He'll have the entire state police force after him."

"No, they are dismissing that because the attacks are too savage. The sheer ferocity is beyond normal explanation."

"Meaning what?"

"Meaning that they are already baffled because a person can't physically mutilate another human being in such fashion. The spreading rumors carry whispers of the supernatural, and that is why the crowd you see there has gathered. The talk of the town is of sacrifice, demons, and witches." She looked pointedly at Angelica and shook her head. "This has the feel of Old Salem coming back again."

"Yeah, but the authorities aren't going to buy any of that. They are going to look for a rational answer. They'll are more likely to call Animal Control than an exorcist."

Anne-Marie pointed to the television screen. A demonstrator in red face paint and devil horns wrapped his arms around a young woman in a slinky Halloween witch outfit. Their lewd laughter delighted the bystanders.

"Tell that to the unruly mob."

"Those people are celebrating the urban legend. The one that you created, remember? They aren't starting a bonfire and burning effigies."

"Because half of them don't know what to think, and the other half are drunk, Angelica. Aiden has them poised on the cusp of terror, and he is waiting for us to provide the fire and lightning show that pushes them over the edge."

"So no more brawls on the front lawn of the school. Don't worry. Tried it. Do not recommend it."

"At least your foolishness brought one positive note along with it. The community is once more showing their willingness to come together in a crisis. Nice to know that hasn't changed over three centuries."

"How so?"

"They have organized a fundraiser for this afternoon to help rebuild the school." Anne-Marie lightly tapped a fingernail against her lip. "I suppose that I am overdue to make an anonymous donation to the town again."

"You make donations?"

"My dear, there are several community facilities that would bear the Carmichael name if the town knew the truth of their benefactor. Does it surprise you that our town library has some of the best funding and resources in New England?"

"I had no idea. I didn't think that you dealt with things like money living all the way out here."

"Have you not found the page of your spell journal to make diamonds rain from the heavens?" She laughed as Angelica's jaw dropped open. "Child, I was a prosperous landowner within my natural lifespan. The only financial sorcery I have ever really needed was three centuries of compounding interest and a wealth manager that doesn't ask too many questions."

"Good to know," said Angelica. "So when should I start hitting you up for an allowance?"

"Consider yourself cut off until we've cleaned up the mess that you have made first," she said as she arched an eyebrow. "Before we can do that, however, you have to finish your recovery. You shouldn't even be out of bed yet. My herbalism skills are formidable, but even they shouldn't have aided you so quickly."

Angelica glanced away nervously. "I guess it was just the leftover magic still in the room like you said before. I feel much better." She lifted her shirt enough for Anne-Marie to see the bandages. Fresh crimson lines ran across the linen wraps, but they weren't nearly as bad as earlier. "They still look kind of gross, but at least you can't directly see what I had for lunch now."

"Disgusting, but optimistic nonetheless," said Anne-Marie. She blew an errant strand of hair from her brow, and a sorrowful shadow crossed her face. "Dark times are upon us, child. Shade has his pieces in play now, and I can feel his power pressing against our own." She removed the bracer she wore on her left arm and scratched at the inflamed scars on her skin. Angelica noticed that those old wounds seemed fresher today than before.

"Any idea what our next move should be? How do we keep Aiden from adding to his body count?"

"I wish I had a good answer to that. I feel as though we have no choice but to react to his schemes. I would love to find a way to surprise him. Put him and Shade back on their heels for a change of pace. We just don't know where he will strike next."

Angelica stared silently at the television screen and watched the costumed townsfolk dancing and laughing behind the muted reporter. She bolted upright. "Yes, we do. The fundraiser. He could dress up like a wizard and walk right through that crowd without a second glance. That's where we get the drop on him."

A smile spread slowly across Anne-Marie's face. "He needs an opportunity to cause a panic. He won't expect us to hide in plain sight waiting for him."

"All you have to do is rip open one of your gateways and we can drag him back here away from the crowd."

"We might need to try something a little more subtle. We'll need to dress casually. While our Guardian outfits might currently blend in, Aiden would spot us even in that costumed crowd. We stand a far better chance of not drawing unwanted attention if we don't charge in looking like a couple of leather-bound goddesses with our hair on fire. We are still trying to maintain a certain level of anonymity, remember?" She smiled wickedly. "Hope you have washed that accursed hoodie of yours."

"We have to hit him hard and fast. Stop him in his tracks before he realizes he's under attack."

"Angelica, we cannot make an overly...explosive display of our abilities with this."

"Well, I don't expect him to come along if we ask nicely. We are going to have to get our hands dirty on this, grandmother." A dark scowl replaced Anne-Marie's grin.

"And what do you plan to do? Rush out there showering the crowd with lightning and hope that you hit Aiden by chance?"

"I can't believe we are having this debate again," shouted Angelica. "We have a chance to kill the one person who wants to bring the dark fleabag, Destroyer of Worlds, to our home and you want to offer him gingerbread cookies to lure him to the witch's cottage?"

"I want to subdue my son."

"He deserves to be ripped to pieces the same way he did to that girl on the news the other night!"

Anne-Marie lowered her head and shook it slowly. "That is exactly the wrong reason, Child. Your heart thirsts for revenge. When will you learn that this power we have been gifted is meant to protect the world? We are not executioners. We are not cold-blooded killers who can do as we please just because we have the might."

"Yeah, I have looked up the definition of the word 'guardian' before." Angelica flopped back into the chair again. "What if we are too subtle and he unleashes hell on those people? There are folks I have known my whole life out there."

"If we have guessed correctly, Aiden will not attack until there is a large enough crowd. He will want to strike fear far and wide. He wants people talking about his actions to spread rumor and paranoia." Anne-Marie knelt down beside her and lifted her chin. "I promise you that he will not catch us flatfooted again."

Angelica gave a weak smile and then stiffened as she looked past Anne-Marie to the television once more. A reporter stood beside the tall blonde teenager that she had seen nearly every day since Kindergarten. The scrapes and bruises were still fresh on Clarissa's face as she stood beside a table with a large poster of Angelica's track team picture. The words 'Have you seen Angelica Brighton' were boldly plastered across the top and bottom.

"Here with us today is one of the students who was on the scene that night, Miss Clarissa Brenner. Can you tell us what you saw?" The reporter held the microphone out to the girl. Clarissa smiled and gave the camera a half-hearted wave as she pushed a strand of her hair up under the black knit cap she wore on her head.

"Ummm, hi," she said as she stared wide-eyed into the camera. "Well, the whole thing was just terrifying. We were riding along, talking, and joking, and then there was a huge boom of thunder. Next thing I knew we were all rolling around and bouncing off of each other. When we finally stopped, those of us that were able started trying to open the emergency windows. Everything smelled like gas and there was broken glass everywhere. I slipped out of the bus and saw the fuel catch fire."

"I guess the fuel spill burned up before it got back to you? Sounds like you all had a lucky break," the reporter said.

"Luck had nothing to do with it. The only reason any of us got out of there alive is because of this girl." She pointed to the photo on her display table. "My missing friend, Angelica, fought something on the lawn that night. I don't understand how exactly, but I know that she saved us all from the explosion."

"She's going to tell everything about us," said Angelica. "She needs to stop talking about that night." She ran her fingers through the white lock of her hair and let her face sink into her hands.

"It's not what she's telling," said Anne-Marie as she touched her shoulder. Angelica looked up as the older woman snapped her fingers. A spark of flame from her fingertips leaped across the room and froze the image on the screen. "It's who. Look."

Angelica glanced at the television, studied the crowd, and gasped. In the shadows that the news camera could barely pierce, Aiden stood among the bystanders, pointedly staring at Clarissa with a toothy grin plastered wickedly across his face.

"We have to go," Angelica said as she hauled herself from her chair once more. As she shouted, Aiden turned directly to the camera and waved. "Oh, no. Can he see us watching?"

"He senses it and is undoubtedly expecting us. We're going to be walking straight into a trap. Again," she added.

"We won't get another chance to know where he will be like this. Please, he's targeting my friend. He is taunting us, telling us that she is his next victim." She wiped the back of her hand across her eyes. "I can't stand by and do nothing."

"Your wounds…"

"Dammit, grandmother," Angelica yelled. "You can't preach to me about being a Guardian and then tell me to stand aside when someone I care about is in danger. And don't even think about telling me to stay behind. You won't be able to take him alone."

"He wasn't always how you have known him. There was a time when he was nothing more than a boy living in a harsh and wild age."

She reached out and took Anne-Marie's hand. "No matter how you try to convince yourself, how much it hurts, he is not your son any longer," she said softly. "There is nothing behind those soulless eyes anymore but hatred and malice."

Anne-Marie chewed her bottom lip as she stared at the frozen screen. Finally, she rose from the floor and smoothed out her skirt. Angelica saw her brow furrow as she shot her a sideways glance.

"Get ready. We leave in five minutes."

*　*　*

Will Brighton dropped to his knees and felt the burn of his breakfast crawling up his throat as he saw the remains of the deer lying at the edge of the property fence. The former Marine has seen some horrible sights as a soldier and was no stranger to finding wild animal remains left behind by a predator as nature would have intended.

But this defied nature.

The poor young buck was scattered in pieces along the outside of the Carmichael Farms fence line. Blood was splashed all over the trees. The animal's tawny pelt was in gory tatters and riddled by wide tears in multiple places. The bites didn't look like those of a feeding predator, but rather as if the deer had been killed out of rage.

The foothills of Alistair's Climb rose ahead of him, lost in the dark shadows of the ancient trees that towered above. Will peered into the thick underbrush, aware that whatever had done this could easily hide mere yards away and he'd never know it until the creature stepped forward. This parcel was what he and Kim jokingly referred to as the uncivilized side of their farm, and Will found his hand settling on the butt of the pistol he wore whenever he came out this way.

As if whatever did this is going to be stopped by my handgun, he thought grimly. He pulled his phone from his pocket and snapped a few quick shots of what was left of the deer and then wiped the back of his sleeve across his mouth.

Will got up, his keen eyes searching the woods as he backed slowly toward his truck parked on the nearby dirt road that meandered through the farm. His fingers brushed the door handle when his blood ran cold, and his pistol was in his hand in a draw so quick that his beloved daughter, Angelica, had she been with him, would have made some sort of crack about gunslingers of the Old West.

Something was there. Will scanned the tree line, but he saw nothing. Not a bird chirped. Not a squirrel chattered. All was quiet. Deathly quiet. Will stood frozen but nothing moved in the shadows.

Still, there was something oddly familiar, yet sinister, about the faint buzz that tickled the edge of his mind. It made him think of Angie and their last walk in the woods before she had gone missing. He struggled again, as he had so many times, to piece together the foggy details of how she had been with him one moment and then vanished when they had gotten separated, but still came up without answers.

He shook the clouds from his mind and jumped into the cab of his truck. He slammed the door shut, and shivered from something more than just the brisk morning air. He tapped his phone lightly against his chin as he watched the trees and then thumbed open his contacts, tapping the name of an old friend who he had spoken to several times recently during the search efforts for Angelica.

"Captain John Harmon speaking," said the gruff voice on the other end.

"Hey, Johnny. It's Will." The whine of sirens in the background made him wince. He hated bothering his neighbor at the precinct.

"Will, how are you holding up, man?" asked John. There was an awkward pause before the officer continued. "I wish I had some news on Angie, but we still haven't heard anything."

"I appreciate that, John. Actually, I was calling to ask a question between neighbors."

"Oh, hell. What did Billy do now?" John asked with an uneasy laugh, referring to his own son and Jamie Brighton's best friend. "You probably heard about Old Man Carter's gate getting busted last week. Guess that apple didn't fall far from the tree, huh? Reminds me of us when we were boys running loose."

Will laughed politely, but his eyes kept watch over the trees. "We sure caused our share of trouble growing up for sure, John. Actually, though, the reason I was really calling was to ask if you had seen any signs around your place of...something big."

John laughed. "Every time I look at my feet and see my belly hanging over my belt. I'm not exactly the team running back anymore."

"Not to be rude, buddy, but I am trying to be serious a second. I got what's left of a deer ripped all to hell out here on my rear property line. Have you or anybody else seen anything? I'm sending you a picture now." Will forwarded the shots he had taken of the site.

"Jesus, Will," said his friend with a low whistle. "Are you sure that was even a deer?"

"Only because I found a snapped antler laying in that mess."

"Danny Blakely called about a missing cow the other day. His would be the nearest farm to yours over on that side of the Climb, but he said it likely just wandered off. Hadn't heard from him to know if he ever found it or not."

"Think that maybe we ought to give someone over in Animal Control a heads up?"

"Judging from these photos you sent, we may want to call the National Guard." John coughed and Will heard the slosh of a drink near the phone's microphone. "Yeah, I'll give a call over there and let them know we may have a big son of a bitch prowling around out that way."

"Thanks, John. I appreciate that. I'm going to make sure that I keep my stock close to home until we hear more."

"Sure thing, Will. Hey, buddy, do me a favor, will you?"

"What's that?"

"Be careful out there. You guys are far enough out of town that help can't get to you in a hurry if you need it, and with....well. Your family has already been through enough lately."

"You guys do the same. Remember that you and Becky aren't too far from our front door. Anyway, I better get going. Stay safe, John."

The two men hung up and Will gave the tree line one last glance as he threw the truck into gear. He pulled off in a cloud of dust, listing in his head everyone he needed to call and warn that a big predator lurked in the forest.

As the truck lights vanished into the distance, the shadows beyond the fence deepened, darkened, and grew.

CHAPTER 8
OUT IN PLAIN SIGHT – PRESENT DAY

George Thorogood growled over the Bluetooth speakers as Ben rinsed the soap suds off the flask that Aiden had given him the other evening after the bar fight. He wasn't even sure why he had held on to it. Something in the back of his mind screamed that he needed to avoid that guy like the plague, but making good decisions in life was still something he had yet to be accused of. Ben liked what George was telling him though. He should probably do his drinking alone from now on, given the choice.

He couldn't put his finger on exactly what it was that creeped him out about the guy. Aiden wasn't anything other than friendly, but he gave off a bad vibe. Take those two Roughnecks in the parking lot. His bar buddy had jumped at the chance to fight them like a....

Like a wolf pouncing on wounded prey, his mind finished. Ben shivered and couldn't fight the urge to look over his shoulder, even though he knew he was being ridiculous. Nope. Nothing there except a days' old basket of unfolded laundry on the floor, and a half-eaten bacon, egg, and cheese biscuit on the kitchen table.

He put the flask into the dish drainer and then reached into the soapy water. Ben cried out and then yanked his hand back as an unseen knife, lost in the bubbles, sliced through his hand.

"Dammit," he said with a hiss. "Hibble karma strikes again." He snatched at the spool of paper towels beside the sink, giving a sharp tug to the loose sheet. Instead, the roll twirled like a top and dumped far more than he wanted straight into the water, ruining them. He laughed in spite of himself as he tore off a piece and wrapped it around his bleeding hand.

His thoughts drifted back to the strange young man. Maybe the guy was just a drifter and he'd never see him again. Hell, might already have left town. Ben remembered though that Aiden said he was related to some of the locals. He sighed. He'd just have to figure out a way to make the guy leave him be.

The sun flashed in the window over the sink and caught the big purple stone on the flask just right. A blinding flash of lavender light shot into the doctor's eyes. He reeled as purple spots jumped and frolicked in his vision.

"Is the whole damn world after me today?" he griped as he snatched the flask from the strainer. He carried it over to the trash can and stomped on the pedal that opened the lid. For some reason though, he couldn't drop the flask in. He looked carefully at the silver metal and the gems that adorned it. He searched his memory for their name. Amethysts? He tried to recall if they were worth anything and shrugged.

Ben lifted his foot and let the lid fall shut. He walked over to the corner of his kitchen and opened up his makeshift liquor cabinet. He looked through the various bottles and finally decided, upon Mr. Thorogood's suggestion, on a label lost toward the back of the shelf. He unscrewed the cap and filled the flask up to the top, and then polished off the last swig remaining in the bottle. He chucked it into the recycling bin against the wall and then joined in the song, terribly off-key, as he stuffed the flask into his back pocket.

"My whole family done give up on me...," Ben warbled as he went off to find his first aid kit.

*   *   *

The crowd milled around as the two women stepped out of the alleyway. The cold breeze made it easy to justify hiding their faces. Angelica wore her Pioneer Vale Minuteman sweatshirt, a black knit beanie, and blue jeans. Anne-Marie had surprised her by donning a simple fleece-lined jacket, with a purple scarf wrapped loosely like a hood over her coppery mane. She couldn't suppress her grin though to see that her teacher still wore the polished black boots of what she had started calling their battle outfits with her dark trousers tucked inside the tops.

Angelica nodded toward the middle of the square where Clarissa handed out flyers to everyone who passed by. "She's safe so far. That's a relief."

"It likely means that the wolf is circling his prey. Be alert. He knows we are coming for him and could spring at any moment. Let's not give him the chance to surprise us." Angelica absently rubbed her stomach and caught the frown that flashed across Anne-Marie's face. "I need you to tell me honestly. Can you do this? I can't watch over you and defend against Aiden too."

"I'm fine," she snapped. "When your son shows his face, I'll be ready. Will you?"

Anne-Marie rolled her eyes. "Need I remind you that all of this is the result of the last time you rushed off against my counsel?"

"No, please don't, and I won't remind you that I figured out where he would show up so that we could put a leash around his neck. I'm going to get closer to Clarissa. You just make sure your pride and joy doesn't get the drop on us." She spun away from her grandmother and blended into the crowd, making her way toward Clarissa's table.

Angelica kept her head down as she pushed through the press of people. She knew she was being childish and that Anne-Marie was right. The construction crew cleaning up the rubble, the fundraising efforts to rebuild the school, and especially all the casts and bandages worn by the students milling about the lawn were all her responsibility. She had been shown the awaiting devastation during her trip to Shade's realm and in her arrogance, she had not only brought it about but had led these people straight into it.

A couple of players from the football team ran past her, one roughly jostling her as they rushed by. Her stomach seized from the sudden bump, and she hissed through her teeth.

"Hey, watch where you are going," she growled.

"I'm so sorry, miss," the boy said as he stopped and turned. He stared a moment as he looked at her face. "Hey, I know you. Aren't you that girl who...."

"Fireworks will begin in just a few minutes, folks," called one of the volunteers over the loudspeaker. Feedback whined in the wake of the announcement, and the young man covered his ears as he turned to the stage. Angelica stole away and vanished back into the crowd before he could return his attention back to her.

How stupid could she be? The worst thing possible was for her to get recognized, and here she was surrounded by the people she passed in the school hallways every day. All someone had to do was yell her name, and Aiden would pounce on her. She needed to get back to the edges of the crowd, find Anne-Marie, and actually listen to her for once.

A firm hand grabbed her shoulder and an icy chill flowed through her body. The wounds in her abdomen came alight with the frigid burn of sinister magic. Her knees wobbled as pain washed over her, but the iron grip of the bony fingers digging into her arm kept her from falling as she was dragged behind a row of parked cars.

"Dear cousin," hissed Aiden in her ear. "I must say that I am surprised to see you out and about so soon after your recent injury." He spun her around, clutching the front of her jacket in his vice-like grip. His eyes seethed with dark energy that danced along glowing red veins that shot through his black corneas.

"How's the shoulder?" she shot back. "You still look a little rosy around the cheeks. Did you get caught on the wrong end of a fireball? Oh, dear, are those electrical burns?"

Aiden snarled and his free hand twisted, his fingers wrapped with coldfire, but Angelica grabbed his wrist. Electric arcs raced up and down her forearm flooding her with the strength to hold him at bay.

"My power equals yours, cousin," she said. Her voice carried the low timbre of rolling thunder as her power manifested within her. "You have no advantage over me."

"You don't want to do this here," Aiden said in a taunting sing-song voice. He smiled and his teeth gleamed. "Think of all the friends you'll endanger." The crowd broke around them both, oblivious to the supernatural power struggle that quaked within their hands.

"You're right. Timing is everything," Angelica said as she saw the last of the crowd move past where she and Aiden stood. The young Guardian's lips pulled back into a wicked grin, and her eyes were lost in blue-white light as she heard the hiss of a bottle rocket firing into the air.

Her blast of lightning threw Aiden across the ground just as the sky lit up with the snap and bang of the first launch of the firework display. Her cousin's howl of pain was lost among the oohs and ahhs of the bystanders. Angelica watched the smoke rise from the fallen apprentice's back as he skidded to a stop across the pavement. The sound of Aiden's teeth as they clacked together was music to her ears. She drew in an eddy of magic that swirled nearby, ready to unleash her full fury on him as he forced his spasming muscles to lift himself away from the ground. Crackling power filled her hands but before she could take a step, a swirl of red hair stormed past her.

"Still not subtle," Anne-Marie called over her shoulder as she marched by and stopped in front of her fallen son. The toe of her boot tapped on the ground in front of his nose.

Aiden shook his lowered head and chuckled. "Hello, mother," he said without looking up.

"Aiden," Anne-Marie said simply. She grabbed her son and hauled him to his feet, holding him at arm's length. Angelica watched the silent stare down, waiting to see who dared to strike first. She cradled a ball of lightning in her palm ready to jump in.

"Is this where we are supposed to fall into each other's arms and forego the enmity of the last three centuries?" he finally asked. "I am afraid you will be sorely disappointed if that is the case."

"She's not here to ask for a backlog of missed Mother's Day cards," said Angelica as she circled behind Aiden. She rolled her eyes at the blank look shot over his shoulder at her with a quizzically raised eyebrow. She snapped her wrists and the air became charged with her withheld power. "You really need to brush up on some pop culture. You're going to miss out on a lot of my jokes."

"I think your fun and games are over, cousin," he said with a sneer and then turned back to his mother. "Do you plan to openly murder me in front of this crowd? Show the world what monsters the legendary Witches truly are?"

"We aren't killing anyone," snapped Anne-Marie. Angelica ignored the pointed look shot in her direction. "Aiden, can you not see through Shade's lies? He has promised dominion to so many others before you but were he to succeed, you will only rule over a burned-out wasteland."

"Been there. Seen it," said Angelica.

"You are not helping," snapped Anne-Marie.

"What? I am agreeing with you."

"You both still miss the grand picture," Aiden replied cooly. Angelica drew back her fist, enshrouded by crackling sparks, but he raised his hands protectively in front of his face and took a step away from the two women. "My lord, Shade, will leave enough people to satiate his hunger. Those who survive will become cattle." He spread his arms wide and cocked his head. "And a Carmichael shall run the farm once more. Ironic, don't you think?"

Coldfire raced up and down his arms, and Anne-Marie jumped, her head whipping back and forth.

"Aiden, you'll reveal us to the world. Quench your flames."

Aiden's smug grin grew wider. "But don't you see, Mother?" His smile melted away and a shadow passed over his face just long enough to cast the ghostly likeness of a wolf across his features. "I don't care who sees."

He lunged forward, the black energy from his hands blasting forth in a bolt of midnight black force. Angelica saw a flash of lavender fire and felt a punch to her chest as Anne-Marie's blast shoved her out of the path. Her mentor's jaw fell open as she watched Aiden's deadly beam race past. Too late, Angelica saw that they had never been the targets of his attack as the coldfire missile hammered into the backs of the fireworks crowd.

Screams of surprise and terror filled the night as the coldfire ripped through the spectators. The gray flames split anew with each person they touched, spreading in a chain reaction that burned its way through the audience. Anne-Marie threw up a series of lavender shields that deflected and diverted the bolts before they could punch any deeper into the throng.

Angelica spun away from the devastation and unleashed a stream of electricity at Aiden. Her enemy let go of his own assault and raised an inky shield of swirling smoke that drew in the girl's magic. Like a growing thunderhead about to burst, the roiling cloud flashed with blue-white flashes of unbridled power as Aiden lifted his arms above his head. The storm between his hands cast a dark shadow over his leering face, the bursts of light reflecting in the consuming black of his eyes.

"Fear the Witches of Pioneer Vale, people!" shouted Aiden. He threw back his head and howled into the rising maelstrom that the outpouring of magic whipped up. With a twist of his hands, as if merely wringing out a towel, Angelica's pent up lightning flashed forward, blowing aside young and old in its path. The arcing power reached out to the construction scaffolding across the lawn that the stage had been built under. Like a twisted snake, the coils of power twisted around the metal framework. Bolts pinged out of the metal like the ricochets of bullets. Chunks of brick exploded into clouds of red dust, and, for a few unlucky souls who stood too close, furrows were ripped through flesh.

Anne-Marie whirled around, the agony of such betrayal stamped on her face as tears ran down her cheeks. "How could you?" she whispered.

Aiden's teeth flashed white under his curled up lip. He stepped forward and grabbed the front of his mother's jacket. "I should ask that question of you first." His free hand pulled backward, and Angelica saw the glint of metal.

Before he could lunge, the shockwave from the thunder harnessed into the palm of her hand boomed, and threw Aiden away from Anne-Marie while her mentor was knocked safely aside. The knife that Aiden held twirled blade over hilt and vanished in a puff of greasy black smoke.

Aiden came out of the tumble and rolled up on his knees. His hand lashed out, but his gaze was beyond Angelica. A wash of energy flowed past her, and he clenched his fist. With a fierce pull, like playing tug of war with an invisible rope, Aiden hauled back. She gathered her magic once more ready to unleash her fury on her kneeling foe, but Aiden threw her a mocking wave as a portal of black smoke swirled around him, and then he was gone.

The wail of screeching metal drowned out the panicked cries of the crowd at her back. Anne-Marie staggered up to her side and leaned on Angelica's shoulder.

"The scaffolding...," she said as she pointed through the terrified throngs. Angelica spun around and gasped.

The metal tower that Aiden had turned her lightning upon wobbled and swayed in slow protest and broke free from its moorings. It pitched forward, casting a shadow that reached toward the scattering people trying to escape, like a giant hammer ready to strike. The crowd erupted in chaos. People screamed in terror as they fought and shoved in search of safety. Angelica held her breath as she watched people running but a sudden movement caught her eye. Two children crouched near the bushes holding each other and crying in the face of the turmoil around them. There was no one else nearby.

She knew that she had no other choice.

Angelica raced past the screaming onlookers and threw her hands into the air. Twin bolts of white-hot lightning lashed out, wrapped around the metal, and caught it in mid-fall. Her magic raced along the beams, and the Guardian felt the brunt of the tower's weight as she held it aloft.

"Somebody grab those kids," she yelled, but the few people who were still close enough to her stood in mute shock. "Please," she said with gritted teeth. "I don't know how long I can hold this." Blood ran from her nose and she staggered as the dizziness from such a mighty outpouring of magic strained her body. The slashes in her stomach sizzled with pain and howled as raw magical energy scorched her shirt. She gritted her teeth and maintained her grip, even as the demands of her power drove her to one knee as the agony coursed through her.

Her hold on the scaffolding wavered and a pipe shook free. It tumbled lazily end over end and bounced on the concrete with a loud bang. Someone from the crowd behind her screamed, and the terror in that cry felt almost tangible as if the raw emotion could manifest into something real.

Something that could be fed upon.

At that moment, the world spun around her, and the lightning roaring forth from her fingertips flickered. The Whisper drifted in and out, not because of her fading consciousness, but because she felt her connection being forcibly sundered. "Not yet," she begged. "They don't deserve this." She saw the two kids watching her, their mouths open in screams that she couldn't hear over the sound of her own pounding heartbeat. A wolf's shadow passed before her on the ground and then faded away before she doubled over, and fell to the concrete.

Boots crunched on the sidewalk beside her as Anne-Marie stepped forward with her arms held high. The wind tore away the scarf around her head and her fiery red hair swirled in the rising gale as lavender flame erupted around her outstretched hands. The bolts of fire shot forth, dancing beneath the falling framework, and held the scaffolding in a cradle of fire, taking up the task that Angelica's own lightning had failed.

A blond-haired blur raced in from the other side of Angelica's hazy vision, ducking low under the framework just above their heads, and dashed toward the two kids. Clarissa took their hands and dragged them into the safety of the parking lot. A woman ran up beside them and threw her arms around the children, showering them with kisses and tears of joy.

"You're clear," shouted Clarissa over her shoulder. Anne-Marie released her magic and the scaffold tumbled to the ground with a teeth-rattling crash. The flashes of dozens of cameras surrounded them, and Anne-Marie shielded her face, hiding her face as best she could. Angelica tried to lose herself within the depths of her hood but when she glanced up, she found herself looking straight into the tear-filled eyes of her lifelong best friend.

"It's really you," Clarissa said. "You're alive."

"Hey, Bumpkin," she said softly.

"We have to go," said Anne-Marie as she took Angelica's arm, helping the girl to her feet. "Aiden is gone, and we aren't safe here anymore." She pointed as several police officers pushed their way through the staring crowd. Angelica noted how the crowd cowered at the mere motion of the woman's hand passing over them.

"This is bad," she muttered.

"Get out of here," said Clarissa, taking her friend's hands. "I'll stall them, but please find me later."

Angelica hugged her, and nearly collapsed into her arms. "You have to play dumb about me for now, though. This is too big to explain."

"Angelica," said Anne-Marie, a touch of panic in her voice.

"Hold it right there," shouted an officer. His hand trembled over the butt of his pistol. "Put your hands where I can see them."

Anne-Marie raised her hands in the air and turned her back to the approaching policemen. She gave Clarissa a quick wink, and then with a roll of her wrists and a flash of purple fire, a portal ripped open around them.

Angelica saw Clarissa's jaw drop open just before they were whisked away. She knew that the police would find no sign of them other than a slightly scorched bit of grass and a hint of the scent of lavender in the air where they had stood a moment before.

*   *   *

The police had asked their questions, taken statements, and generally restored order to the grounds at the school. A large group of people in various witch outfits hollered and cheered as they snapped selfies around the fallen scaffolding and the still smoldering spots on the lawn.

Clarissa hugged herself tightly, trying to ward off the evening chill. Her knees shook as she stared at the hole in the school wall where the Chemistry lab had been. Beside her, the deep scars in the grass where the bus had flipped and slid looked like claw marks of some monster that had torn the ground asunder. The last few days had held one trauma after another, but she took hope in one thing amid the rampant chaos around her.

Angelica was alive.

Not only had she come back from the woods in one piece but was now a part of the great mystery regarding their local urban legend. Twice now, her best friend had come out of nowhere and saved the day with lightning flashing from her fingertips. Clarissa shook her head as she rolled a piece of scaffolding with her toe. If only she could get a few moments with Angelica to get the story behind that.

"Excuse me, Miss Brenner, is it?" said a voice from behind her. She sighed and turned around.

"I already gave all the statements I can give," she said as she looked at the young man in the denim jacket before her. He smiled warmly, but there was something almost sinister in his grin, like a predator sizing up his next meal, that unsettled her. Not a good vibe to get from a plainclothes officer, she thought. "I really don't know anything else about what happened here today, Officer...?"

"Aiden Carmichael," he said. His grin widened as she arched an eyebrow. He grabbed her arm in a steely grip of ice that burned through her jacket. "Allow me to fill you in on some finer details about your friend that you aren't aware of."

CHAPTER 9
LICKING THE WOUNDS – PRESENT DAY

Angelica dropped to her knees on Whisperwind's floor. Her stomach twisted and she coughed up a gout of blood onto the wood boards. "What happened back there?" she croaked. "I couldn't hear the Whisper. I thought I had purged Aiden's poison from my body?"

She leaned on Anne-Marie as the older woman put a steadying arm around her waist and effortlessly held her up. It took some concentration to keep her legs from wobbling beneath her. Angelica nodded her thanks and stepped away. The older woman shook her head.

"No, it wasn't the venom, for I felt it too. At that same moment when the crowd's fear peaked. Shade's might surged strongly enough that he reached across the realms and dampened our magic. He can't silence the Whisper completely, but he can make it more difficult for us to hear if there is enough terror to boost his own strength."

"He's turning the barrier from a brick wall into tissue paper. He's closing in on us."

"The walls that hold him have thinned before, yet even at its most fragile, the Guardians have ever held the wolf at bay." Anne-Marie lifted Angelica's chin so that she could see her piercing eyes full of fire and determination. "We are nowhere near defeated."

"I dreamed of this. When I needed it most, I couldn't find my lightning. This fizzle is going to be another of those prophetic moments, isn't it?"

Anne-Marie hugged her tightly. "Our paths are not set in stone. This is but one more of his tricks to make you fear him. You give Shade power by doubting your own strength. Calm your mind and listen. Tell me what you hear."

Angelica closed her eyes and found the thread, the thrum of power that was like a live wire running through her core. She sighed and nodded.

"It's there. Just like it should be."

"You see. Now you need to leave it be so your body isn't taxed by any further use of your strength. My son will not sit idle for long knowing that he put us on our heels today. We were fortunate that no one was more seriously injured." She ran her fingers through her coppery mane and with a whisk of her hand she opened the fiery lavender portal behind the fireplace that led into Whisperwind's extra-dimensional spaces. "I need to go down to the lab. I think I know of a poultice that will help those who fared the worst."

"Do you have one that'll bring the world back from ashes?" Angelica snapped.

Anne-Marie stopped and turned. Her tired smile melted away into a deep scowl as she looked over her shoulder. Angelica crossed her arms and tapped her foot.

"What did you say?"

"You should have blasted Aiden when you had the chance. I put him down. You could have taken him out." The girl leaned heavily on the nearby chair and yanked up the bottom of her sweatshirt revealing the blood-soaked bandages across her belly. She tore the wrappings loose and threw them on the ground, putting the garish raw gouges in plain view. "After you've had a good look at these, I want you to pull off that bracer you wear on your arm and look at that bastard's fingerprints. Shade left his marks on us while we were actually trying our best to fight him. What do you think he'll do if we go into this halfheartedly? We'll be lucky if we walk away at all. And if that happens, then it's adios, Muchachas."

"How dare you speak to me like that," Anne-Marie growled. Purple fire erupted around her body, but Angelica stumbled forward and grabbed her teacher's wrist, reaching through the flames with her own hand ensconced in a sheath of crackling lightning.

"Every vision they have shown to me, that's the common thread. Everything burned to the ground. Aiden intends to help Shade bring about the end of the world. I feel like I am doing all of the fighting by myself while you keep pining away for your lost son. He's not the baby you bounced on your knee 400 years ago. He is a sadistic murderer who will not stop until our bodies are on the top of the pile. Then it'll be Shade's turn, and we both know how that will turn out."

"Aiden could become our greatest potential ally in the fight against Shade. If we can bring him back to our side, he knows the wolf's mind unlike any other. We have to show him how he is being manipulated."

"He isn't going to turn traitor," Angelica shouted as she pushed the other woman away. "Didn't he make that clear enough to you when he coldfired the crowd? He won't stop. Shade has promised him everything he ever dreamed of and it doesn't make one damn bit of difference if it was all a lie. It's one that he believes and he has the demon's strength behind him to make it happen. You can't keep holding back against him."

She watched as Anne-Marie's hard stare softened, and the proud Guardian lowered her head. "You are asking me to kill my boy, Angelica. I stood right there beside you and watched the smoke from your attack roll from his jacket. And, yes, even though I knew that he was a threat, I hesitated."

"When we first met, you said I was here to help you save the world. Are you sure that I'm not here to help you save yourself?" Angelica took her grandmother's hand and gave it a gentle squeeze. "You carry centuries of guilt on your shoulders. I see how it weighs on you. Maybe all this time, you have held out for a Firstborn to come along and finish the task that you can't bring yourself to do."

"Is this where the student becomes the teacher?" Anne-Marie asked with a tired laugh. Angelica saw pride in the woman's eyes as her grandmother looked up at her. "So many have died in this war. I want only to save one of my children from that black-hearted beast's claws." Silence hung between the two women until a log popped in the fireplace sending a rainbow of sparks into the air.

"And what if one is all you can save?" Angelica finally asked. "If you have to make a choice between him or me, what will you do?"

Anne-Marie shook her head. "Don't ask that question, my dear. I hope never to learn the answer to it."

Angelica looked into the fireplace and then lowered her head. "Guess that makes two of us then."

"Get some rest, my dear, please, while I tend to my work downstairs. We need to recover quickly. I fear Clarissa is still in grave danger. Aiden may have just used her to draw us out before, but I worry that he can use her to divide our protections."

"How do you mean?"

"Until now, he has kept our vigilance focused on your family at the farm. He couldn't attack there because he knew that was the one place we expected him to strike, and he undoubtedly sensed that I had placed certain wards around the property to let me know if he ventured too close. Now, however, he has a second target that he can threaten, and I can't maintain my watch over them both. Using that much magic would eventually take its toll on me and I would be useless when we tried to stop him. With so small an effort he has split our focus. He knows that he can't defeat our combined strength, so he continues to keep us guessing where he will strike next."

Angelica turned and staggered over to the cottage door. "All the more reason we needed to hit him at the festival." She held up her hand as Anne-Marie started to open her mouth in protest. "Forget I said it. Look, I'll be back in a little while. I want to get some air. If it's any consolation," Angelica said as she rested her hand on the door handle, "you looked like a total badass when you were holding up the scaffold. You showed me, at least, what a real Guardian looks like. I'll be back in a little while. I don't think my wounds will let me go too far." She pulled open the old oak door and wandered out into the garden.

*   *   *

Anne-Marie watched the girl sit down on a stone bench among the purple and blue wildflowers, plucking petals and letting them fall aimlessly to the ground. She wanted to step out and take Angelica in her arms, comfort this incredible young woman forced to be brave in the face of such a terrible ordeal for no reason other than that she was Anne-Marie's own blood.

Despite the girl's words, she felt less than heroic. The echoes of people shouting the word 'Witch' over the centuries haunted her still, and it had not stung any less to hear it in the panicked cries of the townsfolk today. More innocents had suffered today because of a battle they didn't even know existed.

Or what it had cost her.

She absently toyed with the amethyst pendant at her neck, feeling as she so often had over the many decades that a glimmer of power pulsed through the simple gem on its gossamer silver chain into her fingers. She fought the urge to rip the stone from her neck and hurl it into the woods, smiling to herself as she thought of how many times over the years that had crossed her mind as well.

But something always stayed her hand, and she felt the reassertion every day. It was the call of destiny, just as her beloved had told her ages past. Too many memories, too many tears, were tied up in that simple piece of jewelry, and she could never lay it aside, or the burden that had come with it, with a clear conscience.

She owed it to all of her fallen children that Shade had stolen from her.

"One last time," she whispered to herself as she watched Angelica coax a squirrel closer to the bench with some berries from a nearby bush. She whirled on her heel and approached the fireplace, the lavender flames leaping once more to the ceiling and then snapping shut as the Guardian passed through the portal into the dark hallway beyond.

*   *   *

Ben lifted his eye away from the microscope and blinked a couple of times. The skin sample taken from one of the burn victims was unlike anything he had ever seen before. It was an uncanny combination of both burned and frozen tissue that simply defied anything he had heard of in his years as a doctor.

Rebecca stuck her head through the doorway. "Need you out here, Ben. We got another madhouse brewing."

"How is this happening again?" he muttered as he followed her into the reception area. Once more, the Emergency Room was full of people sporting various bumps and bruises from the riot that had happened over at the High School. The lobby was a cacophony of shouted questions about patient locations, release times, and diagnoses, but it was the subdued murmurs that whispered from the shadows that caught Hibble's ears. Lightning. Fire. Magic.

The Witch of Pioneer Vale.

Rebecca cleared her throat and drew him from his reverie. "Sorry, what did you ask, Nurse Harmon?"

"I said, do you have any suggestions for how we should treat these strange burns?"

"I've called around to some of the other departments, but they are just as baffled as we are. If we treat it like frostbite the burned tissue doesn't respond. If we treat it like a burn, we damage the frozen skin."

"So that's a resounding 'I have no idea whatsoever'?" The nurse shook her head. "We'll have 'Riot Part Deux' on our hands if that's how I answer the crowd's questions, Doc."

"Well, dammit, Rebecca, then figure out whatever lies you need to tell them to give them a warm, fuzzy feeling. We're in the dark on this right now," Ben snapped. He lowered his head and held out his hand toward her. "I'm sorry. You didn't deserve that."

"It's ok, Ben," she replied. "We're all frazzled by this stuff. We don't know what's going on and everyone is scared. Have you seen any of the videos popping up on social media? Somebody got a really good one of some redhead throwing fireballs around. Here let me pull it up real quick. With the way it's trending right now, it won't be hard to find."

Ben watched the footage as Rebecca held her phone out to him. He let out a low whistle when the screen went black.

"What'd you think?" she asked as she tucked her phone back into her pocket.

"I think somebody had a pretty good special effects budget. Seems pretty hard to swallow that someone got a picture of your local witch."

"Even with so many other people telling the same story? People who were there and are currently in our lobby waiting for us to treat them? What does it take to convince you, Doc?"

"Have her swing by on her broomstick during office hours," he said with a laugh. "Besides, I didn't think witches showed up on film."

"You're thinking of vampires," said the nurse with a roll of her eyes. "But I'll bet those jets of weird purple fire are why we got a full house again. Might even shed some light on what happened at the school the other night."

"You think that redhead blew out the wall of the Chem Lab?"

"Who knows, but my husband, John, told me that the police would love to question that bitch regardless. She disappeared into thin air. Snatched an injured girl that was laying on the ground and nearly grabbed Clarissa Brenner, too."

"Brenner? The same girl who was here the other night?"

"And dented your snoot. Yep. Seems like someone put a bull's-eye on that poor kid. John suspects that redhead might be kidnapping teenage girls. Maybe the fireworks are just part of the show, but you can bet your ass that the police would love to have a chat with her."

"Well, let's set up a stake and grab some lighter fluid," Ben said. "Isn't that how the old witch hunts went down?"

"You don't need to make fun of us, Ben. We aren't a bunch of country hicks and rednecks, Mister Big City."

"Wow, I just can't say the right things tonight. Good to know I haven't lost that talent." Ben plopped down into a chair and grabbed a random chart. He glanced at it and then threw it back onto the stack. "No, I don't think anything of the sort, and especially not of you. I couldn't manage half of what we do here without your help. It's just that Pioneer Vale isn't that big of a town. Somebody has to know who that woman is, and the truth may be closer to normal than a trending viral video suggests. I have never been in a spot in my life where there seemed to be so much that I didn't have a way to explain, or at least make a reasonable excuse for, but I don't think batwings and brimstone are what we are looking at."

Rebecca stared at him for a second and then cracked a hint of a grin. "I'll take that as an apology, half-assed as it may have been. We have a proud heritage in this town. A lot of families go back a long way here."

"Yeah," he snorted. "I just met a guy the other night who says he's a Carmichael."

She frowned. "Well, that's an interesting one. They were an old family, but I thought that name had been married away generations ago. You have to go back to some pretty early colonial records to find them mentioned."

"So you know of them?"

"Sure. John and I spent a couple of weeks archiving town records a few years ago. I love reading up on the history of the old families of the area. A lot of direct descendants are still around, but the Carmichael name vanished a couple hundred years ago, I would guess. Anyway, shouldn't we get back to business? What's our next move, Doc?"

Ben sighed. "I wish I knew, Rebecca. The ones who were standing at the back of the crowd when the ...whatever it was hit are probably going to need skin grafts. Let's go ahead and start writing up some orders so they can get prepared upstairs. That may be our only choice of treatment for these folks."

"That's not going to go over well, Doc," the senior nurse said.

"Well you can let everybody know that I clearly lack the necessary qualifications for making friends," he replied with a quick grin as he made some notes. A flash of purple light caught the corner of his eye as a warm breeze ruffled his hair and then died away. Ben turned and set his clipboard down beside a worn burlap bag sitting on the counter of the Nurse's Station. Hibble's jaw dropped when he saw his name on a slip of paper pinned to the sack. He looked around to see if he spotted anybody who might have left the parcel, but there was nobody close enough at hand.

"Did someone turn on the heater," asked Rebecca. She fanned herself with a file folder. "Where'd that potato sack come from?" She unpinned the note and handed it over to him.

"I swear that this wasn't here two seconds ago. It's like it just showed up by…," He saw the smirk on Rebecca's face. "Don't say it."

"Magic, Doc?"

Ben scowled at her and then slowly unfolded the note. The paper was of fine quality stationery, thick and heavy. The ink shimmered through every spectrum of the rainbow as the doctor read the glittering script. Hibble held the note where Rebecca could look over his shoulder and read along with him.

"Doctor Hibble, your patients suffer from an affliction that modern medicine has not the capacity to heal. Use these ointments on those struck by the strange burns and they shall mend quickly."

"That ink looks like it's alive. I've never seen anything like it," the nurse whispered. She opened up the bag and removed two large mason jars. An iridescent paste swirled inside as if something stirred within the opaque depths. She cracked open the wax seal on the lid, and the smell of lavender and jasmine filled the air. "Reminds me of that time when I was a kid and we found an old jar of canned beets in grandma's cellar that she had forgotten about. At least these smell better than that one did."

"I still wouldn't eat it either way."

"What do we do with this goo?"

Ben studied the glittering note in his hand again and then looked at Rebecca and shrugged his shoulders. "OK, Nurse Harmon, as the resident skeptic here, I am going to give in to your superstitions. Since we don't have any other good ideas on how to treat these patients, and given that your entire town has gone witch crazy, I am left with only one thought."

"And that is?" Rebecca said as she crossed her arms and leaned against the desk.

"Let's see if there is any magic left in the world."

CHAPTER 10
CHANGING OF THE GUARD - 1671

Micah Robillard wiped the sweat from his brow, leaving a streak of soot in its place. His forge bustled in response to the threat of an imminently looming attack by the local natives that had the town in the throes of near panic. He had been tasked by the town council to turn his entire operation toward the general defense. Nails and metal spars for the new wall under construction, and all of the musket balls he could mold now spilled forth from his shop.

He looked over at young Anders Cooke, a lad just starting to grow the fuzz of his first beard, hard at work setting down the next load of fuel beside the furnace for the next run. Micah had taken him on as an apprentice, more as a favor to the boy's newly widowed mother although the young man had proven eager to learn the trade and, in truth, the smith himself wasn't all that much older than the boy. He smiled, happy that he had been able to help provide the beginnings of a trade by which his apprentice could help support his grieving mother.

"Anders," he called over the final echoing clang of his hammer. "Why don't you finish that haul, and go find a bite for lunch? The builders at the wall are calling for those nails we finished this morning, and I wouldn't mind a break from the heat of this place for a few moments." He reached into a pouch at his waist and drew out two silver coins. With an easy flip, he sent them through the air and Anders deftly caught them.

"Two coins, Master Robillard? Lunch for me won't cost nearly so much."

"Not just for you, boy. Use the extra to get your ma one of those meat pies from the Huntsman. I suspect she hasn't eaten much in the last few days and could do with a hot meal." The young man blushed as he pocketed the coins.

"Thank you, sir. I've been worried terribly over her since Pa passed. I know she has been fretting over how we'd get by. I'll do you proud as your apprentice, sir, I swear it."

Micah smiled and ruffled the young man's hair. "I'm sure you will. Off with you now, lad. Just mind you are back and pouring those musket balls before I return though."

"Yessir," said the young man. "Oh, I nearly forgot. A couple of the men brought some of the broken weapons that were collected from the ambush site. Figured that perhaps you could melt down the metal and recast it, I suppose. I left it in that basket over by the anvil."

"Thank you, Anders. I'll give it a look and see what may be useful to us. Now get along and I'll see you soon enough."

His apprentice rushed out of the forge and Micah stared wistfully after him. His own father hadn't been gone from this world all that terribly long either, but it had been sickness rather than a mortal wound that had stolen his da from him. He felt a kinship with Anders and hoped that he could offer as much guidance to the boy as his own father had been to him.

Micah found the basket just as the boy had said. He studied the pieces and saw more than a few items that could likely be put back into service with a little work. He picked a splintered arrow shaft from the pile, noting the squiggles along the face and testing the edge of the metal arrowhead against his thumb. He winced as a thin line of blood appeared on his skin

113

as the razor-sharp edge bit into his skin. Micah cursed and sucked the edge of his thumb as he absently tucked the arrowhead into a pouch on his belt.

"Enough of these stray thoughts," he muttered as he shouldered a large satchel full of freshly forged nails and a bundle of metal strapping bands. He stopped at the threshold of his forge and spared a glance back to the wicker basket. Something nagged at the edge of his thoughts, like a shadow lurking off to the side that disappeared whenever he tried to see it directly. The smith shook his head and figured that if there was anything truly significant, greater minds than his would have come up with the answers already. He started whistling a catchy tune he had heard at the Huntsman a couple of nights ago as he started off to where the remaining men, their ranks thinned, were hard at work on the new fortifications.

*   *   *

Horns blared and drums pounded as the heavily armed troupe rode into town in a formed up column. No battle standards waved before the rugged men as they proudly passed through the newly finished gate. Faces, though grim and scarred, shot grins and nods to the awestruck townsfolk who lined the path. The worn leather of the gloves and saddles, the scuffs on the metal of open blades, and the smoothness of the wooden musket stocks showed that these were seasoned fighting men, and not merely playing as hired guns. The shrill note of a fife broke the air and the column halted except for the two lead riders who continued forward to the platform in the town square.

Abel Harmon stood nervously behind Magistrate Jordan Lucas, Albert Jansen, Preston Mathers, and Constable Clement Owens. He currently served as the spokesman for the outlying farmers in the matters of the town council and had been outvoted when the good doctor had brought up the proposal for hiring soldiers to protect the town from the threat of the neighboring Nipmuc tribe. While Abel couldn't disagree that Pioneer Vale was desperately short on defenses with the recent ambush on the border patrol, as soon as Preston Mathers had offered to put up the funds needed to hire these men, the old farmer knew something was amiss. Lucas and Jansen had jumped on the vote right away. Owens had acted out of practicality for the general good, but when Abel had raised his objection, the others all had pushed ahead for the vote. Though they had tried to appeal to his past service to the crown before coming to this land, Abel still didn't like the turn of events.

The two riders halted before the railing, not bothering to dismount. The lead man leaned forward in his saddle, his eyes carefully studying each of them. The close-cropped hair and the icy steel in those gray eyes reminded Abel what the hard stare of a killer, seen so often during his own soldiering days, looked like. He wondered just where Mathers had found this crew. Jansen withered before the intense glare, and Lucas took a step back as if the hard man would leap from his horse and grab him. Preston, however, stepped forward, his broad smile taking in his wide face.

"Captain Cyrus Forrester, on behalf of the people of Pioneer Vale, I welcome you and your men and would like to personally thank you for coming in our hour of need. I trust your men will find accommodations to their liking as you set up your headquarters within our town."

The man stared coldly at Mathers, drawing out his silence. Preston's broad smile slowly turned into a scowl, but even he eventually began to shift his prodigious weight from foot to foot.

"You must be Mathers," Forrester said at last as he leveled his finger at the moneylender. The stern face broke into a wide grin. "Your hospitality is appreciated, sir, as is the work. Ending the threat of these savages always brings a smile to the faces of my boys here. My thirty men here fight like ten times that number. We have served together for several years so our company works together with uncanny coordination. You will find that the men of my company are well worth the price we ask for our services. Although, when weighed against the safety of your loved ones, we must surely seem a bargain, yes?"

Abel cleared his throat and stepped forward. "That remains to be seen, Captain, and I for one sincerely hope that we find your time here to have been pleasantly wasted with as little fighting as possible. The Nipmuc people have never threatened our community before, and there are those of us who would prefer to see us treat with our neighbors and find out if any recent offenses may have been the result of our own careless negligence to their traditions."

Forrester threw back his head and laughed a hard belly laugh. "Well said, sir. I assure you that we will attend our business and move along just as soon as we are assured that our services are no longer required. We have never once failed the terms of a contract, nor do I intend to begin as such in Pioneer Vale. My men will set up our camp in the vacant lots graciously provided to us by our generous benefactor, Master Mathers, and tomorrow we shall begin our scouting and assessment of the enemy forces.

"Now, if one of you gentlemen would be so kind, where can my lads find a good drink in these parts?"

*　　*　　*

Micah waved at Allison Brenner through the closing door as he stumbled out of the Hirsute Huntsman having stayed far longer than he had ever intended. It was more than just the fact that he had grown up with the serving girl that had kept him close by her side this evening. The taproom had become more raucous than usual with the addition of several of the newly arrived soldiers to the ranks of the patrons. Three drunken brawls had broken out this evening, and while not unheard of, the edge of these scrappers was not so blunt as usual.

Micah sighed as he made his way down the street. He had hoped for a pleasant evening of flirting and good-natured camaraderie with Allison, even if it had been under the baleful glare of her bear of a father. He shuddered sometimes whenever he felt the bar's namesake watching him whenever he chatted with her, but tonight, when his presence would have been most welcome, Marcus was absent and uncomfortably so. Poor Dorothea had held down the house this evening, but her typical sass was subdued. Her head turned with every creak of the taproom door swinging open, only to become crestfallen as someone other than her husband crossed the threshold. Allison and her sister, Tabitha, had little to say tonight but who could tell if it was the mercenary troops or their mother's apprehension spilling over to them.

The young smith shrugged and started down the main road of town back toward his own home. His mother had encouraged him to go off and enjoy himself this evening after his hard day's work with her merry chatter. "You're too young a lad to waste your youth caring for an old cluck when there are plenty of fine young hens preening every time that you walk down the street," she teased as she ushered him out the door. This was usually followed by some banter about her required number of future grandchildren which always made the shy smith scurry away.

A sudden chill shook Micah from his reverie and he glanced around, tearing himself away from his absent-minded musings. The shadow of Preston Mathers' grand house loomed over him, stealing the heat from the night air. He stood transfixed as he stared at the moneylender's home, and shivered as spectral figures seemed to scrabble across the front of the building. The darkness stared back at him, and he imagined that something malevolent kept watch over all who passed by this dismal place. His mind screamed for him to break away and seek out the safety of his own home, but he found his feet unresponsive. Instead of fleeing, Micah found himself drawn closer.

The echo of nearby footsteps made the mesmerized young smith jump and he dashed for cover at the side of Preston's front porch. He crouched down in the bushes not even daring to breathe. The darkness swirled around him, and his skin prickled as every hair stood on end. Fireflies flashed in strangely blinking pairs like the eyes of dozens of unseen animals lurking alongside him.

Preston stormed around the corner of his gate, huffing and puffing. His face was flushed, his brow heavily creased, and his arms pumped at his sides. Patch Erickson loped into view, his easy gait keeping pace with his benefactor. Mathers started to climb the front steps, his shoe stomping the wood tread inches from Micah's face before he turned and poked his finger into Patch's chest.

"That impudent bastard," snarled Preston. "The man didn't even have the courtesy to get off of his blasted horse for me. I am about to make him the wealthiest soldier this side of the Atlantic Ocean and he treats me as though I am but some common merchant. Does he not understand that he will be the general of the mightiest army in history?"

"Seems to me that he already believes that to be the case," said Erickson. "His men do have a well-earned reputation among the seedier spots they frequent."

"Forrester is little more than a bloodthirsty cur who needs brought to heel and taught his place. When do his magnificent soldiers," Preston said with a sneer, "get put to their next test?"

"The scouting he made a point of bringing up today has already been done. You give me the order, and I'll release your proverbial hounds," replied Patch. "Not that it'll prove much of a test of their ability. Riding down a bunch of women and children shouldn't prove too difficult even for his Reavers." A cruel grin broke the man's ferocious demeanor. From his hiding place, Micah shivered. Any sort of smile on the big man's scarred face seemed out of place.

"Which reminds me that we need to speak to him about taking on a more populace-friendly name. If his men are to become the future defenders of my holdings, they need not scare our own, correct?"

Patch shrugged. "I don't know. A little fear makes the rabble step in line a lot faster. Might prove useful."

"They need only to bring back a decisive victory over the Indians for me to garner the necessary support as to why we need them here in the first place. All of which brings my plans closer to fruition."

"I have no doubts that plenty of skins will run red by the time Cyrus has finished his chore."

"Excellent, my boy. Now, while we are on the subject of running down women and children, I have another task for you, my dear friend."

"What would you have me do?" Patch Erickson's voice was forceful and ominous even when the burly brute was trying to be quiet. There was something sinister in the hushed way the normally taciturn man spoke, and how eagerly he rose to such a dastardly topic.

"We have the Carmichaels backed into a corner now. With Anne-Marie in the stockade, and Jeremiah too busy watching over their farm and boys to interfere, we have a clear opportunity to move against them. However, I want her to suffer and stand helpless as her family is fed to the wolves." He grinned to himself. "So to speak. Ride out to their farm, and choose your moment. I trust your judgment in this, my son. I will see to it that Anne-Marie is eventually removed from the board, but not until I have crushed her spirit first."

"My name was drawn to accompany the new patrol. I don't know that I can slip away so easily."

Mathers scratched his chin, looking vacantly past his man. A slow smile spread across his face. "Then perhaps Master Carmichael will find the same call of duty to defend our fair town alongside you."

"But the conscripts have already been selected. Someone would have to drop out."

"Wasn't Magistrate Lucas drawn for your patrol as well? Haven't you heard? Our good friend, Jordan, is about to fall and inflict some serious harm to his knee and won't be able to fulfill his turn." He stared pointedly at the one-eyed brute.

"Do you want this fall to simply release his obligations or leave him with a limp?" Patch cracked his knuckles with the hint of a snarl on his lips.

"As you see fit, my friend, however, do try to remember that Jordan remains our confidante. He must be convincing, but do not turn him away from our good graces. Once done, a new lot shall have to be drawn in his stead. I will arrange for Master Carmichael to fulfill his civic responsibilities."

Patch nodded and shot Preston a grim smile. "While you're at it, maybe you should let his wife know that I am out there keeping watch on her man for her. Might get a confession in exchange for his safety?"

Preston scowled. "I have no intention of offering any Carmichael even a remote semblance of safety, but I appreciate your intentions. Let's waste no more time. Business such as this is best handled swiftly. With Captain Forrester's men at my whim, I shall soon lay claim to far more than just that accursed farm."

"I'd keep my voice down if I were you. Should Cyrus catch wind of your plans, he'll double his fee on you," snorted Erickson.

"If only I had a wall of gold just waiting for me to put to such use," Preston said with a mocking raise of his hand to his forehead. "Whatever he asks in compensation shall pale beside what I am promised, my boy.

Off with you now. You know what needs to be done." He bit down on the end of his clay pipe and waved a dismissive hand at Erickson. The bigger man gave a curt nod and turned back to the street. Preston watched him leave and gave a barely perceptible smile before he opened the front door and went inside his home.

Micah cowered in the shadows. What was Preston up to? He had to go and tell someone that he could trust all that he had just heard, but who? The young smith rushed from the cover of the bushes and dashed through the front gate. He grabbed the post and swung around only to slam into the broad chest of a hulking shape. A flash of white teeth gleamed from the shadows as the young man crashed to the cobblestones. As the figure loomed menacingly over him, Micah cursed himself for not giving Preston's man more time to get away.

"Beware, for I shall defend myself should you seek a fight, Master Erickson," he said as he scrambled back to his feet. He fumbled at his belt for the hammer that he always carried there, but his fingers trembled too much. A dirty hand reached out to him and the bruised and bedraggled face of Marcus Brenner came into the light.

"Oh, make no mistake that I am ready for a fight, boy, but not with you. However, if you ever call me by that name again, I may forget that my daughter adores you." A deep cut encrusted his cheek with dried blood, and a bald patch along his jaw line showed where a tuft of his great beard had been torn away from its roots.

"Master Brenner," Micah gasped as the innkeeper pulled him to his feet. He pumped Marcus' hand in a grateful shake. "I thought that brute had come back around and caught me where I had no business to be, although I feel the need to act quickly now that I have heard the Devil's own whispers."

"Seems as though we have a lot of that going around lately," muttered the big man. "What have you learned, son?"

"The Carmichaels are in terrible danger, Master Brenner," he said as he released the hunter's hand. "Preston has schemes in motion and now a private army to do his bidding. I fear something terrible waits in store for us all."

"Say no more, lad. There is something deeper at work here than any of us are aware of. I have seen things today that will haunt me until I draw my final breath, and we need to get the truth out of someone."

"Well, confronting Mathers won't get us anywhere. His silver tongue has kept him from getting run out of town for years. He holds enough folk of the town in his pockets to deflect any accusation we would bring against him. Who do you suggest we turn to?"

Marcus scratched his beard and then looked up the street toward the stockade. "Run yourself down to Huntsman first. Fetch my wife, and Abel Harmon, if he is there. Then meet me over at the cells.

"I think it's time that we speak to the Witch."

CHAPTER 11
WITH FRIENDS LIKE THESE - 1671

Marcus hissed through his teeth as Dorothea dabbed at the cuts on his face, dipping the rag into a steaming bowl of green liquid that she had brewed up while he had told his tale. "Enough fussing over me, woman. I swear your healing stings worse than the cuts themselves."

"I've not seen you this banged up since that time you brawled with that mountain lion that's now hanging over our headboard," she said as she carefully examined the tear along his cheek. "I hope whoever scarred you this way took a bigger measure."

"The ones that did this won't be getting another chance at me or anyone else. Had that shovel been a stretch further from my reach though, I wouldn't have made it out of that hole. Barely got my fingers on the handle, and then dashed it against the side of that bastard's head. Once I rolled him off of me, I put the blade of it through his neck," Marcus said as he took his wife's hand. He smiled as her stern glare broke and she wrapped her arms around his thick neck. "Easy, woman," he said with a grunt as she squeezed him and lightly kissed the top of his head. "Things are a little more tender than they appear."

Marcus studied their group huddled together in the guard room of the stockade. Micah paced by the entry door chewing on his thumbnail. The smith had brought both Abel Harmon and Jeremiah back from the Huntsman after telling them about his return. They had raced to the stockade while he sat at the small table with his eyes closed, breathing

123

deeply, fighting back the pain he was in. Abel leaned against the wall while Jeremiah stood near the thick cell door. It was the face framed by the tiny window that Marcus now watched. Anne-Marie cleared her throat under his stare.

"Marcus, I am so sorry," she said. "I should never have sent you alone to that evil place. I beg your forgiveness." Her grimy fingers clutched the tiny bars of her window while Jeremiah tried to hold her hand. "I knew it was dangerous and didn't give you enough warning."

"Hush, girl," he said. "I went of my own free will. No one twisted my beard." He absently rubbed the newly bare patch under his cheek. "Well, not at first, anyway."

"Marcus, what you've told us is beyond belief," said Abel. "Monsters of smoke? Dead men rising to attack you?"

"Do you doubt my word, Abel? Do you think these scratches are just from brambles and burrs?"

The old farmer held up his hands. "Of course not, my friend. It's a bit to wrap my head around, but I stand by your words. However, given our present company, what does it all mean?"

Jeremiah whirled around and crossed his thick arms over his chest. "Given present company? Do you think my wife plays us all for fools, Abel?" Marcus rose on weary legs ready to jump between the two farmers, but Micah got there first.

"Easy now, lad," said Abel. "I know you and your wife are good folks. Have been since the day you first arrived in the Vale. I said so before and I'll not change my opinion on it now."

"But?" said Jeremiah.

"But I stand accused of witchcraft and our dear friend barely escaped with his life from an evil that would bring the end of days to us all," said

Anne-Marie. "Leave Abel alone, husband. He has every right to doubt me."

Marcus limped forward. "Put your hackles down, boys. We're all friends here." He turned to each man, satisfied when the iron fell away from Jeremiah's poise and Abel picked up his straw hat and wrung it in his hands. He patted Micah on the shoulder and moved closer to the cell. Jeremiah moved between him and the door, but Marcus looked past his friend.

"Anne-Marie, we all share the sentiment that your family has become as dear as our own," he said, "but there are secrets here that speak to something darker and far more menacing than that foul-tempered moneylender digging for gold in the hills. We took your side in the square and placed our trust in you. I beg you to not let us find it has been misplaced in you."

"And I would speak for my family also," said Micah. "The Carmichael's always dealt fairly with my da in his day, and continue to do right by me and my mother. I am a simple man but based on what I heard between Mathers and his man, as well as Marcus' own story, there is something sinister afoot that we all need fair warning of."

Dorothea stepped forward. "What these overblown windbags are trying to say, girl, are you a part of this storm, or are you our shield against it?"

Marcus towered over his friend and gently, but firmly, pushed the man aside. Jeremiah pushed back at him and stood his ground before the door. "You all say that you stand with my family, and yet you would pin her down to what? A confession that Corbin's charges have merit? That my wife is the monster that Preston's schemes make her out to be?"

"I've hunted these hills for years now, Jeremiah, and have never before felt like I was the one being stalked." He met Anne-Marie's eyes squarely through the bars of the cell door. "I have seen the dead rise up from their resting places and had my face clawed by their icy fingers. I understand where the true monster lies, and I know that you are no friend to the thing that lurks in that deeper cave, yet you risk us all if we don't know what hides in the darkness."

Anne-Marie squeezed Jeremiah's shoulder as he opened his mouth. "You have all endangered your lives or reputations in taking up for me and my family, and I pray that you never regret your kindness to us. You deserve nothing less than my total honesty, for you have been marked now as an enemy to be dealt with by a creature far more vicious than any beast you have known before."

"Tell us what you know of the evil I faced," said Marcus.

Anne-Marie took a deep breath and nodded. "He is Shade, the Father of Nightmares, and is a demon born of war and blood at the dawn of time. He thrives on creating fear and once his power grows strong enough he will try to force his way into our world and claim it for himself. He will slaughter those who oppose him and enslave those too frail to fight back."

"Then the doorway is already swinging open, yes? He is the wolf that nearly ended me in that unholy place?"

Anne-Marie shook her head. "You fought but a shadow of his power," Anne-Marie said with a shake of her fiery tresses.

"Then he casts a mighty nasty shadow." Marcus looked into her eyes and scratched absently at his beard. "You stand against him?"

She nodded. "Literally until my dying day. He cannot fully pass between realms as long as I draw breath."

"Then why did you surrender yourself to the town that is ready to hang you from the nearest tree, lass? You should be off hiding in the hills. Let the bloody preacher call you a witch until Judgment Day."

"I am no witch, Marcus." She stepped away from the door into the middle of her cell and snapped her wrists downward. Tongues of lavender fire twined around her body, winding up from her feet, around her waist, and fanning her hair out behind her. She threw back her head as the tendrils embraced her and lifted her lightly off the ground. The straw pallet and blanket within her cell smoldered, then burst into flame, the wash of heat reducing it to a pile of ash in moments. She looked at each of them with her eyes aflame and her fists wreathed in fire.

The room behind Marcus fell into chaos. Micah grabbed at his shirt and dug his fingers into his arm with an iron grip. He heard Dorothea gasp, speechless for one of the only times in all her years. Jeremiah dashed past him as Abel's frightened cry and a subsequent crash suggested the old man had tripped over some piece of furniture. Marcus, however, stood unflinching before the cell door with his arms crossed over his chest.

"I am a Guardian," Anne-Marie said. Her voice boomed like the roar of a bonfire and rattled the cell door in its frame. "I have vowed to use this power granted to me to protect the world from the darkest of shadows. Mathers is a pawn of the beast and conspires to have me killed to make way for his dark master. I know not how poor Corbin became indentured to Preston." She snapped her wrists again and the fires flickered away and her feet gently touched the floor again. "But I swear on the lives of my children that I am no threat to the good folk of Pioneer Vale."

The hint of a smile played across Marcus' lips. "Let's get you out of this filthy cage then. You aren't guarding much of anything sitting in this cesspool."

"Are you daft?" yelled Abel. Marcus turned to see Jeremiah picking the old farmer from the ruins of the chair that had sat near the fireplace. "You would release her just like that? How can we know that she isn't in league with the creature that attacked you? What if we are all beguiled by honeyed words and a silver tongue?"

"What we just saw is the very reason why we must free her," Marcus said. "These iron bars are not what keeps her within this cage." He bowed his head deeply to Anne-Marie. "It's her integrity. I'm sure that our young smith could attest that with fires as hot as hers, she could have reduced this door to embers if she wanted to, right, son?"

"Hadn't thought about it like that, but yes," said Micah.

"And after fighting that beast in the cave, we need such power alongside us." Marcus took the woman's dainty hand in his massive paw and gave it a squeeze. "If you can look past our skepticism and still stand at our side?"

"There is no other place I would prefer, dear friend," said Anne-Marie. Marcus nodded, smiled, and backed away.

"Then why don't you layabouts set yourselves to the task of getting this damn door open for the lady before our little conspiracy here is discovered?" said Dorothea.

Micah stepped forward and bent his head to the lock. He pulled a set of pincers from his tool belt and began to work on the broken key within. "Mechanism's all fouled up," he muttered. "Mathers did it in when he snapped the key. Guess I'll have to be more direct." He lifted the heavy hammer from the loop at his side, and with one deft practiced swing, smashed the lock from the door with a loud bang.

Abel had found his dropped hat and wrung it in his hands again. He stepped forward and met Anne-Marie as she stepped out of the cell. He spared a glance at Jeremiah and hung his head. "I beg forgiveness from both of you. I am ashamed to have doubted you even for a second."

"You've no need to apologize, old friend," said Jeremiah. The farmer laughed as his wife fell into his embrace. "Trust me when I say that her abilities take some getting used to."

Anne-Marie released her husband after a warm kiss and turned to Marcus. He couldn't help but flinch when she started to raise her hand. She cocked her head and paused.

"Do you trust me?" she asked. Marcus raised an eyebrow but nodded. A wispy lavender flame, softer and less intense than the display she had put on a moment before, bathed her hand from fingertip to her wrist. She placed her palm on his wounded cheek and closed her eyes. A gentle flame enshrouded him, and he waved off Dorothea as she took a step toward him.

Marcus felt the weight of his breathing where Landry had hit him with the ax handle ease. The sting across his cheek where Hollister's filthy nails had raked his flesh soothed and subsided. A foul smell made him glance down at the rip in his trouser leg. A black ichor pumped out of the wound in his calf and boiled away as it hit the floor. The garish wound closed with hardly a scar. He even felt the tickle of hair sprouted anew from the bald patch on his cheek.

"You could have done that as soon as I showed up, lass. We might have spared ourselves all this chattering that we've done, and I'd not have been aching all this time," he said with a hearty laugh as the younger woman removed her hand and let the flames around it die out.

"Might have saved me some herbs too," quipped Dorothea. The others joined in the laughter as she checked his face and then gave him a rough kiss.

One after one, the Guardian took each of his friends' hands in her own, and with each, a curl of flame danced within her eyes. Marcus saw how each stood a little taller and knew that each felt the rush of coiled fire surge through their bodies, invigorated from the woman's embrace. Lastly, she hugged Dorothea. His wife made a soft coo of surprise and then smiled when Anne-Marie let go. The older woman scooped up the rag that she had used on his scrapes and offered it to Anne-Marie. "Mind yer nose, dear."

Anne-Marie took the cloth and wiped away the trickle of blood that ran from her nostril. She wobbled and Marcus took her elbow until the wave of dizziness passed. "This mantle I bear rests heavily on oaths and honor. The flame that just passed between us all is my pledge to each of you that I shall watch after you and your families so long as I may. The road ahead of us all will be treacherous, but I will stand with you against whatever we may face, be it of this world or another."

"Let them come," said Marcus. "I won't hesitate to knock a few ruffians' heads together. Hell, I do it two or three nights a week anyway. Now, given what Micah heard tonight, I think it wise if you both spirit yourselves away to someplace safe."

"I'm not running from my father's land after we only just took ownership. I'll be dead before I let Mathers back inside that accursed hole in the ground," said Jeremiah, "unless it's to plant him there permanently."

"Be careful what you say," said Dorothea. "If I've seen anything from sitting on that tribunal, it's that the others all fear Preston's reach. Don't underestimate him, lad, or you may find yourself falling into his claws the same way that spineless preacher may have done."

"I wish I could speak privately with Corbin," Anne-Marie said. "I suspect that he could turn the tables on Preston if he just had the support."

"Whether he received it or not, I wouldn't trust Reynolds to come to your rescue," said Marcus. "You should heed my words and get away before those two can cause you any more harm."

"I have a place available to me that I may hide until we are ready to face Preston. All I would ask of you is that you act surprised once the word is given that I have escaped my cell. The town will know that I escaped with help, but let none be the wiser who my co-conspirators are. The thing for you each to do now is go back to your normal routines."

"Normal flew out the window with the arrival of that group of ruffians today," said Abel. "Town went from a frightened village to an armed camp in half a day."

"Maybe folks will be less concerned with Anne-Marie's disappearance then," said Micah. "Seems as though we've got bigger matters at hand now with stopping a war with the local Indians, than proving she is a witch."

"Mathers is the key," said Anne-Marie. "He is Shade's man and the true threat to us here. Without his gold, these mercenaries will have no reason to stay, and that will hopefully have given me the time I need to drive Shade back into his dark realm for good."

"I hope you're right, lass, but I'll warn you all," said the old farmer. "I have looked into the eyes of such men before. They are cutthroats. Professional killers that Mathers has invited right into our sitting rooms. He holds the leash so long as his coin keeps them satisfied, but I have seen soldiers go rogue. Their sort can throw down for bloodshed with little enough care for the reason."

"Which makes it so much more important for you all to keep your heads down, and deny any knowledge of tonight. If hired killers are what he has brought, I beg you to do nothing that would give Mathers cause to strike out against you." The redhead lowered her eyes to the floor and wisps of lavender fire rolled around her fingers once more. "Let him keep his hatred aimed at me. I can weather the storm easier than the rest of you."

Jeremiah cleared his throat. "I seem to recall standing by you during a storm at the end of our field when you found these new abilities of yours. What sort of man would I be to not stand with you when the lightning crashes next?"

Marcus snorted. "I can play dumb for you, girl, but make no mistake that if one of those black-hearted bastards threaten one of my own, Mathers'll find my boot so far up his …."

"Not until he catches the broadside of my cast iron pan against the side of his head, husband," interrupted Dorothea. She shot a look at Abel and Micah, her brow raised questioningly.

Micah simply smiled and slapped his smith's hammer into his open hand. All eyes turned to Abel, as the old man plopped down with a weary sigh onto the office table.

"There is a box in a trunk at the foot of my bed, and in that box is an old medal given to me by my commanding officer on the day of my discharge from the Queen's service. The very next day my family and I boarded a ship bound for these shores. That medal is etched with a single word. Valor. I may not have Marcus' brawn or Micah's youth, but you have my courage and honor, madam, or else that accolade is nothing more than a worthless hunk of bronze." The aged farmer took Anne-Marie's hand and gently kissed the back of it.

"Perhaps an old soldier can still show these young ones what a real fight is," he said with a smile.

*   *   *

Shadowy figures slipped out the door of the stockade, hooded all, and looking furtively up and down the street. The late hour favored them for there were no casual bystanders about. In truth, many of the townsfolk had retreated early to their homes with the arrival of the dreaded legion of soldiers that had arrived in an unspoken curfew.

The two largest of the cloaked figures carefully flanked a third and led that one to a horse. The person mounted with practiced grace then reached down, squeezed the hand of one of the other two. With a sharp kick to the flanks, the horse leaped away in a sudden gallop carrying the rider toward the edge of town. The remaining company conferred briefly among themselves and dispersed into the night, swallowed up by the shadows as the conspirators went their separate ways.

From his place at the edge of the town square platform, Captain Cyrus Forrester looked over the worn toes of his boots casually propped up on the rail of the platform in the center of town. He sipped his ale and then wiped the foam from his mustache as he watched the group. An amused smile found his lips as he watched the clumsy getaway. Even though he was newly arrived to Pioneer Vale, the Captain had spent his evening appraising himself of the local gossip, and he felt certain that he knew who had just ridden away into the woods. Though he didn't put any stock into the fire and brimstone stories that he had heard tonight, he knew that the superstitious rubes of the town would stir up easily enough to the news that their local witch appeared to have sympathizers. Perhaps even a coven, he mused to himself. With a little clever embellishment of what he had just seen, he could have that gutless Magistrate send the nervous folk into a panic, willing to pay anything to the man who could keep their boogeymen at bay.

Cyrus threw back the remainder of his drink and rose from his seat. His boots echoed in the night as his heavy tread pounded against the wood steps. He stopped when his eyes fell upon the house at the end of the street, the one belonging to Mathers. The man was shrewd and possessed an inexhaustible source of wealth which Cyrus meant to have as much of as he could swindle. He slipped a dagger from his belt, deftly twirling it between his fingers before smoothly slamming it back home into its sheath. The Captain melted back into the shadows as he made his way back toward his camp, pondering who among his men were the most qualified to pose as experienced witch hunters.

The price for his services had just gone up.

CHAPTER 12
DUTIFUL SERVANTS - 1671

Hoof beats pounded along the dirt road that led to the entry yard of Carmichael Farms. Jeremiah rose from his seat on the porch where he sharpened his hatchet as four burly men and Constable Owens slowed their gallop.

"Where is she, Jeremiah?" said the officer. "Your wife vanished from her cell last night and we have an eyewitness that says he saw her liberated. I have the authority to search the premises for her and Heaven help you if you are found harboring her."

"Morning, Clement," said Jeremiah. "Are you certain that you brought enough men to hunt her down? These aren't your usual deputies. Who have you brought along with you to invade my home?"

"These men are with Captain Forrester's company, hired to safeguard the town from threats," he said as he pointed his finger at the farmer. "Threats of all sorts."

"And I suppose that includes witches?" scoffed Jeremiah.

"These men are particularly skilled in chasing down fugitives and their service has been extended to me in light of your wife's breakout."

"They're mercenaries," Jeremiah spat. "Soldiers bought and paid for by Preston Mathers. The only threat they give a damn about is that the coins might stop jingling."

"Hold your tongue, sir," said Owens. "The town was in dire need after the Indians attacked and it was only through Preston's generosity that we were able to secure these men."

"I'll be damned, Clement. Have you handed the keys to the town over to that pig yet? Well, on my word, gentlemen, you have wasted your time riding all this way. I will freely admit that I visited her at the jail last night, as was my right. But she did not leave in my company."

"Then whose company did she leave in?"

"Constable, if you have misplaced your prisoner, then maybe you should reconsider your ability to perform your office." Jeremiah waved his hand toward the buildings nearby. "Your thugs are free to search, but I tell you truly that she isn't here, and I have nothing to hide."

"Rest assured that we will make certain of that." Owens turned to the leader of his group. "Search every building. Tear the place apart if you have to." The mercenaries dismounted and two went toward the house and the other two went toward the barn. Jeremiah crossed his arms over his chest and glared at the constable.

"Clement, you know that I will seek payment for anything that these men destroy," said Jeremiah. "My wife is quite resourceful, and whatever fool sent you out here to find her should have known better."

Jeremiah heard a shrill cry from the house and his hand tightened around the handle of his hatchet. Aiden and Thomas dashed out of the house, the older boy kept himself protectively between the mercenaries and his younger brother. They bolted toward their father, Thomas in tears, but Aiden seething with anger.

"Da, why are those men going through our house," cried Thomas. His eyes were wide and he nervously rubbed the tail of the stuffed tiger his mother had sewn for him against his bottom lip.

"It's alright, son. They aren't here for us."

"They are looking for mama, aren't they?" asked Aiden. "She has never hurt anyone. They need to leave her alone."

"Settle down, boys." Jeremiah turned and looked at Owens. "These men aren't doing anything but what they were told to do. Like puppets on a string, right Clement?"

"Dammit, Jeremiah you know I don't want to do this," the constable hissed. Clement leaned closer to the farmer and glanced aside to where the mercenaries kicked through hay, turned over baskets, and upset the livestock. "I don't want to believe a word of Reynolds' charges."

"Then why are you here?" Jeremiah shot back.

"Because she stands accused and turned herself over to the town. But this only makes things look worse for her, and don't tell me that you weren't a part of the group that set her loose. You all were seen. Who else helped you? Marcus? Abel? Please don't force me to bring them in on this as well."

"Who was your witness?"

"Does it matter?"

"It does if Mathers' coins line his pocket. Preston has a grudge against my family and will stoop to any depth to try to get his revenge against us. I know you are a man of honor, Clement. Don't let him sway you in this."

"There appears to be a horse missing," called one of the men from the barn door. "Trough full of feed, but no animal in the stall."

Owens turned back to Jeremiah. "Care to elaborate?"

Jeremiah sighed. "She got back here to the farm before I did last night. Marcus Brenner can vouch for me that I was at the Huntsman until the last bell. When I got back home, I put away my team but her mare was already out of its stall. She didn't leave even so much as a note. Guess she wanted to set out before there was any danger to me and the boys as a result of her escape."

He held a straight face as the thoughts of his parting time with his wife was still fresh in his mind. While he had stayed with the Brenners as he said, Anne-Marie had waited for him to return to the farm. She had kept silent watch over the boys, but before she had ridden out, they had a deeply impassioned goodbye in the hayloft of the barn.

"Where would she have gone off to? The Harmon farm? Some other friendly neighbor?"

"Not likely. Clement, you've known my wife for a few years now. Have you ever known her to do anything that would endanger her friends?" He pointedly stared at the man until the constable blushed and shook his head.

"No, of course not."

"But you have your orders." Jeremiah reached out and put his hand on the man's shoulder. "Do yourself a favor, my friend. Ask yourself who is giving those instructions. That alone might be enough to clear away your doubts."

"I have a duty to my office. It doesn't matter what I believe. Your wife has fled from her cell. Her trial. Why would she do that if she was innocent?"

"Perhaps because she felt she was in greater danger by waiting for Preston's justice to clear her name than if she sought vindication on her own terms."

Owens shook his head and then clapped Jeremiah's hand. "I want you to know that I hope for nothing less than the proof coming to light that your Anne-Marie is naught but a loving wife and mother who has been wronged by that conniving moneylender. I am sworn to keep looking for her, though. Please help me bring her home safely, Jeremiah. I swear on my life, that I will not allow harm to come to her that isn't called for."

"I believe you and sincerely appreciate that, Clement," said Jeremiah, "but I don't know where she has spirited herself off to. I can't give her up if I don't know where she hides."

"Not that you would anyway?"

"Not a chance," Jeremiah said with a smile.

The constable shook his head and laughed as the mercenaries regrouped around the two men. "She's not here. Let's head out to the next farm," said one soldier.

"I do have one other task set upon me that I need to perform. With the savages in the area on the rise, we desperately need men to fill in the ranks of the border patrols."

"I thought that's what these soldiers were brought in to protect us from."

"We still need to round out the groups with some of our own men so that we can have enough skirmishers in the event of an attack. More eyes around our borders will mean greater security."

"The Nipmuc are not a threat, Clement. I see them watching us from the tree line from time to time. They wave back when I greet them in kind, but they have never given us any reason to fear them."

"Tell that to the widows and orphans of the men from the border patrol. You risk the future on an uncertain past. For whatever reason, we are not as safe as we once thought."

"And I think you are jumping at the wrong shadows. There is an evil within the Vale these days, Clement, but it sits closer to home than anyone wants to say aloud."

"Yes, yes, everyone knows what a horrible man Preston is, and it's no secret the depth of the hatred you bear for the man." Owens raised his hand as Jeremiah started to open his mouth. "And I don't imply that you are without cause, but the truth of the matter is that Mathers has committed no crime that he could be called to task for. He is despised, arrogant, and selfish, but he can't be run out of town for that alone. Furthermore, we would be nearly defenseless without the men his coin paid from his own pocket brought to bolster our defenses."

"Putting him in a place of strength that once solidified will be impossible to dislodge him from. He secures his own position, not for the betterment or salvation of the town."

"The mercenaries will move along once we have no further need to keep them around. This is why it is so important to have our own folks join up with these newly formed patrols. With a strong young man such as yourself along with the troop, it would help a lot of folks sleep easier at night knowing that we could still rely on our own to keep the town safe. We can't afford another surprise attack. There won't be anyone left to protect if those savages bring the fight to us first."

"Why were our men out near Chatham's Creek anyway? That land is sacred ground to the local tribe. It seems more likely to me that their attack was intended to drive away trespassers. Perhaps instead of sending out a war party, we should try sending a delegation to speak with them first."

"Speak with them? Jeremiah, they are little better than wild animals."

"Says the man who wants to shoot first and ask questions later."

"Are you with us or not, Carmichael," said one of the hired thugs. His fingers danced on the butt of the pistol tucked into the front of his trousers. "Are you willing to stand up for the defense of your town? Either join up with the border patrol or go and hide behind the skirts of the womenfolk."

Jeremiah felt the squeeze of Thomas's small hand in his own and he pulled his boys tight against his sides. He looked back and forth at the staring faces. He knew that if he went along he might have an opportunity to prevent further bloodshed between the people of Pioneer Vale and the

Nipmuc tribe. He could stall or even subvert any scouting parties and just maybe buy Anne-Marie the time she needed to bring to light Preston's schemes before dozens of lives were lost to the madman's plot. He shook his head and sighed.

"Gentlemen, I am with you. You shall never find a more devoted servant than I," he said with a roll of his eyes.

*　　*　　*

Corbin sat in the chair before his cold fireplace. A half-empty bottle of brandy sat on the small table beside him as he swirled yet another round in the glass in his hand. Long shadows played along the floorboards of his small house, and yet he felt more at home in the darkness right now.

Madeline had rebuffed his every attempt to see her. She had been at her husband's side ever since his return. Despite his infirmity, Horace Pritchard had proven himself a fast healer and already hobbled around the town with a cane. Since the ambushed patrol had been brought back to town, the rally cries had been relentless to refill the ranks of the border patrol. Few men had stepped forward, and the gossips were abuzz with talk of conscription.

A light flickered through the small window at the front of the house. Corbin swung his head, scowling at the intrusion. The sight he saw sobered him instantly as his glass fell from his fingers and smashed to pieces on the floor.

A crowd stood outside of his home, torches held aloft and waving. He saw frowns on the shadowy faces of the burly men who leaned on their muskets. A hulking figure, a mountain of a man, limped up the step and hammered on Reynolds' door. Corbin rolled from the seat of his chair and cowered behind it.

"Reynolds," called Horace Pritchard. "Open the door, sir. I need a word with you."

Corbin's nightmare rushed back to him. The terror of that dream, his mad flight through the woods as he escaped the mob, only to find that strange clearing where the monstrous beast attacked him, made him tremble and quake as Pritchard's fist rattled the door in its frame.

The preacher crawled back into his bedroom, ready to flee through the window just as he had in the vision when the most unusual and uncharacteristic thought halted him. What if he didn't run, but instead stood and faced the crowd in answer for his crimes? Could any punishment meted out by Pritchard's hands be worse than what befell him in his nightmare?

The door frame cracked under Pritchard's next barrage. "Reynolds, I know you are within. I saw you stir through your window a moment ago. Do not keep me waiting, sir. Open up the door!"

Corbin drew himself up, straightened his waistcoat, and walked back to the door. A foolish grin and a madcap chuckle came unbidden at the idea that maybe he should duck as soon as he opened it up. He bit his tongue to compose himself and unlatched the bolt. Horace Pritchard glared at him as the man towered over the scrawny clergyman.

"Know why we're here tonight, Reynolds?" Corbin looked past the man and saw the piercing stares of several other hardy men of Pioneer Vale. Patch Erickson stood among them, a wicked grin on his lips as he spat into Reynolds' yard.

"From the cast of your assemblage, I can only assume that you mean to do someone ill will," he replied.

"Only to strike back against such ill as was done first, and that brings me to you."

Corbin felt his stomach quaking, threatening to purge itself as fear tore him apart, but he swallowed the sour taste of the brandy that rose in his throat and nodded. "I am prepared to do what I must, Master Pritchard. What would you have of me?"

Pritchard turned to face the crowd and then back to Reynolds. He clapped the Parson on the arm, engulfing the man's bicep with his meaty hand. Corbin stumbled from the force of the blow even though Pritchard had hardly struck him.

"See there, good folk of Pioneer Vale," bellowed Horace. "Let the rest of you find your courage as our Parson has. Reynolds is exactly the sort of man that the border patrol needs! Steps forward without hesitation to protect those of his flock." The big man reached into a bag held by one of the other townsfolk and pulled out a flintlock pistol, a horn of powder, and a bag of shot. He shoved the items into the preacher's hands. "Thank you for setting your fine example, Parson. If only our town had more men of your stripe. Meet us in the town square tomorrow at midmorning, and we'll make sure you know how to use that piece properly."

Reynolds stood slack-jawed as the crowd slowly wandered away from his home. Patch Erickson hung back until the rest had moved along. He laughed as he swaggered closer to the preacher. A feral smile and the angry red scar on his face gave the man the look of a predator toying with his next meal.

"Oh, for certain, this town needs a few more like you, Reynolds. See you on our rounds." Patch touched the brim of his hat and gave a curt nod before he lazily whirled around and followed Horace Pritchard's recruitment posse.

Corbin looked down at the pistol in his hand as if it were a coiled snake. He had never even held a pistol in his hands before, and yet there was something strangely comforting about the weapon. He pulled a lead ball from the small bag he had been given and rolled it around in the palm of his hand. With one tiny piece of metal so many of his problems could be ended. He shuddered as the dark thought crossed through his mind, but then he laughed at himself.

As if he dared to make so bold an overture, he mused.

Corbin went back inside his home and set the pistol and ammunition on his table. He heard Horace Pritchard's voice boom from down the street as he went to the next home in search of able-bodied recruits. As so often happened, his mind went to Madeline and their unborn child. As he stared at the pistol, Corbin wondered, then prayed, that the cowardice that so marked his soul would die out from his lineage.

*   *   *

"Come in, dearie, before ye catch yer death," said Henna as she dragged Anne-Marie by the hand into Whisperwind's cozy sitting room. A fire blazed merrily in the hearth going through all colors of the rainbow, pausing, she noticed, on violet, almost as if bidding her welcome to the cottage.

"It would appear I am now a fugitive," she said as she allowed herself to be pushed into the comfy chair that she had once caught aflame during her first days as a Guardian.

"Pfft," said Henna. "I'm surprised ye stayed as long as ye did. Had it been me, I'd have burned a hole in the wall as soon as the watch had looked the other way."

"I didn't want to offer them any reason to believe the accusations against me."

"Even though the uncanny truth of it all does hit close to the mark, eh?"

"I don't believe that Reynolds actually knew anything when he set things in motion. His face seemed so haunted the last time we spoke. Has Shade set his claws into that poor man as well? It seems more like a cruel prank at this point."

"Ye know who pulls the preacher's strings, lass, and our true enemy sits in the shadows directing that overstuffed piece of filth. We know not what whispers the old wolf has put in anyone's ears, but surely he puts his pieces on the board."

"We now have a few of our own. I revealed what I am to a few very dear souls, but none save my husband know of you. Should anything happen to me, you still secretly remain in Shade's way."

"I suspected that ye had outside help to get away," Henna said with a nod. "At least that suggests ye didn't have the might to shake the bricks from the walls of that dirty pen, then. That works to yer favor still, but do your friends realize what they've signed up for? Dark times are ahead of us, lass."

"I made them aware of what stakes we play for." She smiled wistfully. "To their credit, that didn't shake them in the least. My hope is that they can hold Preston's schemes in check, while you and I confront Shade and drive him back to whatever pit he crawled from. They are remarkable folk of courage and honor, and are my world."

"What I find remarkable is that yer rescuers didn't bother to bring ye a bit of soap, lass. Were ye kept away in the depths of the outhouse? Do us both a favor, my dear. Peel off those stench-ridden rags and let's draw ye a bath. I'll brew us up some tea so that once ye're washed and a bit less bedraggled we can figure out together how we can best make Old Preston stumble." Henna laughed at her own wit as she whipped her gnarled fingers in a twirl of twinkling green lights. A large wooden tub floated on jade sparkles and settled gently on the floor before the fireplace.

Anne-Marie bit her lip as her mentor went about her tasks. She cleared her throat, and the older woman turned from the fireplace with a steaming kettle in hand. She sighed. "Ye've more to tell, haven't ye?"

"I found the Adversary's shard."

The kettle fell to the floor with a clang and water sloshed across the boards. Anne-Marie clapped her hands and made a twisting motion. In a flash of flame, the puddle dried up before it could run to Henna's lovely rug.

"Are ye sure?" the old woman whispered. Her gnarled hand clutched the edge of the mantle, bracing herself. "We Guardians have searched for generations without success."

"I'm sure," Anne-Marie said with a nod. "It sits within a shrine to the wolf beneath the mountain of Alistair's Climb. I fought the risen dead to escape that place. Shade's power is focused there."

"The wolf grows confident for him to so boldly reveal his might to you. If he no longer feels the need to remain hidden, then ye can wager that he plans to strike at us soon. Remove the only ones who can stand against him." Henna plopped down heavily into her own chair. "All these years. So many lives lost. Could it be that we finally have a chance to take the fight to that creature? How did ye stumble across such a desolate place, my dear?"

"I didn't. Mathers found it first, and Shade has promised him lordship over this land. Preston came to me while I was in jail and confirmed that he had spoken with the demon. He doesn't know, or care, why Shade wants us dead, but he has already made his intentions clear. If we are caught, he will sacrifice us to the Father of Nightmares."

"The magic of the grove will not fall to the likes of Mathers, not that I foresee that gluttonous buffoon stomping through the forest to find us."

"The chase won't come from him. His man, Erickson, does whatever Mathers bids him to. He is cruel and dangerous. To make matters worse, Preston has hired soldiers attending him now, and if they are his to command, then they serve Shade as well. They have come under the guise of defense against the neighboring Indians, but I suspect that Preston brought them to increase his own base of power. He will bring them to bear against the two of us, rather than fight off any war party from the tribesmen."

Henna pursed her lips. "That is far more likely," the wizened witch said. Her eyes flicked over to the feathered and beaded ornaments above her mantle, souvenirs of the old Guardian's younger days. "The forest folk who dwell nearby will fiercely protect their own, but bear no ill will toward the town."

"Then why did they attack the border patrol? The group was slaughtered. Only a few survived."

"I've not an answer for that one, girl, but I suspect more of the wolf's manipulations at work here. Might be one more thing we'll have to take from his hide once we find a way to confront him, and we had best not let down our guard." She cleared her throat. "Go ahead and get cleaned up. There's a trunk in the corner there that should have some clothes ye can have. I'll carry myself out to the garden and give ye some privacy." The old witch pulled herself up and hobbled out the door leaning heavily on her staff.

Anne-Marie placed the dropped kettle back on the hook over the fire and filled the tub from the well pump within the kitchen area. The redhead smiled as she sent a rush of power into the wood slats of the vessel. The tub shimmered with a wispy lavender heat and in a matter of moments, steam rose from the water to the ceiling. She found some fragrant oils on a shelf built into the tub and poured a few drops in. The scent of lilacs filled the room. She pulled off the soiled clothes that she had been wearing since her foray into the mine and looked around. Seeing no bin to put them into, she simply tossed them into the fireplace where they quickly went up in flames. The only thing she kept was the amethyst pendant dangling from its silver chain around her neck.

She slipped into the water, basking in the warmth, and let the aches of the last few days soak away. She scrubbed away the filth and grime that she had acquired both from the fight with Shade's minions as well as the days of her captivity in the town jail. Her mind drifted to Jeremiah and her boys, and she let slip a silent prayer for their safety. The haunting visions she had been subjected to in the Realm of Nightmares lingered still in the dark recesses of her mind. Even though she knew that she could avoid the terrible premonition she had to remain alert and stay one step ahead of the old wolf. She shook her head, submerged herself completely, and finally climbed out of the steaming water.

She had no towel but with a roll of her hands along her bare skin, flames kissed her body and dried her quicker than any cloth could have done. She stretched, reveling in the simple joy of being clean again, and saw the old trunk that Henna had mentioned halfway pushed beneath a table that must have been an antique when Henna was a maiden. The wooden floor sent warmth through the soles of her bare feet as she padded over and pulled the old chest from its hiding spot. A plume of dust rose up and away from her as she lifted the lid. A faint iridescent shimmer rolled across the bands as her fingers touched the old iron latch and a faint shock traveled up her hand that set the hairs on the back of her arm on end.

Anne-Marie gasped when she looked inside. Sitting right on top in a neatly folded pile was the shoulderless white blouse with the ruffle around the bosom and sleeves. She lifted it out and found the black corset with silver trim, purple trousers, with matching half skirt, and the polished black boots that she had found herself wearing upon her trip into the Realm of Nightmares where she had first met Shade.

It was her Guardian's outfit, uniquely tailored for her.

Slowly, she dressed. She felt the confirmation with each piece she pulled on that she was now part of the age-old battle. There was no escaping the destiny that had befallen her since she had first placed her hand upon the black marble slab in the grove so close by. She buckled the black corset, straightened the flowing skirt behind her, and pulled on the polished leather boots. As she stood back to her full height and regarded her reflection in Henna's mirror, she smiled at the confident and fearsome figure that stared back. She kissed the amethyst pendant that Jeremiah had given her and she marched over to the cottage door and boldly threw it open.

Henna sat upon a wooden bench near the woodpile, but Anne-Marie was taken aback as she noticed that her mentor had made a wardrobe change as well. Instead of her customary black shawl that hid her long faded and graying tunic, the old woman wore bracers of studded leather on her wrists. Her shirt was doeskin leather, decorated with beads of turquoise and bloodstone. Her black shawl was replaced by an emerald green cape with feathers and fur along the trim.

"You didn't need to change clothes out in the open air," quipped Anne-Marie. "I would have turned my back to give you your privacy."

"None have tried to peep on me in many a moon, my dear, although, when last someone did, my attire was a little more befitting my heritage. The leather jerkin that I used to wear into battle has grown a mite heavy for my old frame and I haven't your curves to fill it in all the right places anymore." The old woman chuckled as she pulled herself to her feet with her staff. She looked at Anne-Marie and gave a nod of approval. "But don't ye surely look the part of the warrior maiden? Woe to the man or beast that crosses your path."

"Mathers is the only man who needs to fear me, and Shade the only beast." Thunder rumbled in the distant hills as if her words carried her will with them. Dark clouds gathered on the horizon.

"Ye've got a way with your vows, lass. Would it hurt ye to make fewer of them for it seems like bad weather always follows close behind?"

"If it's a storm Shade wants, then let's give it to him," Anne-Marie said. She clenched her fist and a corona of lavender fire surrounded her like a halo.

Henna laughed again and clapped her hands together. "Perhaps that thunder is nothing more than the knocking of that old wolf's knees, knowing what's coming for him, eh? Show me the way to that wretch's hole in the ground, lass. Let's take the lead in this fight for once."

Anne-Marie's smile faded. "I am ready to fight, but I have to warn you. The shrine was consecrated to Shade ages ago, and his evil there is a real thing that can reach out and clutch at your heartstrings. The fallen dead who serve him still may not be all that we would face. We cannot go in there lightly."

Henna took her by the hand and gave it a gentle squeeze. "Child, throughout my years I learned from the bravest men and women that never should I seek out a fight. However, when one comes knocking, ye give it all the hell ye can bring along, and that damnable demon now stands upon my doorstep. Trust in Old Henna."

Anne-Marie watched as her teacher turned and made her way along the trail away from the cottage. She could see the pride of a warrior in the old woman's stride, and the relics in Whisperwind of both Viking and Indian origin left no doubt that Henna must have been formidable in her youth even before she became a Guardian of the Vale.

She only hoped that the old woman still had the same steel in the face of what lay before them.

CHAPTER 13
LIKE LAMBS TO THE SLAUGHTER – PRESENT DAY

Will stepped into the kitchen, pausing at the doorway as he saw Kimberly sitting at the kitchen table. She stared blankly out the window, sparing him only a slight glance as he placed his hand on her shoulder. Her hands were wrapped around the coffee mug that Angie had made for her a few years ago, but no steam rose from the drink.

"Can I warm that up for you?" he asked as he pointed to the cup.

"It would be the fourth time since I poured it. It's been cooked to death already. Just need to throw it out." She placed her hand over his and squeezed it in silent thanks.

"How about you, me, and Jamie head into town later? Grab a couple sandwiches and have a picnic at the park. I think we could all use a little distraction."

"I was going to make a pie to take to Jim and Paula."

"Any news about Clarissa?"

"No, still nothing. No one has seen her since the fundraiser the other day." Kim shook her head and wiped her eyes. "What kind of monster is loose in our town? Angelica, Clarissa, that poor woman they found ripped to pieces a couple of weeks ago. Pioneer Vale doesn't get this kind of trouble."

Will knelt down beside her and drew her into his arms. "I'm not giving up hope on either one of those girls. Angie and Clarissa are both tough as nails. They'll fight to get back to us."

"I know. Trish Robillard made a comment the other day about how each day someone is missing the odds of them being seen again drop. I lost my cool, and ...well, let's just say I don't expect a Christmas card from them this year." Kim got up and walked over to the sink where she emptied out her cup and placed it in the basin. She stared out the window at the empty yard. "She's still alive, Will. Don't ask me how I know, but she's still out there. It feels like something big is coming. All these strange events going on lately are leading up to something... horrible. I don't know what it is, but the girls are somehow a part of it all."

"Can't think like that, honey. You'll spend your days looking over your shoulder instead of enjoying what's right in front of you."

"I don't know what to think anymore." She shrugged. "You should do something with Jamie. I saw him this morning standing outside Angie's door like he wanted to go in but was afraid to."

"Maybe I'll take him with me to check the fence line. Saw some strange tracks out on the north end. Something out near the Climb is chasing all the animals this way."

"Good Lord, not another den of foxes, is it? We got lucky last time that Animal Control was able to relocate them."

"I don't think so. Tracks I saw were a lot bigger than that. I already made a few phone calls, but haven't heard anything back. I want to make sure that nothing dangerous comes down out of those woods."

"I saw some deer running through the south field earlier. Didn't stop to nibble at anything. They were just... running from something." She frowned and grabbed the sponge from the little ceramic dish by the faucet handle. She turned on the faucet and squirted some soap into her mug. "Our own horses have been skittish lately also. Oh, Will, could it be a bear coming down out of the hills?" Her lip trembled and Will knew she was thinking again of their daughter.

"Tracks didn't seem like any bear or even a mountain lion I've ever seen. More like a wolf…"

The crash of broken glass interrupted him as Kim dropped her coffee mug to the floor and turned to face him. Will watched the blood drain from her cheeks. "You saw a wolf?"

"Kim, are you ok," He took her hands and looked them over for cuts. She was trembling like a newborn calf, and he steadied her as she leaned back against the bar. "No, I didn't see one, but if that's what we've got on our hands it's a damn big one. That's why I already told all of the neighbors. More eyes watching out helps us all sleep a little easier. Maybe spare some livestock. Meanwhile, I figure I can go take a look. If he's a loner, then maybe I can put an end to him quickly and easily."

"Or vice versa, Will." She hugged herself and then wrapped her arms around him. "Maybe we should take that trip into town instead. I don't want you and Jamie going out there."

"Kim," Will said as he stroked her long brown hair, "I just want to check around the property lines. Jamie probably won't even have to get out of the truck. I'll grab a couple of rifles and maybe he and I can just do a little target practice."

"OK, Sarge," Kimberly said as she nodded her head and gave him a quick kiss. "Just promise me that you won't try anything heroic. If things seem off, I want both of you to just run, ok? You never know what may be out there." Will saw her eyes glaze over and she shivered once more. He squeezed her tightly, resting his chin on the top of her head while she shook in his arms with her head buried into his chest.

"That's why I'm bringing along my wingman, honey. We'll watch each other's back. Never go on an operation alone. I figure me and him with a couple of guns between us, we won't have anything to worry about." He kissed her on the forehead and started for the door.

"Will," she called to him as his hand turned the knob.

"Yeah, baby?" He watched her hug herself, rubbing her arms as if warding off a chill.

"Take the biggest gun you've got."

*   *   *

Ben couldn't believe his eyes. He stared at the sheaf of reports on his desk that had come back from pathology. Every single patient on who he and Rebecca had used the mysterious salve was showing an unprecedented recovery. Damaged tissue was rejuvenating and repairing itself. The results looked as though even leftover scarring would be minimal. He looked at the small remaining sample he had kept aside, and swirled it in the tiny vial. The viscous goop moved as if it were alive, and there were flashes like purple embers when the light caught it just right. He couldn't wait to get this stuff analyzed. See if it worked on other injuries. The research possibilities were endless. He laughed at himself as he put the glass tube into his desk drawer and locked it. He hadn't been this excited about his work in years. Ben scooped up the papers in front of him and shuffled them into a file folder and dropped the whole packet into his outgoing box. He swiveled around in his chair when a shadow blotted out the light behind him.

"For the love of …," he said as he nearly toppled out of his chair. "You scared the hell out of me."

"Sorry about that, Doc. Just wondering if you were planning on going home tonight?" said Rebecca from the doorway.

"Well, I was but I may have to go get admitted for a heart attack now."

"I wouldn't worry. You'd have to grow a heart first," she said with a grin.

"Touché," he replied. "Let's hope that never happens."

154

"Seriously though, what are you still working on that you didn't bolt for the door at shift change? I think we've both done our time for the day."

"I was just finishing up a few notes. Gathering my thoughts."

"Well, my thoughts are on seeing this place in the rearview mirror," Rebecca said. "Don't stick around too much longer, Ben. Radio says there is a nasty storm brewing up tonight. Rolled up out of nowhere, but looking worse by the minute."

"I will take that under advisement." An awkward silence fell between them and finally Ben cleared his throat. "Rebecca, I just wanted to thank you for all of your help lately. What we did the other day, trying out that salve was…"

"Risky, irresponsible, and might have cost both of us our careers?"

"Well, not to put too fine a point on it, but yeah."

"We did what we thought was for the best. We just got lucky that it paid off." She smiled. "And you are welcome, Doctor Hibble. I better run. John asked me to pick up something for dinner on my way home. See you later."

She disappeared and Ben caught himself grinning from ear to ear. He felt giddy and it dawned on him that he felt something so rare for him it was almost completely unfamiliar.

Pride in himself.

He shook his head, grabbed his bag, and carried a clipboard out to the triage area. With a nod of his head and a few waves to the folk on duty, he slipped out the side entrance into the employee parking lot. He thought about how the quaintness of Pioneer Vale had been the very thing that had lured him here to escape from his past. With the weirdness of the recent weeks, he found that his skepticism was shaken and that the talk of witches and magic seemed less and less like coincidence and superstition. He wasn't sold just yet, but he understood why the locals loved their legend.

A light drizzle fell from the sky already and thunder rumbled as he quickened his pace. He fumbled in his pocket for his keys and dodged a hole in the blacktop slowly filling up with water. A flash of lightning painted the sky into a vibrant lavender and blue vista as the rising sun tried to punch through the clouds ahead of him. Despite the rain, he only saw his day getting better.

His keys slipped from his fingers, bounced off his shoe, and slid along the asphalt until they came to rest on the ground under the bed of his truck. "Dammit," he said as he dropped down and pawed around trying to reach them. His hand splashed in another puddle under his vehicle, and he could feel water soaking into his jeans where his knee touched down. At last, his fingers closed on the ring and he dragged the jingling pile back into his grasp. "Hibble luck ain't gonna kill my buzz today," he said under his breath. He pulled himself up with a grip on the tailgate and tossed his keys into the air.

A boot scuffed behind him and a hand snatched the key ring from the air as they fell. Ben spun around, surprised and outraged when a firm hand grabbed his shoulder. He scowled and then Aiden's mocking laugh rang in his ear.

"Oh, it's you," Hibble said, "Mind giving me those back?"

Aiden lobbed them back, hitting Ben in the chest with them before he leaned up against the side of the truck. The grin on his face sent a shiver down Hibble's spine. "Why so surly, Benjamin? Did you end up in another brawl with a rambunctious teenager?"

"Not yet, knock on wood," Ben said as he rapped his knuckles against the side of his head. The faint smell of sulfur and something worse hit his nose. His stomach churned and bile burned the back of his throat.

"Well, the day is still young, Doctor." As Aiden stepped forward, his frame seemed to swell before Ben's eyes as if the man's muscles grew spontaneously.

As if by magic.

"Look, Aiden," Ben said with a gulp. "I just got off a long shift, and I just want to get home. In fact, I wish you well, but I'm not really looking for a new best friend right now, so I think it's for the best if you...."

"Get in the truck, Ben." Aiden's voice was cold and carried a sinister edge.

"Excuse me? Did you just give me an order?"

"You and I need to take a little ride."

"You are about to get hospital security called on you. Shake my hand and walk away now, so we can end this on good terms."

"I can't simply walk away, Doctor. You see, you and I have a much deeper history than you are aware of." The flash of a snarl crossed the man's face. "Now get in the truck."

Ben started to open his mouth but as he stared at Aiden, a black shadow rippled across the whites of the man's, and the teeth in that feral grin seemed to grow sharper. He fell back until the passenger side mirror struck his shoulder and he grabbed the door handle. He fumbled the keys in the lock when a low growl that rumbled from Aiden's throat ended the debate. The doctor climbed into the passenger seat and slammed the door. A moment later, Aiden slid behind the wheel. Aiden turned and raised an eyebrow, then glanced down at the keys still in Ben's hand. Hibble held them out and they were plucked away.

"What the hell are you?" he asked. His voice cracked as he pushed himself as far away from the driver as he could manage.

"I am something from your worst nightmares, Benjamin, but if you find me frightening, then buckle up." He cocked his head and gave a sly wink as the truck's engine roared to life.

"I've got something that I really want to show you."

* * *

Clarissa's head pounded as she slowly regained consciousness. She blinked but the room was so dark that she couldn't tell if her eyes were open or not. She tried to cough but a strip of cloth was tied securely around her mouth. It tasted like dirt. Her wrists were sore and sticky, and she knew that she must have rubbed her skin raw as she fought against the cords that bit into her flesh. Her arms were wrenched above her head and her shoulders ached from how she had been tied to a cold stone table by that jerk from the fundraiser.

Too late, she chided herself, she had realized that he was not a cop. She remembered the foul smell he gave off, but it was something worse than just bad breath or body odor. She thought about the time she and Angelica had found that dead raccoon when they had been running one day. The summer sun had done its work on the poor animal, but they had smelled it long before they found the carcass.

It was his eyes that had captured her though. Dark flames swirled and danced in the cold irises. Clarissa was drawn in and her will stolen away. She knew that he hadn't needed to force her to leave with him. With a simple request, she had felt compelled to follow him without so much as asking where they were headed.

Her brain was sluggish, and her first thought was that he was some kind of creep, but she realized that her clothes were all in place and hadn't been bothered. Had he just wanted to kidnap her then? Hold her for ransom? Why would he target her family, though? The Brenners were comfortable but hardly rich. No, there had to be another reason why she had been taken, but what?

Something shuffled in the darkness above her head. A low growl rose from the gloom that broke into wicked laughter. Clarissa whimpered and pulled at her bindings but the cords only sank deeper into her skin the harder she pulled at them.

"Please, Child. Keep struggling," said a throaty purring voice. "I do so enjoy watching my prey exercise the futility of their situation." A thick finger covered in bristly hair slid between her skin and the cloth tied around her face. A sharp nail scratched down her cheek. She coughed as her mouth cleared, choking on the horrible smell that she breathed in. It was the same stench that had come from her kidnapper, only it was stronger here.

"My family isn't wealthy. If you guys are doing this for a ransom, you are wasting your time," she gasped.

"I have no need for your money, sweetling," the voice said. Clarissa could sense the speaker slowly circling her. "Your presence here is part of a much more grandiose plan."

"This is about Angelica, isn't it? That's why she suddenly appeared at the school. " There was a snarl at her feet, and the scratch of claws against stone. Clarissa shivered as she felt raw strength and rage roll off of whatever stood at the end of the table. She choked back the urge to scream and prayed that it was too dark for her captor to see how badly she shivered. A moment passed and the dark chuckle returned. The pinpricks of talons grazed up her leg and across her stomach.

"Your dear friend has taken sides against the inescapable. She would try to alter the course of destiny." Hot breath blew across her cheek. "I cannot allow that to happen again."

Clarissa's mind reeled as she imagined every abomination that could be standing so close to her. Black claws, a mouth full of fangs just waiting to tear her apart as she lay helpless were only the beginnings of the dark places her imagination ventured to. She swallowed the lump in her throat and hoped her voice wouldn't shake too much.

"She beat you at the school, didn't she? You were counting on that bus explosion."

"Ahh, but the aftermath of such a tragedy would have been delicious. The weeping of all those parents would have been such sweet music." The voice, almost seductive now, was back at her head again. Circling still, stalking her even though she had nowhere to run. She winced as a droplet of the monster's drool splattered on her arm and burned as it ran down her forearm.

"You'll find the people of this town are made of tougher stuff than that. Pioneer Vale has been through a lot over the years."

"Oh, I am well aware. More so than you could ever imagine, sweetling. Stubborn and foolhardy to the last." Again the teasing point of a claw ran across her cheek, down her neck, almost like a caress. She jerked and tried to pull away, but a powerful grip closed around her throat. "I am a connoisseur of fear, young one. I have feasted upon such delicacies as timeless heroes breaking down into mewling puddles soaked in their own filth. I have tasted the final moments of folk heading into their great unknown. However, I find the terror of children by far the most savory of them all. Such innocent terror untainted by any such false bravado."

"Angelica will come for me. She and the other...witch," she croaked, lacking any other word for the redhead she had seen at the fundraiser that threw purple fire from her hands. Her pulse pounded in her temples as the mighty fingers teasingly squeezed her windpipe. Just as the world seemed to spin away, the rough hands let go and roughly dragged the ragged cloth back over her mouth.

"That, my dear girl, is precisely what I am counting upon." Dim red eyes suddenly flared in the gloom, giving her just enough light to see the monster beside her. Decaying lips pulled back from yellowed teeth while maggots crawled across rotten flesh and denuded bone. As the creature leaned closer its throaty chuckle turned into a fearsome snarl.

From around the gag, Clarissa screamed.

CHAPTER 14
WAYWARD SONS – PRESENT DAY

Ben stood before the entrance to the cave. A low moan came from that dark maw that chilled the doctor's blood. He could only hope that it was just a trick of the wind, but the fact that there wasn't a hint of a breeze didn't set his mind at ease. Aiden stepped up beside him and pressed a flashlight into his hand.

"Do come along, Benjamin. This storm is worsening as we speak, so we should at least get out of the rain." He gave Ben another of those toothy grins that made the hairs on his neck stand up. "Wouldn't want you to catch your death." Aiden stepped forward without hesitation and disappeared into the hole in the granite wall, his derisive laughter echoing from the depths.

Ben looked over his shoulder at the trail they had followed from the road that wound up the side of the Climb. Every instinct screamed for him to turn and run, flag down the first car he could find, and get away from this lunatic. Yet some inexplicable urge, like a whisper in the back of his mind, compelled him to go in. He flicked the switch of the flashlight, reassured by the strong beam that shone forth, and he followed the path into the cave.

Aiden waited just inside the deepest shadows, leaning against the rock with his arms crossed over his chest. Ben's flashlight zipped back and forth as he studied the ancient stone. Support beams ran down the length of the passage ahead. "What is this place? I didn't know there were any old mines near the town."

"This one has been a well-kept secret for many years. This place has a...shall we say, history, that the townsfolk would rather not be privy to."

"No kidding. This place gives me the creeps. Why are we here?"

"Because I have something to show you that I think you'll find quite interesting." Aiden beckoned for him to follow. Water dripped down the walls, and Ben cringed every time he reached out and touched the stone. After several twists and turns, they stepped out of the narrow tunnel into a wider cavern. The vaulted ceiling was lost in the darkness overhead that even Ben's light couldn't seem to pierce. Old tools and other remnants of the working mine were strewn about covered in cobwebs and dust. He took a step toward an old mine cart when he tripped over something hidden in the dirt. He landed hard on his knee and the hard rock of the cavern floor scraped the skin from his palm.

Aiden bent down beside him and picked up a skull from beside the fallen man. Ben saw the spider web of cracks through the surface. Something had struck this man hard enough to shatter the bone. His companion held it aloft and draped his hand dramatically across his own forehead.

"Alas, poor Hollister. I knew him, Benjamin." Aiden chuckled to himself and flippantly tossed the remains over his shoulder.

"You wanted to show me a dead prospector? Some guy killed in a mining accident?"

"Indeed. An accident born of crimson curls and lavender flame."

"I think that guy was dead long before the invention of viral videos if you're referring to that lady from the fundraiser clip. Is there a point to all of this, Aiden?"

"Indulge me a moment longer, my friend," said Aiden. He circled slowly around Ben, his eyes black once more with only flashes of red embers within them. "What if I told you that you had indeed set your eyes upon the legendary Witch of Pioneer Vale? Anne-Marie Carmichael. My mother."

"That's impossible. The Witch legend has been around for hundreds of years." Ben looked for an escape, but Aiden had him so turned around that he couldn't see the tunnel where they had come in from.

"I did tell you that I was older than I looked. I have been set free at last and will not rest until I rip her beating heart out of her chest, and you dear Benjamin, are going to help me." He stopped and crossed his arms over his chest, his weight shifted back on one leg.

"You're insane."

"Oh, indeed have I languished in the throes of madness at her hands, Benjamin. My mother has something of a mean streak toward her children. I have watched her over the decades end the lives of many of them, but let me ask you a question. Have you ever studied your own family tree?"

Ben hoped that if he kept Aiden talking long enough that a way out might appear. "My grandmother kept an old photo album that had a bunch of names and dates scribbled in it. I remember wondering who all those people were. Most of the names didn't seem to have a lot of connections to one another. A lot of different last names. She told me that our family had more than its share of out of wedlock births. Where are you going with all of this?"

"Do you recall the name 'Pritchard' listed anywhere in that old album?"

Ben's brow furrowed. "Sounds familiar, maybe. Yeah, I think I remember that name being on there a long way back. Why?"

"What if I told you that the reason this shabby little town feels so comfortable to you is that you are finally returned from whence you came." He shrugged. "A few generations removed, of course."

"Our meeting in the Huntsman wasn't by chance, was it?"

Aiden raised his hands in the air. "You caught me, Doctor. Our families have a certain history, but their relationship wasn't always as cordial as ours. My mother brought about your legacy of misfortune by calling out a poor misguided priest who tended his flock a little too closely. A sheep in wolf's clothing, if you will." Aiden cackled and slapped his knee.

Ben nearly lost control of his bladder with the startling imagery in Aiden's words. The shadowy creature from his nightmare roared back into his thoughts. "Please, I won't tell a soul about you if you just let me go. I'll forget I ever met you and you can go hunt down your mother."

Aiden stopped laughing and he stared down his thin nose. He grabbed Ben by the shirt collar and yanked the man from the ground with an ease that his frame wouldn't have suggested possible. "On your feet, Doctor. We are nearly at our destination." Aiden dragged him across the wide cavern floor and came to a dark hole in the far wall that led deep into the bowels of the earth. A foul stench rose up on the breeze that wafted from the dark tunnel.

"Whoa," said Ben. "What's down there? It smells like something died."

"A great many things over the centuries, in fact," Aiden hissed in his ear. He threw his arm around Ben's shoulders, gripping him tight even though the doctor tried to twist away. "Down this tunnel, you will at last find freedom from all of the indignities that your family has endured for so many years. At the end of this passageway, you can correct the folly of your ancestor. My dark master can offer you the recognition and respect that you have been denied your entire life." Aiden pushed Ben toward the tunnel and then marched past him. The shadows didn't so much swallow him up as embrace him as one of their own.

Ben spun the flashlight behind him, and could just barely see the mine entrance at the far end of the light. A mad dash to freedom again flashed through his mind, but he once more heard a hush at the edge of his thoughts. The hairs on the back of Ben's neck stood up. His knees knocked together and his stomach turned somersaults in his belly, but instead of a panicked race out of the cave, he turned and faced the foul tunnel. Once again, something tickled the back of his brain that made him go on. He gritted his teeth and descended into the darkness.

The foul miasma of the place gagged him and he tried to breathe through his mouth. The smell was so overpowering, though, that it didn't help. After about ten steps down the sloping hallway, he saw that the walls changed from rough-hewn rock to smooth worked stone. Biers were laid into the walls where burial linens wrapped loosely around blackened bones. Ashes crunched beneath his shoes and he wondered if it was the work of the fires of Hell itself that had done such work.

At last, the tunnel opened up and Ben stepped into the larger room. He stopped when he saw Aiden kneeling on the floor. Something writhed in the darkness ahead of them both and he flicked his flashlight over the other man's shoulder to see what it was. His jaw dropped when he saw Clarissa Brenner tied to a stone altar. She squinted as the light blinded her, and tried to scream around the gag in her mouth.

"What the hell is going on?" Ben rushed over to where Aiden raised his hands above his head. He grabbed the man by the collar and jerked him to his feet. His tormentor whirled around and Ben saw too late the rolling black shadow that coalesced around his friend's hands and the sickly red light that burned around the edges of Aiden's eyes.

"Do not touch me," snarled Aiden. His growl sounded like two starving wolves fighting over a piece of meat. With a sharp backhand, he struck Ben and sent him sprawling onto the cold stone floor.

Ben shook his head, and slowly pushed himself up. He could barely feel his jaw and he spat out a filling that had been knocked loose. He rested on his elbows then stared at the sight of the monstrous wolf statue that leered down from the ceiling caught in the wavering beam of his flashlight.

"Do you have the fortitude to atone for your predecessor's mistakes, Benjamin?" As Aiden drew his hands apart, a swirling storm of ash and flame formed between his fingers. The shapes converged into a knife of the blackest night that hovered in mid-air between them. Red veins of light pulsed like a heartbeat through the blade. Aiden reached forward and grabbed the hilt, then turned toward the altar.

"I don't have a clue what the hell you are talking about." Ben hauled himself back to his feet and stepped closer. "Look, I don't know what you have been through, man, but I am begging you to just let us go." Aiden whirled around and pointed the tip of the wicked knife at his throat.

"Your spineless ancestor forced my mother to give rise to the legend of the Witch of Pioneer Vale. When he accused her of witchcraft, she hid herself away to guard her true nature. My dark master," he said with a wave of his hand to the statue that towered over them, "languished in his exile and was denied from joining us in our world. Now, however, you are offered the chance to atone for the preacher's mistakes. You have brought me this innocent friend of my nemesis, my mother's protégé. With this sacrifice, we shall swing the door open a bit wider for the Father of Nightmares."

"Aiden, you can't be serious. You are talking about killing her," Ben tried to get closer, his eyes darting from the blade in Aiden's hand to the girl on the altar. He saw Clarissa squirm and pulled at the bindings that held her fast as Aiden's cruel intent sank in, but the leather cords at her wrists held her fast. Fresh blood welled from the raw cuts she had already given herself.

"Oh, far worse than that, Benjamin. I am going to torture the absolute hell out of her first. A man of your medical background should know exactly how to inflict the most pain without killing her. Before I release her to Death's embrace, she will scream so loudly that my mother will hear her all the way in her cozy little witch's cottage hidden away in these woods."

"I can't let you do that." Ben swallowed hard, but his mouth was bone dry. The lump in his throat barely moved.

"You cannot stop me, fool. I warn you, Benjamin. Do not choose the wrong side now. Cowardice runs in your blood. I offer you the chance to be feared." Aiden turned his back on him and leaned over Clarissa. He pulled the rag away from her mouth and then ran the point of the blade in his hand teasingly along her cheek and throat. The red veins in the dagger flared with angry crimson. "You are about to become part of history, my dear. A new reign shall come to our world as a result of your death," he said as he leaned closer to her. "But you will scream first."

Clarissa spit in Aiden's face. "Angelica won't let you get away with this. She'll come for me and make you burn."

"I've burned before, my dear. This time when she comes a-hunting me, she will quickly discover that I have the upper hand." He pressed the knife against her shoulder and Clarissa cried out as inky smoke curled up from where the tip pierced her skin. The blood that welled up from the cut turned black and then slithered up the blade, the red veins throbbing as it drank in the girl's life force.

With a great crack and shower of dust, the statue above them writhed, and an unholy crimson light flashed in the stone eyes. Shadows rippled like long-dormant muscle beneath the living rock.

"Leave her alone, you bastard," yelled Hibble. He swung his flashlight at the back of Aiden's head. The metal tube hammered against the man's skull with a dull ringing that echoed eerily around the sepulcher. Aiden staggered and clutched the end of the stone slab. The fiendish blade skittered from his hand and fell to the floor, the bloody tip sinking into the stone. Ben followed with a backhand swing that caught the snarling wizard under the chin. Aiden's teeth clacked together and he tumbled down the steps of the altar. He crashed to the floor on his back.

Ben jumped up the steps to the young woman who looked past him with terror-filled eyes. He followed her gaze upwards and saw the stone sculpture above snarling as it tried to break free from the wall where it was anchored. He ignored the growl above his head and ducked lower as the snapping stone jaws sent a rush of wind over them. Hibble focused only on the cords around Clarissa's wrists. He broke the one closest to him and then turned to her ankles while she untied her other arm.

"Behind you," she yelled, and Hibble whirled around as Aiden regained his feet. The wizard was dazed, and he bled from a deep cut on his chin. Ben ripped away the final bindings and pulled Clarissa from the table. He shoved her to one side and jumped forward to engage their enemy.

Aiden extended his hand as Ben drew back his fist. A blast of midnight black energy hissed through the air and slammed into his chest. Ben felt the air in his lungs burn as the coldfire punched through him and he skidded on his knees across the stone. He gasped but his breath froze in his body as though he were inhaling ice water. He choked and clutched his chest while Aiden slowly turned toward Clarissa.

*   *   *

Clarissa cowered at the edge of the dais as Aiden stepped over Ben's twitching body. She glanced at the statue of the wolf overhead and a chuckling growl shook the cavern. She turned her attention back to her kidnapper. Having nowhere to run, she rose up and squared off as the man approached.

"Now, my pet. I do not wish to keep my master waiting any longer when he is so close to his long-awaited victory. Let us finish what we have started, shall we?" The red-veined knife floated back to his hand and he plucked it from the air. He grinned and deftly twirled the blade in his long bony fingers.

"Finish this," she shouted as she lashed out with her foot catching him squarely in the groin. Aiden staggered, but his clumsy backhand swing hammered the dagger hilt across the girl's face. Clarissa was thrown back and sprawled in the dust. Aiden's shadow rose on the wall in front of her. She knew that she had only a moment before he unleashed his fury on her. She rolled over and scrambled away until her back hit the rock wall.

"That will be the last mistake you ever make," Aiden said as his eyes blazed with flickering black fire. He lifted his empty hand and a swirling maelstrom of magic engulfed it. Clarissa saw his fingers lengthen, his nails extending into talons of black iron. The air shimmered and the temperature plunged.

"Behold, the Nightmare Hand," said Aiden, his voice more of a ghostly keening as if the chorus of a thousand dead men who had fallen to Shade's deadly magic now spoke through the demon's apprentice. He drew back his hand, the air itself quaking with a shrill screech like metal grinding on metal. Clarissa's breath came out in frosty gasps as she frantically dug through the debris around her to find a rock or a stick or anything to defend herself with.

Her fingers closed on a piece of cold pipe lying hidden in the centuries-old dust and scattered bones that littered the room. She snatched it up and was surprised to see an old flintlock pistol in pristine condition.

Aiden's roar blasted her ears, and she had no time to marvel at how the antique weapon came to be here. She only hoped it still worked.

She thumbed back the hammer and squeezed the trigger. The pistol bucked and the boom of the gunshot was the most gratifying sound she had ever heard. Aiden spun around as the lead ball tore through his cheek, burning a line through his skin and spraying his blood across the dais steps. He fell to the ground clutching his face and screaming in rage and pain. As Clarissa clambered back to her feet, the engraved silver nameplate on the side of the pistol glimmered in the flickering lights of the shrine and she read the words:

"To Marcus Brenner,

with gratitude,

from the town of Pioneer Vale"

A howl from the depths of her worst nightmares shook the chamber as the wolf statue twisted around again. The hellish light of its eyes flared and the stone lips curled back around broken fangs. Clarissa screamed when cold fingers suddenly clutched her arm.

*   *   *

"You're ok, Clarissa," Hibble said as he hugged the girl to his chest. He saw the recognition in her eyes and she threw her arms around his neck. He sucked in his breath as she brushed across the scorch mark now emblazoned on the center of his chest.

"We have to get out of here," she cried. The deafening roar of the wolf trying to break loose drowned her words. Ben grabbed her hand and pulled her toward the exit to the mine.

"I promised your parents in the hospital that I would take care of you," he screamed over the snarling cacophony. "I want you to run like hell," He pushed the flashlight into her hand and pushed her toward the tunnel mouth. A rumbling snarl echoed through the chamber, showering them with dust from the cavern ceiling. Ben fell to his knees but waved Clarissa onward. A scream of fury joined the roar of the thrashing sculpture. The shadows parted enough for them to see Aiden rise from the ground. His eyes burned with hatred and malice. The dagger glimmered in his hand as he wiped blood away from the gash in his cheek.

"Go on! Get out of here. I'll buy you whatever time I can," Ben yelled to the girl.

"You can't stop him," Clarissa whispered. She wrung her hands around the barrel of her ancestor's pistol that she clutched to her chest.

"But your friend can. You have to warn them," Hibble said as he cupped the girl's face. A flicker of a smile flashed on his lips. "We need the Witches of Pioneer Vale." He jerked his head toward the exit, and with a quick nod, Clarissa turned and raced up the tunnel. She rounded the bend and disappeared from Ben's sight.

He sighed and turned to see Aiden marching toward him. Black fire wreathed the growling statue of the wolf as it glared down at him with hungry eyes. Hibble squared off and raised his fists as if this was just another bar fight. Given his opponent though, he wondered how bad of an ass kicking he was in for this time.

"Every time I try to make things quick and painless, someone steps forward and mucks it all up for me. One day, I am going to learn to stop being so polite," Aiden said as his knuckles whitened around the dagger hilt. "Perhaps that time is now."

"You won't catch her," Ben said. "That girl is one of the best runners in the state. Your sacrifice just got away, and you'll have to go through me before I let you walk out of this cave."

"Given the precariousness of your situation, Benjamin," Aiden said as he spun the blade into another dance, "you may want to reconsider those words." Aiden threw his arms out wide and his deep chuckle made a sinister harmony with the tumult from the twisted statue above.

Ben stepped forward and took a powerful swing at the man, but a swirling rift of black flame opened in the air behind Aiden and dragged him out of harm's way. Hibble stumbled as his follow-through set him off balance. A second flash of light dazzled his eyes as another mystic doorway opened and Aiden suddenly stood beside him. The dagger in his hand sizzled through the air, a trail of coldfire like a comet's tail behind it, as he plunged the devilish blade into Ben's stomach. He screamed as an icy grip pulled from beyond this world, feeding on his strength and sapping the vitality from him.

"Ahh, Benjamin," Aiden purred in his ear. "THAT sacrifice got away. I had hoped to spare you because of the unfortunate history that our ancestors shared." The smug grin fell away from his face. "However, your screams of terror shall serve just as well in her stead." He placed his palm on Ben's chest and another bolt of searing cold flooded him. The coldfire bounced him against the rock wall behind where he stood. He screamed as his body succumbed to the freezing power that washed through his body. Hibble flailed weakly, but his fist missed Aiden by a wide swath, and he fell to his knees once again.

"Lord Shade," Aiden called out to the wolf statue above the altar. "Taste the pain and fear that your mighty image has instilled in this man. With his blood spilled, let your glory manifest so that together we may hunt down the accursed Guardians."

Ben fought to keep his eyes open as the great wolf head met his gaze once more. The shattering stone deafened him as the massive sculpture broke free from the cavern ceiling and crashed to the floor. Splinters of rock lanced through his skin in a thousand needle-like shards. He shielded his eyes from the billowing clouds of dust but at last, his vision cleared enough to see a massive black form slowly rise out of the broken rock.

Dark as night, swirling like a living fog, the cloud assumed a man-like shape, heavily muscled with black claws, and cold red eyes that bore into Hibble's heart. The creature wavered then fell onto its hands and knees, finally solidifying into the form of a gigantic black wolf. A mournful, frustrated wail filled the chamber, drowning out the slowing thud of Ben's heartbeat pounding in his ears. The great beast approached until it was nose to nose with the doctor.

The fiery eyes gleamed with mockery and scorn. The lips curled back and Ben heard laughter in the throaty growl. The canine snout dipped to the floor and lapped at the blood spreading from the gash in Ben's stomach. The wolf looked at Aiden, delivered a long low rumbling growl, and then loped up the tunnel toward the entrance.

"As you command, my lord," said Aiden as the wolf passed by. Ben clawed at the stone, trying to drag himself away from the man when he knelt down beside him.

"Get away from me," croaked Ben. He tried to push the man away, but his strength spilled out, and his hand slipped in his own blood. Aiden grabbed his hair and yanked his head back.

"I have good news for you, Benjamin. Your family misfortunes are nearly at an end," Aiden said with a hiss.

"The rest of the world's are just beginning."

*   *   *

The black wolf burst from the mine entrance in a blast of gravel and shale. His paws skidded in the rocky soil and threw his head to the sky. The beast's howl shook the trees and sent aloft the few scavenger birds that were still in the area. An unholy red glow filled the creature's eyes and frost formed on the ground where his claws dug into the dirt. His shape shimmered like asphalt on a hot summer day and wisps of black fire rose around him.

From her place in the bushes, Clarissa held her breath, biting her tongue so that she wouldn't scream as the monstrous fiend stepped nearer. She watched his head turn from side to side, sniffing the air in search of something. The ground shook beneath his every step as he stalked from one side of the clearing to the other.

She pressed her hand over the cut on her neck hoping that she could mask the smell of her blood. The young woman nearly screamed as the glowing coals of his eyes turned toward her, and she swore that its lips pulled back in a grin. Another sniff of the air caught the beast's attention and it looked back over its shoulder. The massive wolf turned and raced off into the trees and down the side of the mountain leaving the smell of sulfur in its wake.

Clarissa gasped and trembled as tears ran down her face. She crawled out from under the bushes and rose up on legs so wobbly that she nearly toppled over. Pioneer Vale was in danger and she had to warn somebody. She spied a familiar farm in the distance that peeked through the tree line. She started down the slope of Alistair's Climb, thankful that Carmichael Farms was in the opposite direction of where the demonic wolf had gone. She prayed that she would find Angelica and the redheaded witch there, but, if not, then at least Angelica's dad was both a soldier and a seasoned hunter.

She only hoped they would be enough.

CHAPTER 15
RETRACING STEPS – PRESENT DAY

Will stared at the track in the mud and swallowed hard although his mouth was dry as ash. Definitely canine, but he couldn't imagine the size of the beast that could have left this behind. His hand shook as he tried to measure the print, but the length between his thumb and little finger fell short of the span. If anything, this massive track seemed even larger than the ones he had spotted by the carcass the other day. Worse yet, it was fresh, which meant that a damn big predator was somewhere close by.

"Hey, Dad," said Jamie as he came up the trail with his hunting rifle cradled in his arms. "I need to step behind those bushes over there for a second."

"Better hold it, son. I think we need to circle back toward the truck. Stay close and keep your eyes open for me, ok?" They had driven this morning a couple miles away from the house and parked along the side property line of Carmichael Farms. Alistair's Climb towered nearby, but some instinct had led Will away from the peak, toward the old part of the forest that was still largely untamed. Ancient trees stood like silent sentinels watching over those who found their way beneath their thick boughs.

"Everything alright, Dad? You seem kind of spooked."

"I'm fine, Jamie," said Will, "but I'd feel better if you weren't out here with me right now. Daylight's burning so let's move."

The boy stepped closer, and Will saw his son's eyes widen. His son pointed down at the ground. "Holy cow! Is that from a bear?" He clutched his rifle a little tighter as his head whipped back and forth through the encroaching forest.

"I don't think so, but we aren't going to stick around long enough to find out. Let's march, son." Will's tone was soft but commanding as he gave Jamie a gentle push back toward the trail they had come up.

A low growl rumbled from the trees ahead, and branches cracked away as a horror from Will's deepest nightmares pushed through the bushes. A gigantic wolf blocked their path back to the road and its ferocious snarl sent what few birds remained nearby to wing. Its eyes gleamed with a cold hellish red glow, and the drool that fell from its jaws left plumes of smoke as each drop burned into the fallen leaves. Will was reminded of the state record bull that he had seen at the county fair when he was a boy, but this monster dwarfed that animal. Even at his six-foot-plus height, his eyes weren't level with the wolf's heavily muscled shoulder. He jumped in front of his son, keeping his eyes locked on the creature in front of them. He gripped the shotgun in his hands, wondering if he could get a shot off before it charged.

"Dad," cried Jamie clutching his father's sleeve. His voice was shrill and Will heard the edge of tears as he spoke. "What is that thing?"

"Jamie," Will said, swallowing away the waver in his voice. "I want you to back up slow, son. He might wander off if we don't seem threatening, but if he jumps at me I want you to run like hell for the road. Don't look back, and don't stop until you are in the truck."

As one, they stepped back. The beast growled and moved forward in time with their own retreat, and then paused when they stopped. The wolf lowered his head, digging a deep furrow in the dirt, shifting its weight from side to side as if waiting for them to dash one way or another.

"What's he doing," Jamie whispered.

"I don't know," Will replied. "I've never known an animal to act this way before."

They took another step, and, again the creature matched their pace. The wolf circled to the left and then advanced, deliberately and purposefully angling their path toward the downhill slope that led to an old creek bed. Will tried to move toward more level ground, but the nightmarish creature cut him off. The huge wolf wasn't hunting them. It was herding them.

Their boots splashed through the shallow water of the creek, and into the deeper, older forest on the far bank. The temperature plunged as the thicker canopy of the trees above blocked out all but the most determined rays of sunlight from hitting the forest floor.

A strange tingling sensation warmed Will's back. He glanced over his shoulder and saw a clearing with a polished black slab of stone. With the suddenness of a man dunked into an icy pond, everything rushed back to him. He remembered the details of his brother's disappearance so many years ago. He saw himself beside Angelica when the redheaded witch stepped through a ring of flame in midair. He remembered the sting of the strange woman's purple fire. Like a beacon punching through a thick fog, Will recalled every detail about his daughter's disappearance.

The wolf growled again, and the air in front of it shimmered as if the sound from its maw struck some barrier. The beast rose up on its hind legs and its muscles rippled strangely beneath its skin. Outstretched forelegs twisted and popped. The padded paws elongated, and the iron black claws took the shape of wicked fingers. A gale not unlike the one Will had been caught in on his last trip to the grove kicked up in strength, forcing them to cover their eyes in the hail of dirt and leaves. Lightning flashed and thunder boomed overhead, and the wolf howled as its limbs snapped back to their more normal, yet still terrifying, form. The beast fell back to all fours and bared its wicked fangs.

*   *   *

Anne-Marie cried out and tore away the bracer on her left wrist. Black energy coursed through the veins beneath the scar. Her skin rippled and blistered as smoke rose from her forearm. Although the old injury had never healed, it looked as freshly burned now as it had that day so many decades ago when Shade had grabbed her in the Realm of Nightmares. The pain that shot through her now, however, had never been this intense. It could mean only one thing.

"Shade is coming," she said through gritted teeth. She snatched the glass of water she had been sipping from and poured it over her skin. The tiny deluge did little more than ruin the pages she had been reading at her table. With her free hand, she summoned a globe of lavender fire, but the ball wavered, like a candle sputtering to stay lit. Anne-Marie scowled and closed her eyes. Sweat beaded her brow and her lips curled back over clenched teeth. The flames finally burst into wispy tongues of fire that she sent into a gentle cascade over the ancient wound. The blistering subsided, and the jet black veins faded back to their rosier hue.

Angelica's spell journal fell from her lap to the floor with a thump. The girl cried out as she rolled into a ball and clutched her stomach. The smell of burning flesh filled the room as Anne-Marie stumbled over to the couch in Whisperwind's extra-dimensional library. She raised her arms and bathed her granddaughter in the cleansing flames until the younger woman breathed easier and pulled herself upright. The fires winked out, and Anne-Marie grabbed the edge of the table to steady herself.

Angelica dragged herself from the couch and rushed to her side. The teen snatched a soft cotton towel from the neat stack at the side of the mixing table and wrapped it gently around the scarred tissue of her arm.

"How much power did you pour into that healing? I've never seen you strain this hard," she said.

"It wasn't much at all," Anne-Marie gasped. "I had to struggle to bring my magic to task. Shade is trying to silence the Whisper once more. He intends to attack soon."

"And with neither one of us in the best condition to face him. He sure knows how to pick his moment, doesn't he?"

Anne-Marie nodded. "Something terrible has happened. He's never been this strong a presence in our world. The only way he could be any closer is if we were dead. We need to figure out where he plans to strike."

Angelica's face went white. "He's in the grove. That's where I fought him in my nightmare."

"That's impossible. Even the Father of Nightmares can't see through the glamours that shroud the Widow Stone. The only way he could get through…" She paused and tapped a fingernail against her teeth.

"Is what?"

"Is if someone who had been there before has shown him the way."

*　　*　　*

Will stood in the sunlight that peeked through the clouds in the open meadow. He slowly pumped a shell into his shotgun, flicking the safety off with practiced ease. "Jamie, I want you to keep moving and take a spot behind that black rock. Once I fire the first shot, you follow up with a second from your rifle."

"Can our guns even hurt that thing?" Jamie asked. Will felt the boy shake as he held on to his coat. The boy peeked around his elbow at the monster stalking them. The wolf paced at the clearing's edge, jaws slavering, but hesitant to cross the threshold of the grove.

"We're about to find out. Keep that black stone between you and him and remember to aim for someplace thick enough that you won't miss him." As if that were a difficult feat, mused Will. He fought back a panic-induced chuckle. Jamie's squeezed his wrist and stepped aside, ready to bolt away. The wolf raised its muzzle and swung its head back and forth keeping watch over them both. The creature once again tried to rise on its hind legs and wisps of energy coursed through the wolf's frame.

"Jamie, run now," shouted Will as he raised his gun to his shoulder and drew his sight on the writhing beast in front of him. His eyes met the burning gaze of the rage-filled fiend before him. The former Marine paused in mute shock as plumes of black fire rolled across the creature's back. The leaves above it burst into flame as the monster thrashed around. Will steadied the barrel and squeezed the trigger, the mighty boom echoing through the clearing.

The wolf leaped and rolled to the side, as the slug whizzed harmlessly past. The beast crouched and was ready to spring when the zing of Jamie's rifle shot cracked past the former Marine's ear. Will worked the shotgun's pump, loading another round. The shell clicked into place, but too late he saw the enormous beast already launching itself into the air. He squinted down the barrel once more, but he knew that he moved too slowly. Behind him, he heard Jamie's piercing scream as black death rushed toward them.

A flash of purple light and the roar of bonfire washed through the clearing. A shockwave knocked Will aside and out of the path of the creature's lunge. The monstrous wolf was thrown to the ground. It skidded in the soft soil as its claws raked the dirt. Will rolled away, looking up in time to see Angelica step out of a blazing wreath of purple fire that hung in the air above the black stone that dominated the clearing. She dropped lightly to the ground, followed by the redheaded witch that had taken her away. A blinding glare made him cover his eyes, but his jaw dropped when he saw through his fingers that his daughter's hands were encircled by crackling white lightning.

He saw Angelica drape an arm protectively around her brother, twirling him behind her as she loosed a lance of white fire at the scrambling wolf. The bolt wrapped around the beast and hurled him through the air toward the edge of the clearing where it slammed into a might oak with an ominous crack. The creature was slow to get up, but it whipped its head around to the women who took to the front line.

The redhead was surrounded in a corona of raging flame and two bursts of lavender fire poured from her outstretched palms. Her blasts punched into the roaring wolf, rolling him through the brush and setting the nearby bushes ablaze. With a shrill yelp, the creature raced off into the underbrush.

"Don't let him get away. We have to stop him!" shouted Anne-Marie as her lavender flames dimmed around her. She stumbled and a trickle of blood dripped from her nose. She nearly fell but Will caught her and held her steady. She thanked him with a silent nod.

"You ok, kid?" Angelica asked. Will turned and saw his daughter grab her brother and squeeze him tightly to her. Tears welled up in his eyes and he raced over to them and grabbed her by the shoulders. He just looked into her brown eyes, and then engulfed her in a massive bear hug for the first time in weeks.

"Angie! It's really you. You're alive! I thought I'd never see you again."

"I don't think you were supposed to, Dad," she said. "You don't understand what's going on. We have to hurry before Shade escapes." She gently pushed her father away, but Will held firm.

"Now hold on just a minute, young lady. I didn't just get you back to have you chase off after some mutant Hound of the Baskervilles. It's time I got some answers and then we're going to go hunt that thing down together."

*   *   *

"It's too late," said Anne-Marie as she returned from the tree line. "He's already gone. Slipped away before we could cage him." She glanced over at Jamie, who stared at her with his mouth agape. She gave the boy a wink, and gently lifted his chin with her finger. She then turned to face Will.

"Whatever tricks you played on me are over," Will said to her as she walked over. "You took my little girl from me. I remember everything now."

"Then you should recall how I told you that the fate of the world depended on us stopping the forces of evil. You have no idea how fortunate you are to be alive. Did you think you could stop the Father of Nightmares with an ordinary bullet?"

"Father of Nightmares? You mean that wolf? I don't get it."

"Dad," Angelica said, "What are you even doing out here? How did you find your way back?"

"That thing herded us here. Kept us backing up until we stumbled into the grove."

"Shade used his own magic to draw the path from your hidden memories, the dark playground that he is master of. Once you breached the veil that surrounds this place, the demon knew that I would sense him."

"And that we would come running," Angelica added. "I don't get it though. Why would he risk drawing us out on home ground though? Shade knows he wouldn't stand a chance of beating us here alone."

"It was a message," said Anne-Marie. "Or rather an invitation. He was daring us to face him. He pushed us to react and now wants us to chase him to his own battleground."

"Then let's give him what he wants," Angelica growled. Lightning crackled as she clenched her fists, and thunder rumbled in the sky.

"Angelica, look at us," said Anne-Marie. "Our powers are weakened just by his presence, your stomach is bleeding through again, and we need to see your brother and father to safety first."

"We can't let him hurt anyone else. Where would he go next? Would he charge straight into town and go on a rampage?"

"I think we already know the answer to that." She waved a hand at Will and Jamie. "He drove these two here to us, leaving the farm virtually empty."

"Virtually," said Will, "but not entirely, you mean. Kim is there all alone."

Anne-Marie nodded. "And the Father of Nightmares is undoubtedly racing there to meet my son so that when we come rushing to the rescue he can finally make his play to destroy us both. We risk the end of times, Child."

"Shade and Aiden are going to attack my mom. This is what you have been trying to prepare me for. This isn't about anger or revenge anymore. It's about saving the people we love."

The corner of Anne-Marie's mouth curled up and flames danced in her eyes. "And at last you know what it means to be a Guardian."

"We have to get there as fast as we can," said Angelica. "Time to rip open one of your portals."

"Stand back," said Anne-Marie. Flames surrounded her hands and she drew her clenched fists slowly apart. A rip in the air burst to life, but it wavered and sputtered. Some unseen resistance fought against her. She poured all of her might into the effort but her magic flickered and died out.

"What's the matter?" asked Angelica.

"I can't open the gateway straight to the farm. Shade's growing strength blocks me from taking us directly there."

"My truck is close by," offered Will. "But it's still a bit of a drive. If we move out now, maybe we can still get there in time."

Anne-Marie bit her lip in frustration but stopped when she saw Angelica's scowl. The young woman, the co-captain of Pioneer Vale High's cross country track team, knelt down and began deliberately tightening the laces on her shoes.

"How close can you get me?" Angelica asked.

*   *   *

Vines and roots writhed and clutched at her feet, tripping her up as Clarissa stumbled through the tree line. Her knee slammed into a stone, but the bolt of pain that shot up her leg was still dwarfed by the searing agony that wracked her body from the cut at her throat where the black dagger had pierced her. The shadows twisted behind her, spectral fingers reaching forward reluctant to let her escape. The howl of a wolf echoed in the woods behind her and she dragged herself back to her feet.

The farmhouse ahead brought a sigh of weary relief to her face, but it was the terror that lay behind that gave her the strength to chew away the distance to the front porch. She fell again as her feet hit the front step and she scraped the skin from her knee as she skidded across the rough boards. The screen door burst open and gentle hands took her by the shoulders.

"Clarissa," cried Kim. "Oh my God, is it really you? Sweetheart, are you ok?"

Clarissa squeezed the woman tight as her heart thudded in her chest. "Angelica is alive," she gasped as tears streamed down her face, "but we're all in danger."

"Come inside and let me call your parents, and then the police. Oh, honey, we've been worried sick." Kim pulled her to her feet and dragged her by the hand into the foyer of the Carmichael farmhouse.

Clarissa caught a glimpse of movement from the corner of her eye and saw Aiden walking up the driveway toward the porch. His wavy chestnut hair flowed behind him, caught by the winds of the approaching storm. She yelped and dug her fingers into Kim's arm. "That's him," she screamed. "He's the one who took me."

The man's eyes darkened, but he maintained his steady pace and slowly raised his hand. It shimmered like the highway during the summer heat, and when he punched forward toward them, a wave of concussive force blasted the women back through the door of the farmhouse. Clarissa heard a loud crack and felt the warm rush of blood from her nose as she careened off the door frame. She felt Kim's arms wrap around her, but the power of the blow threw the two women down the hallway, tripping over one another until they collapsed in a tangled heap. The thump of the man's boots on the porch shook away their dizziness as his dark shadow blotted out the light streaming through the doorway.

Aiden cracked his knuckles, sparing a glance over his shoulder before he leaned against the jamb, and crossed his arms over his chest. His grin mocked them as the women slowly pushed away from the floor. Their breath came out in puffs as a chill rolled off of him.

"Mrs. Brighton, I presume," he said in a throaty whisper. "My name is Aiden Carmichael. You have no idea how pleased I am to make your acquaintance at last."

CHAPTER 16
TRAITORS IN OUR MIDST - 1671

"I believe this covers the next sortie, Captain," said Patch as he opened the lid of the small wooden chest on the back of the wagon. The gold within the box gleamed as brightly in the torchlight as the host of weapons carried by Forrester's soldiers around him. "How soon can Preston expect results?"

"Tell our benefactor that the next phase of his plan has already been...executed," Cyrus said with a laugh. "I expect the news shall reach the town in short order, Master Erickson." The mercenary closed the chest and fastened the lock. He waved to two of his men who carried it away toward their own supply wagon nearby. "And here I thought my boys were bloodthirsty. What you and Mathers have outlined has even some of my hardiest men off-balance."

"I trust you aren't having a change of heart on me, Cyrus," said Patch. Forrester saw the torches flickering in the icy blackness of that piercing uncovered eye. "It would upset me terribly if I were forced to take a more direct hand in the leadership of your Reavers."

Cyrus frowned. "You just keep the coins coming, big man. I had hoped for a bit of honest fighting, but we're cut for wholesale slaughter if that's what you want. Blood's on your hands for today's work though." Patch took a step closer, and Forrester held out his hand to stay his men from drawing weapons. To Forrester's chagrin, Erickson didn't even spare them a second glance but squared up nose to nose with him.

"You were hired to start a war, Captain. In order to gain the town's support, there are certain unsavory things that must be done. You and your men knew what they signed up for, and you have been well paid already without having fulfilled your end of the bargain."

"And what of the fact that we now pursue your escaped witch? The hunt for such devil spawn was not in our original contract. Although my men have engaged in such activity before, the risks of fighting her conjurations are far greater than butchering a lot of buckskin-clad brutes. Should any of my soldiers die to her sorcery, men of such training and experience won't be easy to replace. When do I see the bump in pay for this new enterprise?"

Patch snorted. "That woman is no more devil spawned than you are, you opportunistic thug. Bring her to me and I will see you are fairly paid, but she is little more than a bounty to be had. Be wary, Captain. I will not endure any more attempts to alter the terms of our arrangements. "

Forrester locked glares with Erickson, who didn't flinch despite being surrounded by Cyrus' own men. He felt a chill flow into his body as he met that single dark eye, and Forrester swore at that moment that something from beyond this world stared back at him. His every instinct told him that he had fallen in with something far more dangerous than he had bargained for.

Cyrus threw his head back and let his bellowing laugh echo into the night. He turned his back to Patch, waving his arms out wide, encouraging his men to join in his mirth. The volume rose, turning the heads of a few townsfolk further up the street. Suddenly, Forrester spun around, the knife from his belt sheath already in his hand, only to find that Erickson already loomed over him. Mathers' man swatted his blade away and lashed out with ungodly reflexes.

Sparks of light exploded in Cyrus' eyes as Patch closed his crushing fingers around his throat. He clawed at the brute's hand, raking flesh and drawing rivulets of blood that ran down Patch's wrist, but the iron grip was relentless. He gasped for air and his vision faded. The pointed tip of Erickson's own knife poked against his stomach. The smell of brandy tickled his nose as Patch leaned closer and Erickson's bared teeth were close enough that he could bite Forrester's face. With an effortless heave, Patch hurled the mercenary back into the arms of his men.

"Dead men can't spend gold, Captain, but attack me again and we'll find out which of these fine men standing around us wouldn't mind adding your considerable share to their own. Shall we put their loyalty to the test?"

"Stand down, lads," croaked Cyrus as he rubbed his neck. The soldiers helped him back to his feet and slowly took their hands away from half-drawn weapons. He straightened his leather vest, then he coughed and spat. He bowed his head curtly toward Patch.

"Damn shame you throw in with Mathers, Erickson. We could make one hell of a fortune if you joined up with us."

"Do as you are told and you will still have it, Cyrus," growled Patch. "As soon as the town hears of the next unprovoked act of Indian aggression, Preston will call for immediate retaliation. Have your men ready, for the fight you have been waiting for is upon us," said Erickson. He studied the assembled soldiers, gave a parting sneer, then turned and walked away.

Forrester's second, a rugged blond man with a scraggly goatee, approached him. The young officer carried his pistol cocked and ready in his hand. "Say the word and I shall put one in his back, sir."

Cyrus waved a dismissive hand. "Put it away, Carter. I shudder to think what you'd bring down upon us all were you to miss, son. Get the men quartered for the night. I want equipment checks at dawn. Any trouble receiving those new supplies?"

"No, sir. Our smith from down the coast met with Dasher and Marshall precisely as you had instructed. It was far enough outside of the town that none of the residents caught wind of them. The squad had what they needed in time and left a few more bits of damning evidence around the site."

"Good. Survivors, I trust?"

"One, sir. Injured but able to sit a horse. She was last seen on horseback riding toward the town as fast as she was able."

"Then we are in motion. Get the rest of the weapons and ammunition distributed to our outliers. Mathers also apparently had some new livery made up for us, so see to it that our men are dressed out. Once that rider reaches the town, Preston shall have the final incentive he needs to incense the town enough to rise against the natives. He'll finally have his war." He rubbed his neck again as he watched Erickson's hulking figure disappear into the shadows near Preston Mathers' estate.

"Reckon that one's half demon, do you, sir?" said the younger soldier.

Forrester snorted. "No demon there, son, although it wouldn't surprise me to hear he worked for one. No, my boy, I think Master Erickson is nothing more than one incredibly tough son of a bitch. Enough of that for now. You and the men have your orders. Hop to them."

The soldiers broke up their gathering, commands were given, and the men fell to their chores as instructed. So focused were they on their duties that they failed to hear the faint rustling in the nearby bushes.

*   *   *

As the soldiers dispersed, Micah Robillard finally breathed again. How the mercenaries couldn't hear his teeth chattering or his knees knocking as he once more became an unwitting spy was beyond his reckoning.

The young blacksmith slipped back through the bushes the way he had come. He looked toward the Hirsute Huntsman, knowing Marcus and Abel were still there. He hoped that the two of them would have some idea what to make of this new information.

"I swear on my life," Micah muttered as he ran down the street, "that when this business is behind us, I will never eavesdrop on another soul."

*   *   *

Marcus shut the door to his drawing-room in his family's quarters above the Huntsman while Abel poured the shaken smith a drink from Brenner's private stock. The young man tried not to slosh the potent liquor, but he couldn't hold his hands steady.

"Take a breath, son," he said as he plopped his massive hand on Micah's shoulder. "That drink takes me some time to brew to that potency and I won't have it wasted on my tabletop. You are among friends here."

Micah threw back the whiskey and coughed. He wiped his mouth with the back of his hand and then waggled two fingers at Abel to give him a refill. The old farmer obliged as he studied the young man's face.

"Tell us what you heard, slowly and with all the detail that you can remember," said Abel.

"Mathers hired those mercenaries to start a bloody war," said the blacksmith. "I would wager that the ambushed patrol wasn't attacked by the local tribe, but rather they were set upon by these soldiers all to turn the town against our neighbors so that we would welcome the attack on the Nipmuc people."

Marcus brought two more glasses to the table and poured drinks for all three of them. He raised an eyebrow as Micah threw that one back also.

Abel swirled the amber liquid in his glass, deep in thought. "It certainly seems like the sort of dastardly plot that fits along with Preston's character. None of the men who survived the ambush have said anything to suggest it wasn't the Nipmuc warriors though. The bodies had been removed from the battle site when our folk went out there to bring back our fallen. We are left as always with nothing to bring against Preston and prove that the attack was anything other than what it appeared to be."

A log cracked in the fireplace as the three men sat in silence. "Maybe we do," said Micah as he stiffened and fumbled at a pouch on his belt. He took something out and slammed his hand down on the table. "Here's our proof. It has stared me right in the face this whole time and I was too daft to know it." He raised his hand away from a broken arrow shaft with the metal head gleaming in the firelight of the room.

"I don't follow you, son," said Marcus. He picked up the arrowhead and ran his thumb along the edge. A line of blood rose from his skin and he sucked his thumb into his mouth.

"That arrowhead is forged metal. The native people make their weapons out of bone or flint."

"Who's to say they haven't upgraded? We know they keep watch on us from the fringes of the forest. What if they saw us using metal tools and decided to step up? If they were planning to attack," said Abel as he raised a hand to halt Micah's imminent protest, "and I'm not saying that they are, it would make sense for them to improve their equipment, wouldn't it?"

Micah shook his head. "Do you see those squiggles on the face of the metal? My father taught me about them when he was teaching me the trade. You will find those same markings on all of the other weapons that

192

were carried back to my forge after the attack. Master blacksmiths use them to sign their work. It advertises their craftsmanship and marks it as their own."

"Like branding livestock?" asked Marcus as he handed the piece back to the young man.

"Exactly. These weapons were made at another forge, and I would wager that it was the same smith that I overheard Forrester and his man speaking of. Weapons crafted by a smith from another town, purchased by Mathers, and delivered to the mercenaries so that they could stage the attack on our men."

"Preston's sparing no expense to cause all of this trouble," said Abel. He shook his head and threw back his drink.

"Well, he does have a wall of gold that he has been chipping away at for who knows how long," added Marcus. "I still don't understand what Preston stands to gain from starting a war in the first place, though?" He scratched at his beard.

"If we fail to convince anyone else about the truth of his hired guns, it will be too easy for him to spin a tale of his foresight saving the town," said Micah. "He'll be praised as our savior despite everyone knowing that he does nothing without an underlying motive."

"If Pioneer Vale wins the war," said Marcus, "then he can come forward as the hero of the town who brought in these soldiers to protect us. The tribe would be driven from the surrounding lands, and he would become the wealthiest landowner on these shores."

"And in command of a private army on his payroll to enforce his rule over Pioneer Vale," said Abel. "He could become a king and none could stand against him. How many men would you say are at Forrester's beck and call?"

Micah shook his head. "Only about thirty in town, but Forrester said they had outliers. Probably the ones who attacked the patrol in the first place. They said that there was another attack somewhere today, though. We need to find out how many more men the Reavers have and where they are encamped."

"But even if we knew that, Pioneer Vale doesn't have the manpower to take on even the thirty trained soldiers that are already here. We'd have to find allies somewhere." Marcus pounded his fist on the table, making the shot glasses jump and roll. The three men sat in silence when a grin crept across Abel's face.

"The enemy of our enemy might just be our friend," he said. "Surely the nearby tribes have enough able bodies to help us stand against a common threat, right?"

"We'd have to send someone to propose an alliance. Does anyone in town even know how to speak their language?" asked Marcus. "And what if they refused anyway?"

"Or what if we beat the mercenaries but then they turn against us after?" asked Micah.

Abel nodded. "That could still be a distinct possibility. We must hope that they will understand the greater good to be had in defeating the danger to us all, and keep Mathers from becoming our monarch."

Again, the three men sat in silence, an unspoken question hanging in the air between them. Finally, Marcus shivered and set the three shot glasses back up, pouring one more round into each.

"Are we missing where the true threat truly lies? What if the soldiers are but a distraction for that thing down in the mine that Anne-Marie stands to protect us against. With war at our doorstep, maybe there is no scenario where Shade loses unless she can drive him back to whatever hell he crawled from."

"All the more reason for us to do our part here, and give her one less concern to draw away her attention," said Micah. "Let us fight the battle that she may win the war."

Allison threw open the door to the drawing-room, her cheeks flushed. Shouts from the streets followed up the stairs behind her. "Trouble outside, Da. We may need you downstairs."

The three men jumped from their seats and raced through the common room, joining the rest of the patrons who spilled out into the street. The crowd parted before Marcus as the brawny hunter shouldered his way through Abel and Micah following in his wake. He jumped from the porch of his tavern and moved to see what had happened.

A small pony lay in the dirt. Blood ran down its flank as three arrows waved drunkenly in the air. The animal's eyes stared blankly as it had breathed its last in delivering its rider into town. A small figure, a mop of dirty blond hair matted to the side of her face, lay beside the fallen mount. The girl's clothes were splattered with blood, but none could see if it was her own or another's. One of the townsmen and his wife knelt by the fallen child's side and were gently wiping away the gore that streaked her face.

"That's little Lizzie McBride," said Abel as he caught up to Marcus. "I traded some turnips to her father just three days ago."

"Theirs is one of the outermost farms, isn't it?" asked Micah.

"Aye. They settled in right at the foothills." The old farmer met Marcus' stare. "Right at the border of the natives' land."

The girl groaned, weak and delirious. "Mama...Papa," she moaned. "The Nipmuc..."

"My God," breathed Marcus. "They've murdered an innocent family."

"The Indians have lashed out at us once more," called Erickson from the outskirts of the crowd. The one-eyed enforcer stepped from the shadows into the ring of lanterns as the people surrounded the child. "This girl's own words damn those savages."

"That son of a bitch," said Micah as he stepped forward, the arrowhead still in his hand. Marcus and Abel grabbed the young man and held him back. The smith's words were bitten back by the subtle shake of Brenner's head. He raised his finger to his lips. Micah turned to the old farmer who leaned forward.

"Hold your position, son. We still don't know the odds against us." Micah's face flushed but he held his tongue and tucked the arrowhead back into the pouch at his waist.

Forrester walked into the circle from the direction of his men's camp. All eyes turned toward the Captain as he knelt down, pulled off his black leather glove, and placed his hand on the girl's brow. He bowed his head, but only Marcus saw the way his lips turned into a smirk beneath the broad brim of his hat. At last, the soldier stood and shared a nod with Erickson. Cyrus pulled his glove back on, making a fist once it fit to his satisfaction.

"People of Pioneer Vale. Your peaceful way of life has been threatened by those who would slaughter your children in their beds." Forrester's voice was low and even but carried to the far reaches of the terrified bystanders. "This is the reason my men have been asked to come.

"And the time has come for us to earn our pay."

*   *   *

Preston chuckled to himself as he let the curtain fall back across his window. The uproar had begun and he savored the cries for vengeance that now carried through the streets. The war to wipe out the accursed native population was imminent. Patch and Forrester had preyed upon the crowd's underlying fear and now drummed up their fury for blood. Although he didn't necessarily care much for Captain Forrester, the man's methods were undeniably thorough at what he had been hired for.

He smiled at the ominous shadows that crept and danced along the walls of his study. He yawned and snatched up the snifter of brandy in front of him, downing the fiery drink in a single gulp. Mathers let loose a thunderous belch and then wiped his sleeve across his mouth. He arched his back and lazily stretched his fingers toward the ceiling. He scratched his belly and decided to venture into the kitchen and see if there were any scraps of the mutton remaining from dinner before he retired for the night.

Tomorrow he would ride out to the shrine and inform Lord Shade of this latest development. The old wolf would undoubtedly reward him for setting the pieces into play while he basked in whatever nether hell he came from. All that remained was to squeeze the life from Anne-Marie Carmichael and the elusive old crone that his dark ally was so obsessed with.

An icy breeze blew through the room, chilling him to the bone. The shadows swooped from the walls to surround him, spinning him, shoving him, and dragging their frigid talons across his flesh. Mathers cried out in terror as they twisted between his legs, tangled his footing, and dropped him to the floor with a heavy crash. The flames in the hearth roared up the chimney then turned from cozy orange and red, to a chilling blue-black that sucked the warmth from the room. He crawled back to his hands and knees just as a shadow shaped like a giant wolf stepped from the dark fire before him. Glistening fangs dripped beneath eyes like embers, as Shade emerged into Preston's home.

"Our chance is upon us, my faithful servant," growled a voice in the darkness. "Even now, my enemies make their way to my shrine. Make haste and get yourself there so that we may spring our trap." A throaty chuckle rumbled from the spectral figure. "The moment of my arrival is imminent."

"Of course, my lord. Allow me to find my man, and he can go and...."

"There isn't time," snarled the shape. The wolf's carrion breath blew hot against Mathers' cheek as the creature paced before him like an animal trapped in a cage. "You must go there now. This is a crucial moment in the tapestry of fate. With those bothersome women destroyed, my rise can begin."

"Our rise, you mean. I will rule in your stead as promised." Preston swallowed hard as the shape froze and turned its head slowly in his direction. His blood ran cold as those burning eyes narrowed and burned into his heart. The low rumble rose from a warning purr to a predator's growl.

"Forgive me, my lord. I will make my way immediately," Preston stammered. Black claws reached forward and caressed his cheek tenderly, then lashed out and grabbed his throat in a crushing grip of ice.

"Do not fail me, Mathers."

The shadows melted away and Preston fell back to the floor, his breath coming in shallow gasps as the pressure left his neck. He pulled himself to his feet and rushed over to his desk. He yanked open the side drawer and snatched up the pistol that he kept there. He hugged the weapon against his chest, as lightning flashed through the windows, and the distant howl of a wolf carried through the night air.

CHAPTER 17
THROWN TO THE WOLVES - 1671

The rambunctious laughter of children at play roused the young man from sleep. He smiled at the joyful sounds of their little village already going about their daily tasks. He kicked away his fur blanket and rose from his pallet. He pulled on his doeskin trousers and slid his feet into leather moccasins but the air was warm enough that he grabbed a soft fur-trimmed vest instead of his heavier beaded shirt. He caught his reflection in the looking glass, an heirloom passed down in his family for generations, given by fur traders to one of his ancestors. He rubbed his scalp, bald but for his sleek black topknot that hung down between his shoulders, and he ran his fingers through it to make it seem less apparent that he had just rolled out of his bed.

The fit warrior, his wiry frame toned from endless days of running, hunting, and fishing, threw back the hide flap to his wigwam and stretched. He silently thanked the Great Spirit as the morning sun warmed his tanned skin. He splashed some water on his face from a nearby catch basin and padded over to the cook fire. Breakfast would be over soon and he had no doubt that he was due for a lecture. He sighed. It wouldn't be the first time that Grandfather had scolded him for rising late again.

"Good morning, Kitchi," said a young woman who stirred a cook pot. She filled a bowl with a wooden ladle and handed it to him with both hands. The aroma of honey and crushed pine nuts made Kitchi's stomach growl, and he took a deep sniff of the porridge.

199

"Hmmm, smells like your famous stinkberry stew, again, Alawa." He winked and tousled the girl's long black hair.

"That's probably just the rancid rabbit you brought back, oh, mighty hunter," she teased back. "Are you off to see the shaman?"

"I had better. We don't want that old grizzly bear wandering into camp for his own meal."

"I made this for him because of the stories he told us yesterday." Alawa pulled a lovely braided bracelet made from wildflowers from a small sack she wore at her waist and held it up for his inspection. "I wanted to thank him but didn't know what I could give that he didn't have already. Do you think he will like it?"

"That is lovely work and I think he will be deeply honored. Why don't you hold on to it until tonight and I will call you forth at the circle so that you may give it to him? Since you are in such a generous mood, hand me a second bowl of these carp droppings you call breakfast so that I can make sure he doesn't venture in and scare all of you little ones."

"I am only three summers younger than you, O Wise One," Alawa said with a laugh. She handed him a second wooden bowl and blushed as she dipped her head in a small bow. A shout from a couple of younger boys whose wrestling match had resulted in a bloody lip drew her away.

Kitchi beamed, overcome with joy from the sense of community that his people shared with each other. All worked hand in hand for the good of the entire tribe. His father had impressed upon him years ago to never let any of his people lack for anything unless the hardship was shared by all. There was no one higher than another in their village. Kitchi had taken those words to heart, and he hoped he had done his ancestors proud. There was an abundance of food, and his people were happy and thriving.

As Kitchi made his way between the birch bark homes they lived in, his people both young and old smiled and waved as he passed. He reached the edge of the camp, pausing but a moment as he looked into the deep bushes where a barely perceptible trail led into the lush canopy of trees. He walked softly, his steps falling without a sound as he delicately balanced the two bowls. The trail was short and he quickly smelled the wood smoke and the scent of herbs that his grandfather, the tribe's shaman, burned when he sought a vision from the spirits. As he crept toward the birch wood abode, he spied the old man sitting cross-legged in front of a wispy fire. The man's skin was so dark and weathered that he blended into the trees beyond and would have escaped notice if not for his stark white hair. Although the old man's eyes were closed, Kitchi had no misconception that he had crept up on the aged shaman unaware.

"Do I welcome you for breakfast or lunch?" said the old man.

"Forgive me, Grandfather. I stayed up late staring at the stars when others were at rest."

"I think you were staring instead at that pretty Alawa. She slowed you down with her doe eyes again." The shaman faced him and smiled. Even after all these years Kitchi still wondered at how clearly the old man's milky white eyes could see through him. Whispers often said that the shaman had traded his worldly vision for sight into the beyond.

"If you wanted your meals hot more often then you could consider moving back to camp instead of living all the way out among the briar patches. You would probably be more comfortable as well. My home has more than enough room since Father passed." Kitchi sat down beside the wizened old man and held out one of the bowls. His grandfather took the porridge, breathed deeply, and then took a sip.

"You are a young man and soon to start a family of your own, my son. You are the future of our people and I am a relic of another age."

"You are still our respected elder. We look to you for guidance."

"I have set down my old roots here. Besides, there are things that I can see more clearly when away from daily distractions. A dark cloud looms above us, my son," said the old man.

Kitchi glanced up at the blue sky peeking through the leaves above. "The skies are clear and blue, Grandfather. The spirits are playing games with you today. It occurred to me that you and I haven't been fishing together for some time. Why don't we go down to the river later and…?"

"Maheegan comes for us," the shaman said. "I saw this in my dreams. Even now his claws reach toward our camp."

"The Black Wolf? Grandfather, do not treat me as though I am still a child frightened by your campfire stories of evil spirits and old legends."

"No, Kitchi. You are Chieftain's Son, and the future leader of our tribe, but I tell you that there will be none left for you to watch over if you do not heed my warning." The old man's hand grabbed his wrist with surprising strength. "Blood will soon be shed in our home."

"You dwell too much in old myths, Grandfather. Our people are at peace. The settlers from across the ocean leave us alone, and even the neighboring tribes have kept the old alliances. The rivers run heavy with fish, the forests with game, and the cook pots are full." He laughed. "If Maheegan comes, we'll spare him a few morsels to keep him quiet."

"It is not fish or deer the dark spirit will feast upon. His allies will tear our people apart, and the wolf will devour our very world."

"I think you have sat too long in the sun, Grandfather. Our scouts have seen no sign of any such danger."

The thunderous crack of the settlers' favored weapon broke the quiet tranquility of the forest. More shots fired in rapid succession followed by a piercing scream of terror had Kitchi on his feet, scattering their breakfast bowls at his feet. His grandfather grabbed the leg of his trousers, and he looked down into the milky white eyes that stared into his soul.

"Take my bow," his grandfather said as he pointed his finger behind him. "Save all that you can, my son."

Kitchi saw the worn wooden bow leaning against his grandfather's wigwam, freshly strung, as if the old man had anticipated some danger today. He snatched up the weapon and threw the quiver of arrows over his shoulder as he dashed through the forest back toward the camp. He leaped over rocks and fallen trees, like a racing deer, fleet of foot, and silent as a summer wind. The thunder of horses roared in his ears as he closed the distance and slipped in behind the charging riders.

The men were dressed in hard leather, and Kitchi gasped as he saw the black head of a snarling wolf emblazoned upon the yellow banner carried by one of the marauders. The ground was already covered in blood and several of his people, men and women alike, stared sightlessly into the morning sky. Fire and smoke belched from the weapons that the frightful soldiers carried and he watched sprays of crimson erupt from his friends with each booming retort. The sight of a nearby horseman riding after a fleeing child drove him to action.

He held the respect of his people not simply because he was the only son of the late Chief. Kitchi was well known as the tribe's greatest hunter, and one of the deadliest archers among the Nations. He sprang lightly onto a rock, his line of sight on the rider clear and unobstructed. With practiced ease, Chieftain's Son smoothly drew back an arrow and released the bowstring with a twang. The cutlass in the rider's hand swung high into the air as he rode in for the kill, but the razor-sharp flint arrowhead found the unarmored place beneath the man's armpit and threw the soldier from his mount. A gout of pink foam fountained from the soldier's mouth as his pierced lung filled with blood.

Kitchi dropped to a kneeling position and let fly two more arrows, each shaft finding and taking down another rider. He cried out though as

Chogan, a fine warrior that he had grown up beside, was slashed from shoulder to groin. Machk, the strongest man of their tribe, raised his war club high above a rider who had been dragged from his mount, but the man unleashed the thunder of the weapon in his hand, blowing a hole in his friend's chest. The war club fell from limp fingers as he toppled over. All around him, his people raced around in blind panic and the young warrior knew he couldn't save them all.

A woman splattered with blood raced toward him, as a man with a lewd grin plastered across his face pursued her. Kitchi leaped from the rock as the man rode by and tackled him to the ground. He yanked the bone-handled hunting knife from the sheath at the soldier's waist and buried it into the brute's throat, the spurt of blood painting Kitchi's face. The woman screamed as he rose up, dripping in gore. She tried to flee, but he grabbed her as she tried to run past him.

"Hurit," he yelled to her as he swung her behind the shelter of a birch bark hut. The terror in her eyes vanished as she recognized him.

"Kitchi," the woman sobbed, "they swooped down on us like hawks on field mice. We never even heard them coming. My poor husband's head burst like a melon with the first thunder strike."

"Take the trail to Deer Run Hollow. Take anyone that you find as you go and I will send everyone I can save toward you. Lead them to the caves behind the waterfall. You must hurry." The woman nodded blankly and hurried off as Kitchi found his grandfather's bow and nocked another arrow. He spun back into the chaos around him. A brute with a long beard spied him and turned his horse, bearing down on him as he raised his sword high above his head. Kitchi lifted his bow, but his aim was rushed and his arrow only grazed the barbaric man's neck. He dove but felt the fiery slice of the rider's weapon crease his shoulder. Knowing he had only seconds before the pounding horse turned and the rider came back to finish him off, he desperately rolled across the grass. He rose to his knees, ignoring the agony in his shoulder as he drew back another arrow, trying to hold it steady against the waves of pain. As the rider grinned at him and shouted something in his guttural language, Kitchi's eyes fell upon an item lying in the blood-soaked grass.

It was a bracelet of wildflowers, broken and trampled, their blue and purple dotted with streaks of red.

Kitchi's rage surged in his breast. The pain in his shoulder was pushed away and he leveled his arrow at the charging horseman's leering face. The din of the battle around him faded to distant echoes as he heard nothing other than the sound of his own breathing. He released the string, feeling the familiar tickle of the wind on his cheek as the arrow's fletching brushed past. The warrior spun around in search of his next foe before the arrow had even found its mark. Kitchi was already drawing back his next shot when the rider's lifeless body hit the ground with the shaft still quivering in his eye socket.

A hand from under a pile of hides grabbed his ankle. Kitchi dropped to his knees ready to grapple when he saw the soft brown eyes that had warmed his heart earlier peeking out from the stack of furs. Tears streamed down the girl's face, and her lips trembled as she saw the terrifying visage of Chieftain's Son covered in blood.

"Alawa," he cried as he dragged the girl out of her hiding place and hugged her tight. "I thought you were lost. You can't stay here. We have to get you to safety." He took her by the wrist and tried to drag her away, but the girl pulled against his grip.

"Not yet," she cried out. Alawa threw back the hides and revealed three small children huddling there. Kitchi cried out in relief and he threw his arms around each of them, relieved to see their dirty little faces.

"Hurit waits at the Deer Run trail. Run like little rabbits. Dart back and forth to escape the jaws of these foxes that will snap at you. Go!" The little ones bolted away, but Alawa paused. She turned quickly and stood up on her toes, stretching to reach him. Tenderly, she kissed Kitchi before she raced after the little ones in her care.

Chieftain's Son watched them as they fled, covering their escape as they ran for safety. Satisfied that they had made it to the tree line, the warrior rushed to see who was left. He ducked and dodged the riders as he ran through the burning camp. He found two more of his hunters, fierce warriors garishly wounded. He found folk cringing in terror from the acrid stench of smoke and blood in the air. Kitchi directed them all to the far edge of the field where he hoped Hurit still awaited as he had instructed. With a whooping war cry, Kitchi sprinted through the middle of a group of the riders, calling their attention to him and away from his remaining people that ran for their lives. He smiled grimly as he heard the sounds of angry pursuit behind him, and leaped over a fallen tree trunk and into the thick underbrush.

*　　*　　*

Cyrus Forrester rode lazily through the trees of the woods. He smiled as the screams of terror reverberated from the savages' camp. He knew his men would do just as they were ordered. Decimate, but do not exterminate. He wasn't sure what game Preston was playing at, but so long as the flow of gold kept coming his way he didn't much care.

He had to admit that there was a certain beauty to this land. It was wild and rugged, but serene and tranquil. Maybe once he had finished subjugating the locals, he could convince Mathers into giving him a few acres and set himself up as a land baron. Enslave a few of the native women, force the broken warriors to serve as field hands. Could make for a lovely retirement, he mused.

The trail he was on opened up and he saw a lone Indian sitting in front of the coals of dying fire. The man was ancient with snow-white hair and skin like tree bark. He lifted his head and looked at Cyrus with milky eyes. He raised a gnarled finger, pointing it at Cyrus, and chattered something in his nonsensical language.

"My apologies, sir," said Forrester as he drew a pistol from his belt, "but I'm simply afraid that there isn't a place for you on my future estate."

*   *   *

Outraged shouts fell into the distance as Kitchi raced through the trees. He knew that the mounted soldiers couldn't ride through the dense woods as quickly as he could dart and dash along the hidden pathways. He only had to lose them and then he could circle back to make sure the others had made it to the waterfall. He had to try to reach his grandfather first and lead him to safety though. He angled his mad dash toward the old shaman's grove.

Kitchi burst through the brush in time to see a single horseman pointing his thunder weapon at his grandfather's chest. The rider glanced up at him and smiled wickedly. Without looking back to his target, the stick in his hand roared like an enraged bear and his grandfather was thrown back against the ground. Blood ran from the old man's chest and mouth as he struggled to rise up on his elbows.

"No," screamed Kitchi as he raised his bow and drew back in one fluid motion. The rider pulled a second weapon from his belt and pointed it at Kitchi. Arrow thrummed and fire roared at the same time, with both hitting their mark. Kitchi spun around as his shoulder exploded in pain. Both rider and horse screamed as Kitchi's shot pierced the man's thigh and pinned his leg to the saddle. The man's mount reared and raced from the clearing, stealing away the young warrior's vengeance.

Kitchi dropped his bow and scrambled to the shaman's side. He took the old man's blood-soaked hand in his own and he knew that his Grandfather's last moments were upon him.

"The black wolf is on the rise, my son."

"Be still. Let me bandage you up." His grandfather gently took his hands in his own and smiled weakly.

"I never tell you how proud I am of you, my son." The dying shaman weakly poked Kitchi in the chest. "You have the strength to lead our people against Maheegan and his soldiers."

Tears ran down Kitchi's face as he stroked the old man's silky white hair. "You cannot leave me alone, Grandfather. I don't know how to begin this fight."

The old man coughed and blood ran from his mouth. "Seek out the Guardian. The Viking's Daughter. She has guarded the vale for many winters."

"You speak of stories from when I was still a boy. How can I know if she even lives?"

"Maheegan draws closer, but he has not arrived yet. This is the ancient pact that tells me a Guardian watches over us still." The old man's gnarled fingers slid down his grandson's chest, leaving crimson streaks as they fell slack into the grass. The milky white eyes found Kitchi's once more, still staring into a distance that Chieftain's Son couldn't follow.

"You must find her before the wolf does."

CHAPTER 18
DESTINY UNHINGED - 1671

Rain hammered down and turned the winding trail up Alistair's Climb into mud. The trees overhanging the side path to the mine offered little in the way of shelter from the deluge, but a canopy of lavender flame turned the water to steam and kept the two cloaked figures dry as they plodded toward the tunnel entrance. They stepped inside just as another crash of thunder shook the heavens as if warning away the two Guardians from the task that they set about.

"Watch your step through here," Anne-Marie said as her flames winked out. "The explosion from before sent all manner of debris flying around and footing could be treacherous."

"Mind yerself, girl," chuckled Henna. "I may be old but once I was rather fleet of foot when there was less winter in my hair." The old woman was surrounded by her telltale twinkling green motes that she directed down the mine shaft to light their way in. The fire that Anne-Marie kept in the palm of her hand warmed them as they descended through the twists and turns, but when they reached the entrance to the main cavern Henna shivered and pulled her shawl tighter around her bony shoulders.

"You can feel him close by, can't you?" she asked. "There is a foulness in the air, stronger now than when I was last here. I'd wager we can smell Shade's reek now that he is less concerned with hiding himself and pushes even harder at the walls of our world."

"Aye, that's certainly a possibility, lass," Henna said as she slowly paced around the overturned worktable. A thin smile creased her wrinkled face as she kicked a boot across the floor toward her student. "Or it could just be the ripening of those two ruffians that ye left behind when ye escaped."

"We should burn their bodies while we're here. They rose against poor Marcus when he tried to help me. He could have been killed and his blood would have been on my hands."

Henna turned and faced her. The old witch's foot tapped slowly on the cold stone floor. "Did yer own magic drag those poor souls back from the nethers to make them stand again? Was it yer own mind that set them against the woodsman?"

"No, of course not, but...."

"But nothing, lass," Henna snapped. It was the harshest tone of voice that Anne-Marie had ever heard her mentor speak. "Ye know as well as any whose hand is at fault here, but ye had no idea that Shade would direct his power that way."

"I was so frantic to get away from this place that it never occurred to me that they would pose any further threat, even though I had seen for myself in the shrine below that he could raise the dead to fight for him."

"And what expense of dark energy has that move cost our enemy? Ye know how weak broad strokes of power render us. The same holds true for the wolf, and even more so as he has to reach across the realms. The terror he inflicts upon the town with threats of war breeds strength in him, but he still needs time to retreat and recover after such a vulgar display."

"Then what does he gain to have attacked Marcus in the first place?" She plucked up a chunk of gold ore from the workbench and frowned. Lavender flame burst from her palm and melted the precious metal from the stone that held it. She poured it into a small cup, then brushed the remaining dust and ash from her hands. "Why waste so much magic against someone who isn't even a player in this fight?"

"How do ye know that Master Brenner has no role yet to play? Are ye so proficient now in our art that ye know the ways of destiny upon us all?" Anne-Marie opened her mouth but the old woman placed a hand gently on her shoulder. "Shade's ploy was twofold and that is why we need to be ever so careful in our coming steps, lass. First, he has exposed the common folk to the reality of magic. By confronting your friend, he has let the cat out of the proverbial bag about us. He forced your hand to reveal the truth about yourself to those ye hold dear. Friends though they may be, Shade has gambled that the seeds of fear and distrust have been planted for him to sow later on."

"Then his gamble failed. My friends embraced me after I confessed to what I am. They are each possessed of sincere courage that Shade will never corrupt."

"Then the second consequence is the real danger."

"And that is?"

Henna waved her hands around at the cave. "The cagey bastard has pulled all the right strings so that the chips have ever fallen to his favor. All of his manipulations, from luring Mathers with promises of wealth to the attack on Marcus, have reached their peak. He has now brought the only two people who bar his entry down to this unholy place. We are the lambs walking literally into the wolf's den."

Anne-Marie's heart sank. Her head dropped for a moment, but then she shook her fiery mane and looked up at Henna with fierce determination in her eyes. "My friends will not suffer another moment of his intimidation. Henna, you should leave."

"Are ye daft, lass? That was too far a march for me to turn away so soon. And what would be my gain? If I leave and the wolf ends you here, how many more years may I keep him at bay until I breathe my last? I am old and weary, Child, and I take affront to the idea of dying huddled in my bed. On my feet with a foe before me is how I will leave when my days must end. Besides," she said with a mischievous gleam in her eye, "have ye a clue what even needs to be done?"

"Do you?" Anne-Marie retorted with a smile.

"Of course not, which is all the more reason that we go together. Might be that one keeps the other from doing something addle-brained that sets the whole damn world aflame." She squeezed her student's hand and cackled gleefully, but Anne-Marie saw eyes full of pride and determination looking back at her. Henna turned solemn once more. "Come, my dear. Let's finish this business once and for all."

Anne-Marie pointed to the darkest recesses at the back of the cavern, and Henna's twinkling lights whipped through the shadows until the gaping maw that led to the shrine yawned into view. They walked over together and paused at the entrance. A chill breeze blew up from the tunnel, swirled around the two women, and then clutched at their skirts before howling back down into the confines of the ancient corridor. Henna said something softly under her breath that wisped out in puffs of cold air.

"What was that?" asked Anne-Marie.

"Just an old prayer my people used to say to the Old Gods before going into battle," she said. Her infectious grin found her face once more. "No harm in asking for all the help we can get at this point." With a shake of her head, the old woman stepped forward into the tunnel. Anne-Marie followed close behind her, both women oblivious to the flickering light that glimmered from the mine entrance.

Anne-Marie stood vigilant as Henna studied the soot-stained walls and stepped past the charred remains that littered the floor of the shrine. "Ye certainly were thorough in taking down his minions. Turned yerself into a walking bonfire, did ye?"

"I'd say there was still some measure of precision. I just used a bigger fireball."

"Ye lofted a boulder at a mosquito, but ye got the job done," Henna quipped.

A low growl rumbled from the darkness ahead, and torches sprang to life around the chamber. Anne-Marie was unmoved by the burst of light, but she caught Henna as the old woman stepped back with a gasp. The shadows melted away from the leering statue of the Father of Nightmares snarling at them from high above.

An old wooden chest sat upon the blood-stained altar, and as with Anne-Marie's previous visit, the lid creaked open of its own accord. The pale yellow crystal once again rose from the velvet pillow that it sat upon. It began a slow spin as the ghastly light from its depths pierced the surrounding gloom. The silhouette of Shade's visage pressed against the gem and his mocking laughter echoed throughout the chamber.

"And what have I done to deserve such a delightful gift?" said the demon. "I have always dreamed that the two of you would have to be dragged before me in chains, and yet here you walk so freely into my reach."

"Hello, wolf," said Henna. The Guardian leaned upon her walking stick. "Ye'll pardon me if I don't give ye a scratch behind yer lice-ridden ears. It has been ages, but it seems we have finally arrived at the same place where we first met."

Anne-Marie turned to her teacher. "First met? You said that the Guardians had never been able to find this place before. How could you have seen the shrine?"

Henna sighed deeply as she stared at the image within the crystal. "At the time, I had no inkling of where he had taken me, but, as he promises all of us, we see shadows of events yet to come."

"Your own Ascension," Anne-Marie said. "Shade brought you here when you accepted the mantle of Guardian." Henna nodded.

"A place of special significance among her own visions," added Shade. "Just as your own dreamscape rushes toward you now."

"Not if we stop you first," Anne-Marie said. She snapped her wrists and blossoms of purple flame wrapped around her forearms. "All of your lies will fall apart and we will drive your threat from this world."

Shade's dark laughter shook the walls. Pebbles from the ceiling cascaded on the women from above. Bones rattled across the floor as the very ground shook with the reverberations. The eyes of the wolf statue began to glow with a hellish red light and the carved fur rippled as if real sinews lie beneath the rock.

"Would you like to tell her, crone, or shall I?" growled the demon. Henna looked up and met the gaze of the statue with surprising calm. She sat down on a large rock that lay near the altar and turned to face her student.

"Shade's visions are facets of our own destinies. Like yerself, I was shown the deaths of those I loved. I tried to stop things from falling into place along his terrible path, but I found time and again that the tale was written long before its time had come to pass. I failed to change the sights with which the demon had tormented me all those years.

"And today, here in this place, is where I die." Henna looked at her and found a sad smile.

Anne-Marie felt as though she had been punched in the stomach. "You can't believe for a moment that what Shade has told you is true. He knows how close we are to defeating him."

"You will stand against him without me. I have been haunted by this place since I was younger than you are now." She smiled at Anne-Marie then pointed her gnarled finger back at the tunnel. "I'll be haunted by it no longer."

Anne-Marie whirled and saw a blur of motion in the shadows. She opened herself fully to the Whisper and channeled the raw magic into a shield of lavender fire around her teacher. Every bit of power she could draw through her body was poured forth into a conflagration of heat and flame that rushed back toward the entry corridor. The blaze revealed the creeping form of Preston Mathers standing with a pistol leveled at the old woman, but the sudden flash of light and fire dashed him against the rock wall. The inferno rolled over him and the powder in his pistol ignited. The gunshot careened off the wall, ricocheting harmlessly away from his target.

"It's true," Mathers whimpered. "You really are a witch." He fumbled with the pistol in his hand, trying to pluck another lead ball from the pocket of his coat, but Anne-Marie succumbed to her rage. She stepped forward and a vicious snarl crossed her face. She clenched her fist in the air, and the flintlock pistol burst into flame. The metal ran red and the wood stock reduced to embers in Preston's hand. He yelped and dropped the burning ashes to the floor, tripping over some of the bones as he backed away. Anne-Marie wrapped herself in a shroud of flame and floated across the floor toward him.

"Oh yes, you were unwittingly right about me, Preston, but the only soul I seek to torment is yours for all the harm that you have inflicted on Pioneer Vale," she roared with the force of an erupting volcano. She let the lavender fires not merely dance behind her eyes but engulf them so that her face seemed like something that hid the doorway to Hell itself. "And on my family. Run for your life, dog. No matter where you hide I shall still come for you."

Anne-Marie launched a fireball from her hand that struck and scorched the stone at Mathers' feet. The man let out a pitiful cry as he turned and lumbered back up the tunnel. She started to give chase when she was thrown to the ground by a howl of pure rage. She rolled to her side with balls of flame clutched in her palms.

The giant statue writhed along the wall. Cracks appeared along the sides of the stone carving, pulsing with that same reddish glow that filled the piercing eyes. "What have you done, witch?" growled Shade. "No mere mortal has the power to tear fate from its moorings." The ghastly light from the yellow crystal stabbed forth at her, twisting as it raced across the distance between the altar and where Anne-Marie crouched. The tendril reared back ready to strike her down when a green flash of light cut through it like a blade dispelling the dark energy.

Henna stepped from the shadows along the sidewall, her hands bathed in her own mystic power. "Ye've answered yer own question, wolf. Anne-Marie Carmichael is no mere mortal. She is a warrior Guardian unlike any that has been called to serve in ages." Henna looked over her shoulder at Anne-Marie as she rose from the dirt. The old woman gave her a quick wink. "She is the Witch of Pioneer Vale."

The menacing growl became a soft chuckle. "So be it. You have thwarted the end I have promised to the crone, but there are forces in motion that even you won't be able to stop entirely. As you have seen for yourself, many are the visions that I deal out to those who dare oppose me.

"Which one will you try to stop next?"

The ground shook again, and dirt rained down once more from the ceiling. A fissure opened up in the floor and spread a spider web of cracks towards them. Anne-Marie grabbed Henna by the arm and dragged her teacher back into the tunnel. Shade's laughter boomed from the shrine behind them as they staggered back to the main cavern. With flames at the ready, she searched for signs of Preston, but the coward had apparently fled the mine.

"Slowly, lass," said Henna. "The old wolf isn't going to drop the roof upon his own head. Give an old woman a chance to catch her breath."

"We haven't time. Shade is about to strike. His threat about the visions was not an idle one. He'll come at me next."

"But how could we possibly know which nightmare could become real?"

Anne-Marie chewed her bottom lip and her hand slipped to the amethyst pendant she wore around her neck. Her eyes went wide as she realized she knew the answer. She grabbed Henna's shoulders and felt her heart lurch within her breast.

"We have to get back to the grove right away." Without another word, she rushed for the entrance to the mine as Henna spared one final glance back at the tunnel to the shrine.

"She's coming for ye, Shade. That one will not rest until she has yer pelt hanging on her wall." She spat at the tunnel entrance but jumped as two red coals of light peered like eyes out of the darkness below. She turned and hurried after Anne-Marie, but the haunting laughter that echoed after simply left her....

CHAPTER 19
GUARDIAN – PRESENT DAY

Cold.

That was the only thing that went through Ben's mind. The cold stone floor beneath him. The chill breeze that blew across his bare skin. The frosty puddle of his own cooling blood dripping from the wound that Aiden's devilish dagger had ripped open in his stomach.

The icy fingers of death that waved mockingly at the corners of his awareness.

Ben fumbled around in the pitch black, his hands slick and sticky, but they finally closed upon the flashlight that Aiden had batted away. He clicked the button and the beam of light drove away the encroaching shadows. He swallowed hard, letting the searing pain remind him that he was still very much alive.

He had to get up. Clarissa Brenner and who knew how many others were in danger because of his own gullibility. Lured in by Aiden's false pretense of friendship, he had released a monster into the world. All the failures and dodged responsibilities of his life came crashing down on him. A strange humming tickled the edge of his mind and suddenly he saw flashes of memories that, while not of his own life, showed him the tangled skein of a long woven tapestry of misfortune and tragedy his family had been subject to.

It was time to cut that thread.

He shook his head to clear the dizziness that accompanied his blood loss and assessed the seriousness of his injury. The stab was clean, but the edges were blackened already with decaying tissue. He rolled over and felt a lump in his back pocket. With a quiet chuckle, he pulled out the flask Aiden had given to him, uncorked it, and took a quick pull before pouring a splash of the liquor over his wound. He hissed as the alcohol burned him both inside and out, but he knew it would cleanse the wound for now. The amethyst stone inset into the stainless steel flashed with an inner fire as he set the flask beside him.

He struggled to sit up, leaning his back against a barrow inset into the wall. A skull regarded him with a look that almost resembled surprise, and Ben laughed.

"Believe me, pal. I'm just as shocked as you are at this point. Don't suppose anyone dropped a first aid kit beside that antique bang stick, by chance?"

The skull simply sat motionless.

"Guess I got to do this one myself then. Is there a doctor in the house?" He laughed again, unsure if his mind was desperately seeking a way to cope with the day's events or if he was losing his sanity.

Ben took another sip from the flask and ripped the sleeve of his flannel shirt. The effort from pulling the fabric apart made a fresh explosion of pain blossom across his abdomen, but he gritted his teeth and fashioned a crude bandage. Satisfied that he would make it out of the cave at least, he drained the last few drops from the flask and slid it back into his pocket. He pulled himself to his feet, holding onto the wall as the room spun around him. He was wobbly but more than determined to get out of the mine. He grabbed an old shovel handle as a makeshift cane and Ben found himself outside a few minutes later. The kiss of the mountain air on his cheek and the warmth of the midday sun had never felt so good.

"Where to now, Hibble?" he asked himself. Alistair's Climb towered into the sky behind him. Town was a few miles on the other side of the mountain, but he was in no condition to make such a hike. His truck was parked at the bottom of the hill but his keys were long gone, either lost in the depths below or taken by Aiden. He looked down the trail to the far side of the clearing and saw fields peeking back at him through the breaks in the tree cover.

Ben knew the local geography well enough to recognize where he was, and, given the players involved, he knew that Carmichael Farms was about to be ground zero for the battle to come. He only hoped he wasn't too late to stand against Aiden and his dark master. He placed his hand over the bloody bandage around his midsection and started through the forest and down the mountain slope toward the peaceful homestead.

*　　*　　*

Aiden closed the front door and sneered as he turned to face the two women before him. "Be it ever so humble...," he purred. "I love what you've done with the place."

Kimberly stood in front of Clarissa, pushing the girl toward the kitchen entrance. "Clarissa, run," she shouted. She grabbed a vase from the hall table and threw it at the man. Aiden flicked his fingers and casually deflected the missile into the wall with a crash. His other hand shot forward, swirling black vapors writhing around his fist. A chilling numbness flowed through Kim's body. She couldn't get her legs to move, and her lungs ached as the air temperature plunged in the room.

Clarissa shrieked in her ear and tugged on her sleeve. A menacing growl from the kitchen whipped her head around. She gasped as a monstrous black wolf squeezed through the doorway into the foyer from the back entrance and trapped the two women between man and beast. Kim met the glowing red eyes, and hugged the girl against her, for she recognized the creature that glared at her. The horror of her nightmare came to life as she watched the saliva drip from razor-sharp fangs. Slow rising plumes of smoke rose from where the drops fell and burned holes into the wooden floor. The beast crouched, muscles coiled, and ready to leap as the muzzle curled back in a vicious snarl.

"What do you want with us?" Kimberly asked over her shoulder to Aiden. She backed Clarissa against the wall, determined that these two would have to go through her first. She doubted that they would have much trouble, however. Aiden lunged forward and grabbed her by her long hair. Kim cried out as he wrenched her neck back and leaned in close.

"I want to leave a crystal clear message for your darling daughter by splashing your blood upon these walls," he growled. His voice was a harsh, but mesmerizing, whisper. "Then, while my dark master over there gnaws on your bones, I intend to rip that little bitch's still-beating heart from her chest and present it to my mother."

"I don't understand any of this," she said. "Where is my daughter? Did you take her from us?"

"Your Angelica has fallen in with poor company, I'm afraid. She has had a taste of power and has sadly evolved into one of those foolish heroic types who thinks that she can charge in and save the day. Like my accursed mother, she now thinks herself invincible." His fingernail traced teasingly down the line of her throat. She pulled away from his touch, but his hand tightened the pull of her hair. "Let me assure you that she is not."

Kimberly felt a ripple of energy flow through his fingers and she was thrown back against the wall. She rebounded from the blow and fell forward when he punched her in the stomach with his fist encircled by that strange black fire. Her insides twisted and burned, writhed and froze as the magic energy tore through her. She dropped into a ball on the floor, clutching her stomach and retching.

Clarissa jumped in front of her. Through the girl's legs, Kim saw the stranger square off against her. The beast by the kitchen door watched, swaying its weight from foot to foot. "Why do you even think that Angelica will show up?" yelled Clarissa. "She knows that you are just setting a trap for her and your mom."

"Dear girl, such is the fallacy of the heroic mindset. The overwhelming compulsion to rush headlong into danger to save those too foolish to steer clear of it." He chuckled and brushed his sleeves. "I can't tell you how grateful I am to have avoided that ridiculous obligation that my mother thrust upon all of the others."

"It's called courage, jerk, and of course you have no clue what that's about."

"I found intelligence to be more useful."

"And yet you're too stupid to realize that even if you kill us, they will hunt you down. You won't gain anything except having a pair of really pissed off witches who want nothing less than to kick your ass into the nightmare world you crawled from." Clarissa jumped back, nearly tripping over Kim when Aiden drew back his hand. He paused, however, and let out a grim chuckle.

"The Witches of Pioneer Vale," he said with a sneer, "are about to find themselves dragged into a hell of their own making. I will rid the world of the Guardians once and for all. When they have breathed their last, then my master's reign over this world can begin. Regrettably, Child, you won't be around to endure it."

Kim rose to her feet and pulled Clarissa back against her. From the side of the room, the wolf snarled and bared its fangs. The beast's muscles rippled beneath its fur. Canine paws flexed and dug furrows into the wooden floor, like a bull pawing the ground before a charge. The wolf barked a staccato noise that sounded like laughter, then, with a sudden spring, the nightmarish creature threw itself into the air at the crouching women. Kim and Clarissa screamed as the shadow of death approached, but their cries were lost in a sudden deafening rumble of thunder.

A blast of lightning sizzled through the air and slammed into the leaping monster's flank. The wolf was spun in a circle and slammed its head against the wall. Kim whirled around to see Angelica standing in the doorway with her hand outstretched. Without pause, her daughter whipped her other fist at Aiden and released a second bolt that hammered the man in the chest and blew him back through the stair railing. He shrieked as a broken spindle pierced his body, and blood poured from his side.

*   *   *

Angelica stood like a warrior goddess as lightning wrapped around her body in a scintillating shield of raw power. Her hair danced wildly around her face, billowing in the current that surrounded her. Her breathing was even despite her mad dash down the slope of Alistair's Climb where Anne-Marie's portal had carried her and her hazel eyes crackled with blue-white elemental force. Blood soaked her shirt and ran in a trickle from her nose, but the ferocity in her eyes defied any hint that she was injured.

The wolf scrambled back to its feet and shook its head. It growled at first but the noise turned into a soft whine as it looked her way. The beast paced warily, with its tail tucked between its legs, and its lips pulled back over yellowed fangs.

"Get the hell away from them, Shade," Angelica roared. Her voice boomed with the might of a storm, the magic in her fists built up with another blinding charge. She took a bold step forward and the wolf cowered before the blinding fury that turned predator to prey.

"Angie?" Kimberly cried. "Is it really you?"

"Nice entrance, Hick," Clarissa shouted. Angelica shot a glance over her shoulder at her loved ones, giving a brief nod before turning back to her foes.

The demon bared his fangs and made a snarling call to Aiden who struggled to rise up from the tangle of broken wood he was enmeshed in. "And so the little witch arrives at last," he said through gritted teeth as he rose from the debris. He pulled the jagged piece of wood from his side and pressed his hand against the wound. He sent a pulse of coldfire into his body to staunch the bleeding, brushed splinters from his clothes, and then cocked his head at her.

"It's Guardian, you bastard, and you won't slip away in a puff of smoke from me this time." Angelica raised her hands above her head and a blinding ball of lightning grew between her palms. And then just as suddenly it flickered, resurged, and then disappeared.

"I have no intention of slipping away this time, cousin," laughed Aiden as he watched the girl snap her hands over and over again without releasing so much as a spark. "And now that your magic has failed you, I can promise that neither shall you."

The wolf's eyes flashed with inky darkness and it tried once more to stand on its hind legs. Its paws elongated, splitting into fingers, claws lengthening at the end of black fingers. Shade wobbled as reshaping bones snapped, and forelegs thickened into arms. Ragged trousers misted into being around him and his threadbare cloak fell from his shoulders as he finally rose to his full towering height. Angelica's backed away as the Father of Nightmares rose before her just as he had weeks ago in her dream of the destroyed farmhouse.

"You impertinent whelp," snarled Shade. He threw back his head and howled in glee. "What have we to fear of you now?"

"Well, I sent your boy running once before, Fluffy," she said with a jerk of her thumb toward Aiden. "How much help do you really think he is going to be?" She let her other hand fall behind her back hoping that her mother caught on that she was pointing toward a small stand near the front door that held some gardening tools. The scuff of movement behind her brought a smile to her lips.

"Ah, Cousin," said Aiden as he stepped up beside the demon. "Just as before at our last battle, your foolish steps have led you down the very road you were warned about. Once again you have rushed in alone and have overestimated your chances of survival. And this time, without your magic to save you," he said with bared teeth, "the world will lose one of its precious Guardians."

"You are wrong about two key things though, Aiden," she said as she flashed a mischievous grin at the pair. "First of all, I'm not alone this time." She snapped her fingers and ducked as the small shovel that Kim swung cut through the air. The blade smacked Aiden hard in the jaw, and a jet of blood erupted from his busted lips.

Shade roared and a dark writhing cloud of mist swirled around his head as he drew back his taloned hand. Kim shrunk back and brandished the puny weapon as the Father of Nightmares towered above her. Rage blazed in the coals of his eyes. Shade's claws slashed down as Angelica stepped between the demon and her mother. She caught his wrist in a crackling white-hot glove of magical power. Thunder rattled the windows of the house as lightning crackled to life around her once more.

"And secondly," Angelica continued with a smirk, "I was faking the whole time about that last fizzle." She punched the demon in the stomach with her free hand, unleashing a blast that launched him back into his apprentice. They crashed to the floor together in a tumble of arms and legs. She hugged her mother quickly, then jerked her head toward the kitchen doorway. "Get out of here now. The cavalry is on its way."

Kim nodded and dropped the shovel with a clatter to the floor. "You've got some explaining to do, young lady," she said. She gave Angelica a quick kiss on the cheek. "Clarissa, let's go." The two women leaned on each other as they dashed through the doorway out of sight. The screen door banged and they were gone.

Angelica smiled in relief and turned back to her foes disentangling themselves from one another. She bit her lip and hoped that the cavalry really was closing in. It didn't matter though. The fight was here and now, and two of the people she cared most about in this world were safe. For now, at least. She fell into a fighting stance, snapped her wrists to the floor, and once more reveled in the power that thrummed through her body.

Shade threw Aiden aside, and scrambled to all fours, before slowly rising back to his full height. Angelica watched the demon tremble with fury, coldfire roiling behind his eyes as he glared at her. Aiden groaned as he pulled himself back to his feet, and shambled beside his master. She saw fear in his eyes as he gave the monster beside him a quick glance.

"You boys ready for round two?" she asked. She was light on the balls of her feet, poised like a boxer ready for the next strike.

"There will not be a third, whelp," snarled Shade. He punched his fist into the air, and dark energy swirled from the tips of his claws down the length of his arm. Aiden followed suit but the power he wielded lacked the same intensity as the demon's. His hand was bathed in a similar, yet not quite as intense, power. "Fear me, Guardian," growled the wolf.

"Not a chance," said Angelica. She dipped her chin, her eyes locked on her enemies through the wisps of her bangs. She fanned them away with a quick puff of air and threw up two distinct shields of blue-white fire as twin blasts of black energy erupted toward her. The temperature

226

plunged as the coldfire raged through the room, but Angelica planted her feet and shoved back. The Whisper of the Guardian was an angelic choir in her soul, reaching a crescendo of beauty against the darkness she faced. She amplified her defenses, fueled by the Elder's might that filled her, and she actually pushed a step closer to her adversaries.

"This isn't possible," yelled Aiden. "How can she stand against our combined might?" Shade snarled and grabbed the front of his apprentice's shirt. With a mighty heave, he tossed him across the foyer to crash beside the front door of the farmhouse. The demon suddenly dropped his attack, and the coldfire drew back into a wreath around the beast as he crossed his arms over his chest. The air bulged around the wolf's hulking frame, and he glanced up at Angelica with a toothy smile as a globe of malevolent magic surged around him. He threw back his head, snapped his arms out wide, and released the shockwave that built up around his body.

Angelica had only half a second to wonder if her shields would save her.

*   *   *

Kimberly and Clarissa sprinted down the gravel driveway when they were thrown to the ground by the explosion behind them. Tires squealed dangerously close to their heads as Will's truck skidded to a halt. The farmer jumped from the cab and fell to his knees. Kim shivered in his arms as the farmhouse blew apart in a black fireball of wood and glass.

"Angie was still in there," Kim shrieked. "Will, our daughter was in there!" She paused when a tall woman clad in leather and frills with fiery copper hair, leaped from the bed of the truck, and stared in horror at the smoking ruins of the farmhouse.

"Angelica," the redhead whispered as she covered her mouth with a trembling hand. She rushed forward but Kim jumped to her feet and stood in her way.   Lavender fire danced in the woman's eyes, and she scowled. "Get out of my way, Kimberly," the stranger told her.

"Anne-Marie, let us help," said Will. "We can back you up."

Kim grabbed the leather bracer the woman wore around her wrist. She ignored the wince of pain and held her fast. "We have to find Angie. I didn't just get my daughter back only to lose her again."

"You will only be a target and a distraction. I haven't the time to explain this to you now." Anne-Marie jerked her wrist loose from the woman's grasp and made a clenching motion with her fist. A lavender cage of fire sprang up around Kim as the witch marched past. "William, get your family to safety. This battle isn't over yet," she said as she ran toward the black smoke.

Kim turned to her husband and Will just shrugged and shook his head.

"I don't think that woman knows how to leave a good first impression," he said.

CHAPTER 20
BEFORE I WAKE - 1671

"I don't see why I am needed to skulk about in the woods," griped Corbin. "I am a preacher, not a soldier."

"Try being a silent one then," snarled Patch Erickson. "If there are any of those bloodthirsty savages around, you'll bring them straight down on us all."

Jeremiah winced at every snapped twig and muttered curse as the border patrol lumbered through the forest. Of the six men recruited for today's team, he was the most skilled in woodsmanship, with Erickson being a close second. Along with Reynolds, they had a candlemaker, a leatherworker, and a tailor, good souls all, but not the hardiest for the detail they had been assigned to. Of course, the most suitable had either died in the ambush or were recovering from their wounds. And just what were the odds that he and Mathers' man would have their lots drawn together? Jeremiah suspected manipulations at work and was uneasy every time Erickson came too close. He felt as though he needed to put a closer watch on Patch than the surrounding terrain.

"Speak not another word," hissed Jonathan Proudman, the candlemaker who had been selected to lead this party. He was the oldest of the men drafted into the patrol, and someone had decreed that his age made him a capable leader. The man had no sooner scolded them when he stepped on a fallen tree branch. In the hushed forest, the snap sounded like a church bell clanging to their ears.

They all froze and sweat ran down Proudman's face. As one, they all listened for the slightest sound, but there were only screeching birds and scampering squirrels fleeing from their path. Jeremiah gripped his hatchet tightly. He knew that if any natives were nearby the only whispers that might give them away would be their laughter at the incompetent group that he had been stuck with. After a few agonizing moments, the lead man waved his hand in dismissal.

"I believe we are clear for now. Why don't we take a short rest and then we'll continue on. The evening is upon us and I, for one, am ready to get back inside the town walls." The other townsmen sighed and groaned, dropping their packs heavily into piles of leaves. Jeremiah shook his head as he put his back against a mighty oak tree.

Patch stood near Jeremiah, still gripping his pistol. "If the savages find us, we'll all be dead men with this lot," he muttered.

"We've not seen any signs along this edge of town. The closest of the local tribes live in the other direction. We are nothing more than a rearguard here."

"Only rear I intend to guard is my own, farmhand," Patch growled. "Anything goes down out here, and you can bet that I will fight tooth and nail to reach safety. I would strongly advise you to do the same."

"What I will choose to do is none of your concern, Erickson. We all stand better chances if we hold together." Patch glared at him, but Jeremiah met his gaze without flinching. Erickson snorted and turned away.

Corbin tripped over a fallen log and crashed into the bushes. "Curse all of this anyway," snapped Reynolds as he reached out and grabbed a branch to pull himself up. He yanked away the foliage and shrieked as a dark-skinned young man appeared behind the leaves. He held a fine bow and crouched low as he watched the patrol scrambling to their feet. The young warrior said something in his language, and the bow in his hands shook as he strained to draw back the string.

"They'll murder us all," shouted Reynolds, and he bolted off into the woods.

"Corbin, wait," yelled Jeremiah and he held his hands up and out to the man before him. The farmer saw that the Indian's vest was already covered in blood and his struggle with the bow was clearly due to his own injury. "Hold your fire, men," he called over his shoulder to his fellow patrolman. "He's frightened and injured and is no threat to us."

"Tell that to the Parson," quipped Christopher Downs, the town's leatherworker. "I imagine he's halfway to the coast now."

Jeremiah ignored the jibe. He dropped his hatchet and stepped slowly toward the young warrior. "I don't know if you can understand my words, but there is no reason for us to fight." The brave swallowed hard, his narrowed eyes darting back and forth among the men, but his hands relaxed the half-drawn bowstring and he stepped toward the farmer. Jeremiah saw the man look past him and his dark eyes grew wide once again. The Indian raised his bow again, but his shoulder failed him and it dropped from his hands into the grass.

The shadow of an arm extending crossed the ground in front of Jeremiah. He whirled around and struck Patch's wrist, driving the man's arm high into the air as the pistol shot boomed into the air. Erickson growled and shoved him away with his free hand, but he rolled his shoulder out of reach. He countered with a hard right hook that caught Erickson under the chin and spun the big man halfway around. When Jeremiah whirled around the young man had vanished into the woods.

"You stupid bastard," he yelled. "You just pissed away our chance to work this all out."

"His people slaughtered a score of our own men, Carmichael," said Patch. The two men squared off, each grabbing the other until Jeremiah shoved Mathers' thug away from him.

"Easy, lads," said Proudman. His voice was but a squeak and he wiped his brow with a dainty handkerchief he pulled from his jacket. "We've all had a fright here, but we are all still alive."

"For now," snarled Patch as he locked icy glares with Jeremiah. He spat blood on the ground at his feet. "And you will never lay your hands on me again, do you understand?"

"Do you think that you can stay here and guard the rest of our 'soldiers' while I go find the Parson?" asked Jeremiah.

"You shouldn't go off alone," said Proudman. "That Indian was probably an advance scout and proof that the town is being watched. Take Downs with you at least."

Jeremiah's cold stare still burned fiercely against Erickson's. "No, sir. I believe I am safer on my own." He snatched his hatchet up from the ground where he had dropped it and went into the bushes after Corbin.

"Stubborn fool will end up killed by the savages yet, mark my words," said the group leader. Patch eyed the dropped bow and arrows that the young warrior had dropped when he ran off. A cold smile found his face as he caressed the smooth wood of the bow.

"I'm off to use the bushes, gentlemen. I won't be long," the enforcer called over his shoulder as he slipped into the shadows of the ancient tree boughs.

*   *   *

Corbin raced blindly through the woods. Every shadow, each rustling leaf was surely a raider ready to jump out and slit his throat. His heart hammered in his chest as he plunged deeper into the surrounding woods. An unseen tree root tangled his feet and Reynolds tumbled across the grass, his eyes growing wide as he watched his Bible fly from the pocket of his jacket and into the nearby underbrush. The preacher pushed himself from the grass, grimacing as the scrapes in his palms bled. He shuffled over to the bushes and plucked the book from where it had fallen.

"How did you come here?" he muttered. "I had thought you were safe at home by my bedside."

He looked around the grove in which he had found himself, wondering if he had at least fled in the proper direction of the town. He stepped around a tree and gasped as the rising moonlight gleamed off of the polished black slab that had haunted his dreams for weeks now. The memories of his horrible nightmare surged in his thoughts and he fell back against the trunk, frantically searching for the hellish gleaming eyes of the beast that stalked him in his sleep.

"No, no, NO," he whimpered as he stormed over to the stone. "This can't be happening." A twig snapped in the trees to his left, and he shrieked in terror. A black shadow moved stealthily along the tree line. The lurker's frame was well built and far larger than Corbin's own. He raised his patrol pistol but his hands shook so violently that he knew he didn't have a prayer of making an accurate shot.

"What are you?" Reynolds demanded. "Torment me no longer, fiend. If you would have me then come along and end this. I will not live in fear of you for the rest of my days."

Jeremiah Carmichael stepped forward, and Corbin didn't know if he should be relieved or not. The man's face was a mask of fury as he glanced around the grove. He carried his hatchet in his hand, gripping it so tightly that the white of his knuckles was clear even with only the light of the moon above. The farmer held his hands out before him as he saw the Parson trying to take aim on him.

"Easy, Corbin. I am no threat to you here, but we need to rejoin the others and return you to town before it grows any darker." Corbin saw the man look past him, seeing the slab, and the farmer's eyes went wide, and the blood drained from his face.

"You feel it too, don't you, Jeremiah? There is something wicked here," said Corbin as he watched Jeremiah's eyes dart around. "It's as if we have walked straight into a ..." The preacher's words trailed off as the farmer simply nodded.

"A nightmare," Jeremiah finished for him. "My wife has described this place to me many times. We must leave now."

"Did she see the wolf too?"

Jeremiah's jaw dropped open. "You know of the beast?"

Reynolds spun around, clutching his hands to the side of his head. His reason threatened to leave him and the laughter that ripped from his lungs filled the empty woods with an almost hysterical, madcap ring.

"Oh," he said as he threw his arms out wide, "I should know of the beast far better than any, and yet I in my arrogance failed to realize just how real he was. You shouldn't have followed after me, Carmichael, for I fear that you have only damned yourself by seeking to bring me back. Please, Jeremiah, leave me to the demon and you may yet be able to free your wife from the true monster of Pioneer Vale."

The preacher threw his pistol to the ground and raged around the grove. He kicked at rocks, threw fallen sticks, and cursed to the heavens above. He looked into the bushes but still didn't see the glowing eyes that haunted his thoughts. He whirled around once more to find Jeremiah close upon him, and the burly farmer grabbed him by the jacket with a fierce shake.

"Get hold of yourself, man. We need to move now, and I don't need you splintering apart until we make it back to town. Maybe once we get

GUARDIAN

there, we can put aside our disagreements and you can help me save Anne-Marie from the baseless accusations that you made against her."

"I have no quarrel with you or your wife, Master Carmichael," said Corbin as he cackled. Did something just stir in the bushes he mused? The idea of their imminent dismemberment by some demonic creature seemed somehow absurd to him and he shook with laughter. "Her predicament was brought to my attention by a concerned member of our congregation."

"You mean that you were fed lies by Preston Mathers," said the scowling farmer. He pulled back his arm and his backhand slap rocked Corbin's jaw. Despite the stars that danced before his eyes, Reynolds staggered but somehow kept his feet.

"You dare strike a servant of the Most Holy?"

"What does Mathers have over you, Corbin? I may never have been one to come shake your hand whenever we crossed paths, but I never believed you were a wicked man. My wife is on the run now, her location held secret even from me, and for what? So that Preston can grow both his power and wealth in this new world? Stand against him, man!"

Corbin looked the farmer in the face and found his wits returning to him. Reynolds felt a sudden rush of envy, daring to dream that he could become more like this man who he had wronged. He realized at that moment how much he admired Jeremiah. For his compassion. For his courage. For his integrity.

"Forgive me, Jeremiah. He knows a secret of mine that could prove disastrous to another that I care deeply about. He has threatened me with betraying my confidence if I do not act as he instructs. Your dear Anne-Marie…"

"Is innocent…."

"…Is in grave danger. Mathers wants her dead, for some reason unknown to me. I have no proof of any witchcraft created by her hand, but

235

there are things, including this place, that call to something not of our world, and I am terrified by it. Preston and your wife are somehow tangled together in a feud that is beyond any rational explanation."

"Corbin, you have the power to expose Preston and put an end to his schemes. You can clear my wife's name of the unjust accusation."

"And then what of me? I would be run out of town and the one who shares my indiscretion would be in jeopardy. You ask me to trade your heart's love for my own."

"Corbin," Jeremiah said as he reached out and placed his hand on his shoulder. "You are as much a victim in this as any. I do not ask you to sacrifice anything. I ask only that you do the right thing. Tell the townsfolk that you made a mistake about my wife and that there is no evidence of what she has been accused of. Let them know how Preston moves against us all."

Corbin's eyes looked past the farmer and froze as the shadows capered in the moonlight around something crouching within the tree line. A dark figure rose up, powerful and threatening. Reynolds knew that death approached them.

"Jeremiah, beware," the preacher shouted and he reached out to push the man toward the cover of the black stone slab.

*   *   *

Jeremiah grabbed the Parson's arm and instinctively threw the man to the ground when he lunged forward. The bushes rustled behind them and he whirled around. Ice filled his veins and time slowed to a crawl. Although he had never seen this moment himself, Anne-Marie had described it to him in vivid detail. The stone slab gleamed behind him as he held his hatchet in his raised hand against a man with whom he had struggled falling to the ground. He looked now into the bushes where he knew his death awaited.

The sudden twang of a bowstring filled the air, and Jeremiah's eyes went wide in shock. A hammering blow thudded into his chest and he looked down to see the shaft of a quivering arrow. He tasted blood and a strange gurgle rattled within him as he drew a breath. A second thrum filled the night and another arrow took him in the stomach. Jeremiah collapsed to the ground staring as blood spread across his shirt.

*   *   *

"No," Corbin screamed as he crawled over to the fallen man and placed his hands on his chest. "This isn't supposed to be your end. Tell me what to do," he sobbed as Jeremiah weakly looked up at him. The farmer gave a gentle squeeze to Reynolds' hand and wheezed as he looked into his soul.

"Save...her..., Parson," Jeremiah gasped. His stare fell away, forever gazing into the night sky as his eyes glazed over.

Corbin snatched up the man's fallen hatchet and brandished it in a two-handed grip as Patch Erickson stepped from the shadows with another arrow nocked and ready.

"You might want to set that hatchet down, Parson. Preston won't be too pleased with you as it is when I tell him how you nearly revealed his plans. Your moment of fleeting virtue could have us all swinging from the gallows before dawn because you couldn't keep your mouth shut. Once you get back to town, report that we found him with these arrows in him and I gave chase after his killer."

"You murdered him."

"No, Parson," Patch said as he grabbed the front of the preacher's jacket and dragged Corbin nose to nose with him. "You did. I just pulled back the bowstring. All I did was tie up a loose end."

"You will go to the flames for this, Erickson."

"One of these days, perhaps, Parson, but right now there's somewhere else I need to go first. I have to go peek in on a dead man's children." A wicked grin crossed his face. "Hope I get there before the savages do."

Corbin's jaw dropped open. "How could you be so cruel? Those boys have done nothing. Why would you endanger them?"

"I just told you, Parson," Patch said. The blood from his own busted lip was smeared across his teeth making his smile even more devilish.

"I'm tying up loose ends."

CHAPTER 21
ONLY A BAD DREAM — PRESENT DAY

Angelica groaned as she pushed away pieces of burnt wood, drywall, and siding that Shade's blast had buried her under. She choked on the dust and thick black smoke that hung in the air. Cuts and scrapes from thousands of pieces of flying debris dotted her skin, but her shields had kept her alive. Her temples throbbed, blood flowed freely from her nose, and the wounds in her stomach were ablaze, but there was no time to rest. Biting through the pain that wracked her body, the young woman got back on her feet.

Through the haze, she saw a figure lying on the ground nearby. The smoke cleared enough for her to see Aiden sit up, clearly dazed, but far less banged up than she had managed. She stumbled toward him, but he saw her coming and dragged himself up to one knee. He raised his hand with his palm outstretched toward her, but before he could summon his magic Angelica grabbed the front of his shirt and punched him as hard as she could, flattening him back to the ground.

"Shade's a clever bastard. Threw you toward the front door so you wouldn't get blown through a wall when he popped his cork." She stomped on his hand and enjoyed both the crunch of his fingers under her boot heel and his resultant cry. "Where's Fleabag run off to?" she said as she looked around. As the landscape came into view, the sight that loomed out of the darkness dropped her to her knees.

The farmhouse was a blackened ruin. All that remained of the home she had known her entire life was a charred section of the front porch, and a piece of the frame where the front door had stood. The screen door hung from a single hinge and squealed mournfully in the light breeze. The bed where she and her mother had planted flowers every year was gutted. The corn stalks in the field closest to the house were lit like torches, a beacon to any passersby that Carmichael Farms had once stood here. Tears welled up in her eyes, for she had seen this horrific landscape before.

In a nightmare.

The shadows writhed beyond the corner of the broken porch. The mist swirled, rolled, and took on a towering shape. The smoke thickened and Shade strode forth amid a cloud of embers and ash. He stretched his powerful limbs and howled into the sky. As the echoes rolled from the nearby hills, the Father of Nightmares turned his hellish gaze on her.

"Right on cue," Angelica muttered. Aiden cradled his hand as he limped over to Shade's side. The wolf rumbled with a disapproving growl, and Angelica smirked at how Aiden squirmed under his master's scrutiny. The demon shook his head and then slowly turned back toward her and grinned. He held his arms out wide and cocked his head.

"Your despair delights me, Guardian, but you have delayed me for the last time," said Shade. "The barrier between my realm and yours is all but dissolved. There remain only the gossamer threads of you and your wretched mentor that hold me from my full strength."

"Glad to still be a pain in your ass, Furball," Angelica shot back. The world spun around her as she opened herself up to her magic. Her knees shook and she didn't know if her legs would support her through what was to come. With Shade so close, the Whisper of the Elder carried a darker melody as if the power was now tainted by his corruption.

"I beg you to allow me the privilege, Master," said Aiden. "This one has caused me so much personal injury, that it would be my sincere pleasure to remove her for you." Shade simply nodded his head, but Aiden cackled and capered back and forth on his feet. The man raised his hand and several pieces of splintered wood from the farmhouse rubble lifted above the ground. Coldfire swirled around the ends, chiseling through the wood, and made half a dozen fire-hardened spears that hovered at Aiden's whim.

Angelica raised a wavering shield, but Shade snapped his fist shut and it crushed it in a spray of sparks. The slashes across her abdomen sizzled with a blaze of soul-stealing fire. She fell to her knees with her arms draped over her stomach and trembled as she was paralyzed by unearthly coldness. She raised her head to see the demon wagging a finger at her.

"Your magic will not save you this time, sweetling." The glow in his eyes flashed with hatred, and he looked over his shoulder to Aiden. "Kill her."

Angelica fought against Shade's walls, reaching for her magic with sheer willpower, but the demon's might was relentless. Defenseless and in agony, she watched Aiden draw back his arm. The spears began to spin in a slow spiral, like a drill revving up to speed. Knowing she had only a split second to protect herself, she threw herself wide to the forces of magic hoping to hear even the slightest note of the Whisper.

But all was silent.

"Time to die, cousin," said Aiden. Coldfire turned his eyes to midnight once more. He threw his arm forward and the spears hurtled toward her. A sudden breeze fanned her hair and the air ripped open in front of her in a wash of lavender fire. The missiles swept into the portal and vanished. A second hole opened behind her and they dropped harmlessly back onto the scorched lawn.

"Don't you two ever tire of saying that?" said Anne-Marie as she sauntered out of the smoke. "I mean, you haven't gotten it right yet." The Witch of Pioneer Vale crossed her arms over her corset. The amethyst pendant at her throat gleamed with a light of its own as a shroud of her signature magic enveloped the woman.

"Mother," said Aiden. He threw his arms in the air and turned away. "Of course you make your timely entrance."

Shade roared and dropped to all fours. His great claws ripped the ground when he pawed like a bull and then rushed toward Anne-Marie. The Guardian touched her thumbs together and rolled her palms toward him. A fan of purple flame caught Shade in mid-charge stopping him in his tracks. His cloak smoldered, and the smell of burnt hair filled the air as the demon fell to the ground, yowling and rolling in pain.

Angelica felt the surge of magic as her connection was restored. She pulled herself up and hurried to her teacher's side. "About time you got here," she said. "Was dad afraid of getting a speeding ticket or something?"

Anne-Marie ignored her jibe. "Aiden, you have to see now that Shade can't win this battle. I beg you, son. Come home with me."

Angelica's jaw dropped. "Are you kidding me? He just blew up the house and tried to skewer me with a bunch of sharpened two by fours!"

"Ah, dissension in the ranks," chuckled Aiden. "Come home as what, mother? Your prisoner for another three centuries? I don't think so." A ball of coldfire grew between his hands, the swirling deadly energy pulsed as his mother sadly lowered her head.

Angelica moved first and threw a quick burst of lightning at her cousin, but Shade's arm reached out and threw a shield in front of his apprentice, deflecting the cascade that arced from the girl's hand. Aiden threw his hands forward, and a burst of black magic shot toward his mother who swirled her arms in a wide circle creating a fiery shield of her own.

Chaos erupted as they closed upon one another. Lightning and fire flashed in streaks through the air. Sprays of black venom and freezing winds splashed against mystical barriers. The sky rumbled and the ground quaked. Black clouds rolled upon themselves and trees were uprooted as elemental forces waged war on the tiny New England farm.

*　　*　　*

Angelica wrapped herself in a cloak of light and disappeared from view long enough to run to Aiden's side. She dropped her camouflage and, forgoing magic, went for a solid punch to the man's jaw. He dropped to one knee but slipped loose a bolt of black magic that thudded into her shoulder. The blast picked her up and spun her around in the air. She crashed and rolled along the ground and sent her spinning her through the air to crash and roll along the ground.

She groaned as she got back to her feet. Angelica couldn't remember ever being in such pain. Her gouged stomach burned, her shoulder felt numb, and her head pounded from the strain of her magic use. She saw Aiden rise, unsteady and running the back of his hand over his cheek where she had struck him. She saw fear in his eyes as he looked at her, and knew that he didn't have a lot of fight left in him.

"You do enjoy your sucker punches, Cousin," he said. "But had you used your magic instead of brute force, you might have won the battle."

"I'll keep that in mind," she said as she snapped her wrists. Lightning filled her hands once more, but before she could renew the fight, Shade's ear-splitting roar turned her head.

*　　*　　*

Anne-Marie spun a full circle, dodged a swipe of Shade's claws, and fired a bolt of eldritch fire into the demon's side. He tumbled head over tail across the debris-filled lawn, but the Father of Nightmares came out of his tumble with smoke trailing from his ribs and a snarl of pure hate plastered across his face. With a slash of his hand, the ground beneath her feet split, and she stumbled to one side. She leaped to one side, narrowly avoiding the gouge in the earth, and fell heavily to the ground. She scrambled to face her old adversary, desperate to raise her defenses.

A thin wall of fire burst before her eyes just as Shade coiled his mighty legs and sprang across the distance. She felt his bulk slam into the shield and he slapped aside the flimsy shield with his black claws. His hands slammed her shoulders to the ground and his slavering teeth snapped inches away from her face

"I will rain hell upon you and your whole accursed family, witch," roared the demon as he threw back his head. His muscled arms and barrel chest bristled with power and he howled into the sky.

*　　*　　*

Angelica seized upon a sudden idea that his words gave her. "You want rain, you've got it, Furball," she shouted. She planted her feet and threw her arms to the heavens. Lightning poured from her widespread fingers. The brilliance around her was blinding as her magic seeded the clouds above and the sky flashed across every color of the rainbow in the grip of the girl's power.

A gray storm cloud above rippled and glazed over, gleaming like a mirror in the sky. Cracks shot through the face of it and as Angelica dropped sharply to one knee, the jangle of shattering glass filled the air. She seized the lightning like reins in her hand and dragged down a deluge of razor-sharp shards. The growl that had been in the wolf's throat changed to a whine and then a scream as dozens of tiny daggers punched relentlessly through his hide.

Anne-Marie sent a bolt of fire into his stomach and crawled out from under the writhing demon. She paused and picked up one of the shards from the ground. Her eyes widened. "Are these...?"

"Made it rain diamonds from the sky," Angelica said. The cloak of lightning around her slowly fell away but her voice carried the roll of thunder and her eyes still burned with white-hot intensity as she watched Shade struggle to lift himself from the ground. "Now we finish him."

Before she could take a step, a powerful blast hammered her in the back and threw her to the ground. A boot pressed down on her neck and she was able to twist her head just enough to see Aiden looming above her. His fist was gloved in coldfire, and his eyes had become pure ebony with scarlet striations. He threw a second bolt at Anne-Marie who narrowly managed to block with her shield, but she was still rocked backward by the attack.

"I will suffer no more of your little surprises," he yelled as streams of coldfire lanced down into her back. She writhed under his foot, but his magic stole her strength. "Rise, my Lord Shade. Destroy my mother as I kill the last of the Firstborn."

A grey mist surrounded Shade and the dozens of punctures in his skin began to close. He rose to his feet and slowly approached Anne-Marie. He reached down and grabbed her by the throat, lifting her effortlessly into the air. "You've no idea how much I will enjoy this, bitch," he growled as he drew back his black claws.

A shot rang out, and Shade's face lurched to the side as a chunk of his rotting cheek exploded into the air. Anne-Marie broke free from his grip and jumped away from him. A second shot followed and punched the demon in the stomach, although the bullet didn't pierce his thick hide. Anne-Marie hit the wolf with a stream of fire that rolled him across the yard. Through the curtains of ash that hung in the air, Will and Jamie stepped forward already chambering their next shots.

Angelica heard a sharp whistle and felt the pressure of Aiden's foot lift enough for her to turn her head. Clarissa stepped into view, swinging a piece of broken pipe like a baseball bat at Aiden's head. His jaw crunched and several teeth rocketed from his mouth. He landed on his back on the ground, blood flowing freely from his mouth.

With his magic broken, she pushed herself back to her feet and let the Whisper envelop her once more. Her eyes shimmered with power once more and she hurled a double blast of lightning that launched Aiden into the trunk of a nearby tree. As he lay still, Angelica released her power and fell weakly against Clarissa.

"Thanks, for the save, Bumpkin," she said as she hugged Clarissa.

"Looked like you needed a hand."

"Angie," came a cry from behind them. Angelica turned to see her mom race through the smoke toward her. She grabbed her mother in her arms and squeezed tightly. "Oh, honey, are you ok?"

"I'll survive," Angelica said. She noticed her mom was streaked with lines of soot. "What happened to you?"

"I ran through the bars of the purple cage that woman put me into. I told her she wasn't going to keep me away from you."

"Heads up, gang," yelled Will. "Job's not done yet."

All heads turned as Shade snarled from his knees. His pelt was singed in several places and black ichor oozed from the wounds that peppered his body. Angelica walked over to Anne-Marie and stared hard at the demon. "Are you ready to do this?"

"I've been waiting for you, dear."

The two women each snapped their wrists and called their respective elemental forces to the ready as they advanced. Will and Jamie fell in beside them with weapons raised as they took aim at the monster in their yard.

"For ages past, you have tormented this world, Shade," said Anne-Marie. "Your reign of terror ends today."

"Any last words, Fleabag?" asked Angelica. Shade's head bowed and his shoulders quaked. His lips curled back in a smile, and his mocking laugh built to a terrifying peak.

"I have one last torment to inflict, sweetling," he snarled. The demon rolled from his kneeling position and snatched up one of the sharpened stakes that Aiden had made. He grinned at the Guardians as his heavily muscled arm pulled back. With a smooth throw, the demonic Father of Nightmares hurled his makeshift spear with supernatural force.

*   *   *

Kim went cold as the terrible beast turned to face her with his arm drawn back. Everything slowed at that moment and she viewed the world with a clarity that she had never known before. She saw the grinning snarl on the demon's face. She heard her daughter's scream of terror as it rang in her ears. She smelled the very air burning as a hole ripped open in front of her and the redheaded witch jumped though, pushing her aside.

A spray of blood splashed across Kim's face, and she met the eyes of the woman who had stolen her daughter. She was stunned for they were not the cold eyes of the witch of legend, but the loving eyes of a mother protecting her children. She caught Anne-Marie as the Guardian fell forward, a crimson smear spreading across the white of the woman's sleeveless blouse. The point of the stake that punched through her corset wavered inches from her own chest. She lowered Anne-Marie to the ground as gently as she could.

"You saved me," Kim said. "My nightmare…"

"Was just a bad dream," said Anne-Marie through clenched teeth. She softly touched the woman's cheek, before her eyes rolled back in her head, while around them the world turned upside down.

*   *   *

"NO!" screamed Angelica as she saw her grandmother collapse. Lightning poured through her as rage siphoned raw magical energy from all around. Arcs of electricity shot from the ends of her fingertips, her cry of anguish was deafening thunder, and her feet set the grass ablaze where she stood. She channeled a blast of magic at Shade, but he threw up his own swirling black shield that held the relentless torrent of energy at bay.

"One down, sweetling," he howled over the raging white fire that hammered away at his defenses. "Sleep well tonight for I'll see you soon enough in your dreams."

Will fired his shotgun, chambered another shell, and fired again, but the slugs ricocheted off the shield with a whining ping. Shade retreated to stand beside Aiden's still form, and ripped open a gateway of howling cold that swept across them both, whisking them away from the battle.

Angelica's lightning receded with a lingering rumble and she ran to her mother's side, falling on the ground beside her mentor. She took Anne-Marie's hand from her mom and held it to her chest. "Don't do this to me," she shouted. "I need you here."

"Angelica," Anne-Marie said. Her eyes fluttered open and she gave the faintest squeeze to the girl's hand. "You must let me go, Child."

"Not a chance," Angelica growled. She placed her hands beside the garish wound, but the Whisper was faint. The explosive outpouring of power from her last attack against Shade left her weak and with little more charge than if she had rubbed her socks across the carpet. "Don't fizzle out on me now," she cried.

"This is your fight now, my dear," Anne-Marie said. Each word was a struggle. "You have earned your place. Finish the battle, Guardian."

"Not without you," she shouted. Angelica gritted her teeth and found a different hum to the thread of her magic. It was her own strength, the power of her own life force that was open to her. Without hesitation, she grabbed the cord and jerked as if she had grabbed a power cable. Lightning shot from her hand and wrapped Anne-Marie's abdomen in a cage of fire. "I won't let you die."

"Then millions of others will. You must stop Shade."

"Let me help." They all whirled to see a weak and wounded man leaning heavily on the shattered porch column.

"Doctor Hibble," cried Clarissa. She ran over to the man and threw her arms around him. He winced as she squeezed him, but hugged her back. "You made it out of that cave."

The doctor stumbled forward, blood trickling from dozens of cuts and scrapes, but most noticeably soaking through a ragged shirt wrapped tightly around his stomach. "Aiden was behind this, wasn't he?"

"You know him?" asked Angelica. Her face paled as she traded her vitality for Anne-Marie's. Sweat poured from her brow, but she held a steady flow of magic into the injured woman.

The doctor dropped heavily to his knees beside the women. He stared for a moment and rubbed his jaw then began to examine the injury. He gently rolled Anne-Marie more to her side as he studied the entry wound then nodded. "Yeah, unfortunately, I got myself tangled up with that son of a bitch," he muttered as he leaned closer to her. "Stay with us, ma'am. Can you tell me your name?"

"I am the bitch that Aiden is the son of." Hibble's eyes widened but he couldn't hold back a smile.

"So there's still some life in you yet? Good, let's keep it that way. That makes you Mrs. Carmichael, I presume."

Anne-Marie nodded weakly, and a feeble delirious chuckle broke from her lips along with a thin red bubble that dribbled down her cheek. Her eyes focused in a moment of clarity and she cocked her head as she studied the man's face. "There is something familiar about you, Doctor."

"Well, if you're really his mother then apparently your family and mine go way, way back," Ben replied. "Aiden pretended to be a friend, but before I knew what he was I unwittingly helped him set loose something out of a nightmare."

Angelica tensed up at his words. Her arm shook and she struggled to keep from toppling over. "It's going to get worse without her help."

He nodded and his eyebrows raised as he saw the electricity that leaped from her fingertips. "You two really are witches?"

"Guardians," said Angelica and Anne-Marie in unison.

"Right, my mistake," said Ben. He reached toward the stake but hesitated as sparks danced and circled around Anne-Marie's abdomen. "You're going to have to cut the power, Miss. I can't get in there with a live wire kicking."

Angelica nodded and her hand trembled as the sparks fell away. She collapsed to one side, gasping as the strain fell over her. Blood that had been held inside the wound gushed out and spilled across the grass. Anne-Marie's eyelids shut only the barest rise of her chest gave any sign that she still lived.

"Can you save her?" Angelica asked.

"I'm going to do everything that I can to help her. Gentlemen," he called out to Will and Jamie. "Find me some towels, curtains, or the shirts off your backs if that's all you've got so we can slow this bleeding. One of you ladies, find a phone and get us an ambulance out here now." Hibble looked Angelica in the eye as the others all scattered. "I've got this. You have to stop that monster. It's up to you to save us all."

Angelica kissed Anne-Marie's forehead and then rose on shaky legs. She paused a moment and then gave a quick hug to the doctor. She looked once more at Clarissa and her family racing about their tasks. She knew she had to go or else she risked losing them next.

"There is a gateway to Shade's world that I think they will try to take control of. I need to get there first. I just hope this works." Angelica slapped her palms together then made a ripping gesture. Her arms quaked as she fought to rip open a hole in space, as she had seen her mentor do so many times before. Her lips curled back in a feral snarl, and white-hot lightning danced once more in her eyes. A tiny tear in space opened between her hands but slammed shut. She gasped and shook her head.

"What happened?" asked the doctor.

"That's harder than it looks," she muttered. "It's too much. Too soon. I'm wiped out." She looked off in the distance and saw their horses milling about in the field, set free from the corral when the house exploded. "Maybe I can still catch a ride, though. Tell them goodbye for me, Doc." Angelica called to her horse, Bonnie, and swung up onto the mare's back. She held her hand over the horse's rump and a current flowed through the animal. Blue sparks shot from Bonnie's hooves and they raced away, vanishing into the forest trails.

*   *   *

"Wish I could say that was the strangest thing I've seen today," muttered Hibble.

"All we could find were some blankets we kept in the barn," said Will as he and Jamie rushed up with their arms draped.

"Ambulance is on the way," said Kim as she returned to Ben's side. "Clarissa is calling her father from the truck. Where's Angie?"

"She has her own role to play in this. Those blankets will do fine for now. I'm going to need you three to listen closely and do everything I say if we are going to keep this woman alive." He frowned as he took one of the offered blankets and ripped a long strip from it.

"Our very lives may depend on it."

*   *   *

"I can't do this alone," said Angelica as she stood before the polished black slab of the Widow Stone. The marble gleamed under the moonlight in the grove. "I don't have a clue how to stand against them by myself." The forest was silent except for crickets chirping. An owl hooted in the night. At least, she mused, there wasn't the howl of a wolf this time.

Angelica paced around the stone slab in frustration. She kicked a rock and screamed into the sky, thunder echoing the rage inside of her. At last, she fell to the ground and dug her fingers into the patch of wildflowers beneath her hands. And then her breath caught in her throat.

She stared at the crumpled petals of two flowers in her palm. One was a bold and vibrant lavender and the other was bright blue laced with white veins. A soft warmth spread across her back, and she felt her aches and pains fade away. A smile crept to her lips as she sensed the otherworldly Elder Guardian approach her.

"It was always about her and me, wasn't it? All the other Firstborns were just window dressing to bring us to this moment. Did you hinge the fate of the world on the random presence of two flower patches?" She turned and shielded her eyes from the blazing intensity of swirling purple fire and blue-white lightning that stepped into the clearing. The Elder Guardian was shaped more like a man this time rather than the scintillating ball of energy that she had encountered before in her bedroom at Whisperwind.

"Far less of this is as random as it appears," the being said, his powerful words reverberated both in her mind and the grove. "The moment fast approaches where a great turning point shall be reached. It is within your power as my champion to chart destiny's course. You have done so already, just as your teacher, my most devoted and resolute defender, has done many times throughout her service. I need you to be ready, however, young one. The hardships that await you must not be taken lightly."

Angelica rose to her feet and stared into the entity's dazzling face. She held her arms to the sides, her eyes blazed once more with her telltale signature as lightning enveloped her from head to toe. The bloody and soiled clothes that she wore burned away and as the swirling eddies of power receded, she stood in the leather jacket and black trousers that were her own Guardian outfit. She held out her hand, looking once more at the petals before she tucked them into her pocket.

"Tell me what I need to do," she said.

"Long have the Guardians kept watch over this realm for me as I sought the hiding place of my enemy. I have always prayed that one day your sacrifice would no longer be necessary, but I fear I must impose upon you some while longer."

"I never had the impression that I was about to get fired," Angelica replied. "Killed maybe, but never fired." The bones of the earth beneath her feet shook as if the world itself laughed at her joke.

"Your courage is inspiring, young one. However, before you heedlessly race off across the realms to resume your fight, hear my words.

"There is something you must do first if you hope to win this battle."

CHAPTER 22
HELL HATH NO FURY - 1671

The moon stood as a silent sentinel over the surrounding forest. Its pale light stood watch over the still form lying in the shadow of the black stone slab. Anne-Marie burst through the tree line into the grove. Her knees buckled and she fell to the ground at the sight laid out before her. Shade's vision from her visit to the Father of Nightmares bleak realm had changed from a worrisome dream to a cruel reality.

"NO," she screamed as she threw her head back and released a column of purple fire into the night sky. The eruption of her anger crisped the leaves from the nearby trees and set ablaze the scrub brush that grew too close to the clearing. The flames flickered and died out as tears ran freely down her cheeks. She crawled over to Jeremiah's body and cradled his head.

"Someone's at least laid him out properly," said Henna as the old woman came up softly behind her. "Oh, my sweet girl, I am so sorry for ye. Your man deserved so much better than this."

"Was this his destiny?" Anne-Marie growled. Her tears fell upon Jeremiah's face and her hand trembled as she touched the arrow protruding from his chest. "Why couldn't I change this one? That bastard showed me what he had planned, and I could have stopped it."

"Ye had no inkling of when those terrible events might transpire. We both made the mistake of thinking that if we carried the fight directly to the wolf, we might prevent all his workings. The fault is not yours, lass. It is mine for not sharing my own experiences with what the monster brought to us."

Anne-Marie stroked her love's brow and gently kissed his cold lips. She rose and wiped her cheeks before turning to her teacher. "My tears must wait. Whoever did this can't be too far gone, and I mean to have his head on a platter."

"Sweet girl," said Henna, " ye've been to the literal gates of Hell tonight. I'll stand and mourn with ye, and we'll save the fight for another day."

A branch snapped in the bushes nearby, and a shadowy form lumbered around in the darkness. Anne-Marie spun around, her hands already alight. "Show yourself," she yelled and fired a blast of flame into the forest. The tree boughs ignited like a torch, throwing embers down on a young man of the local tribe. He staggered into the clearing with a startled cry. His eyes were glassy, and with a sideways glance at the burning branches overhead, he fell to his knees.

Blood oozed from a black wound in his shoulder and matted the fur trim of his vest. He tried to catch himself but his arms were too weak to hold him up and he fell on his face in the grass. He raised his head and reached a hand out to Henna. He muttered something in his elegant language before his strength gave out and he collapsed. Anne-Marie held another ball of magic at the ready, but Henna grabbed her wrist. With a flash of green light, she extinguished her fire.

"Stay yer hand, lass. We aren't in danger from this lad." The old woman hobbled over to the fallen man and rolled him over on his back. She held her hand over the wounds in his shoulder, and green twinkling motes spun from her fingertips, floating like snowflakes over the wound. A lead ball pushed up out of his flesh, and then new muscle and skin grew over. The cut of a blade pulled itself shut and closed with little more than a thin white scar in its wake.

The man's eyes fluttered and then opened. He rubbed his arm, eyeing Henna askance for a moment before saying a few soft words that would have been taken as "Thank you" in any language. The old woman nodded her head and replied to the Indian in his own dialect.

"You speak his language?" She took a step toward the young warrior with fire renewed in the palm of her hand. "Ask him what happened here." Henna pulled herself back to her feet with her staff. She raised her finger and frowned at her. The warrior also regained his feet, his words a clear challenge to Anne-Marie. He dropped into a fighting stance, but Henna threw her other hand out toward him, and a dazzling wall of green sparks stopped his charge.

"Both of ye stop this nonsense," she shouted. "Oh, but this'll be too bothersome with me telling ye two back and forth what is being said. Here." Henna blew a few twinkling green spirals into the air that spun in tight pirouettes around the three of them and then vanished.

"Now, then," said Henna. "Let's start anew, shall we?"

Anne-Marie pushed past her teacher. "For the sake of your own soul, tell me that those are not your arrows sticking from my dead husband's chest," she yelled.

"Try a wee bit of diplomacy, lass," said Henna with a roll of her eyes.

The young man lowered his head and shook it. "I am Kitchi, future Chieftain of the Nipmuc people. They are my arrows, but not by my hand. This man was dear to you?'

"He was my husband, and I will hunt down whoever did this to him."

Kitchi bowed his head. "I am deeply sorry for you. I fear that we have both suffered great losses this day for many lives were taken by the soldiers of Maheegan."

"Who the hell is Maheegan?" said Anne-Marie. "Stop wasting my time, warrior."

"Maheegan is the Black Wolf," he said. "He is a monster of ancient legend, and today soldiers carried flags of yellow with the beast's head sewn upon it."

"Shade," gasped Anne-Marie as she turned to Henna. "It's true then that he has an army to clear his path now."

"Preston's mercenaries attacked their village." The old Guardian leaned heavily upon her staff and bowed her head.

"Their leader killed my grandfather, our shaman. With his dying breath, he told me that to fight a myth, I must locate a legendary warrior from another of his old stories. I must seek out the Viking's Daughter"

Anne-Marie shook her head. "I'm sorry. That means nothing to me."

"It does to me," said Henna. "Your Grandfather. Was he called Ahanu?"

Kitchi smiled sadly. "As a younger man, he answered to He Who Laughs, yes."

"And indeed he could," Henna said, her eyes growing distant for a moment. "I knew him well, although I doubt he ever thought of me as a hero of legend. More like a thorn in his rump. He named me Viking's Daughter in jest, for my people were of such heritage, but that was ages past." Anne-Marie raised an eyebrow, but Henna just held up her arms, showing again the leather wrist guards that she had put on before leaving Whisperwind.

"He also called you Guardian. I mean no disrespect, but aren't your fighting days behind you? You seem too...revered?" Kitchi blushed as Henna burst into laughter.

"Well spoken, lad. Clever way to say 'old'," Henna said. She jerked her thumb toward Anne-Marie. "I leave the fighting to this one now."

"And I am more than ready to give it all the hell I can bring along," Anne-Marie said with a cold smile at Henna. "When I learn who is responsible for this I will rip the bastard's heart out, just as he has done to me." The tears that rolled down her cheeks sizzled as they fell into the purple flames that engulfed her forearms. Kitchi fell to one knee before her and placed a fist over his chest.

"My people know you, Firehair," the warrior said. "We have watched you work the land beside your fallen husband and your sons. You are a woman of good heart, and his kindness has fallen upon me this day. Allow me to offer whatever help I may."

"His kindness? What do you mean?"

"Maheegan's men would have taken my life today as well if not for your husband's bravery. I would have been killed by the same villain one who did this to him."

"Ye saw his killer?" asked Henna. "How long were ye crouched in those bushes, boy?"

"Please, you must tell me who it was," said Anne-Marie. Her flames winked out and she took Kitchi's hands in her own. "I will nail his hide to Shade's altar myself."

"There were two men here when he fell. The first was a coward, but he made no threat to your husband. He cried in warning when the murderer made himself known."

"That doesn't tell me much. Who was the second?"

"He attacked from the bushes using my own bow that I had dropped when your man saved my life. He was like a bear, large and fierce. He only had one eye, the other hidden behind black cloth."

"Patch Erickson," Anne-Marie gasped. She turned to Henna, and the fires blossomed in her eyes anew. "Then Preston is behind this dirty work. I shall burn him to the ground for this."

Henna looked past her. "Where did these men go after they...?" Her words trailed off and she waved her hand toward Jeremiah.

"The one eye laughed as he left. He found a stray horse grazing nearby and rode off in the direction of your home, Firehair. The other man placed your fallen warrior as you have found him and said words to the Great Spirit before he left back toward the group of scouts from your town."

"Rode toward the farm?" Anne-Marie's eyes widened as another memory of her first encounter with Shade flitted through her memory. "Oh, Henna! The second nightmare! The one with the boys. Erickson stole my horse and is going after my children! He was the one who rode past me in the dream realm."

Henna took her hands in her own. "Lass, we need to go with Kitchi to his people. There's a war a-brewing and only we can keep it from happening. My heart breaks for ye, my girl, but how can ye hope to get to yer farm in time? That brute was on the move as soon as this shaft found its mark on your poor Jeremiah. Even with a swift horse, he has too much of a head start on ye. The old wolf's tricks have taken ye down the path he showed at your first meeting. Ye'd need a magic doorway to step between the grove and yer farm in time, my dear."

Anne-Marie turned and stared at her teacher. "That's exactly what I need. Oh, Henna, you may have just saved my boys from that devil." She knelt down and tenderly kissed Jeremiah's forehead, then gently tousled her husband's chestnut hair one last time.

The Guardian walked over to the shining black slab, watching the moonlight gleam off the polished surface. As she stared into the depths,

259

she saw stars whirling in a cosmic dance that had commenced at the dawn of time. The Whisper of the Elder rose to a tumultuous melody that shook her very core. She reached deep into her heart and tethered all of her grief for her husband and fury toward Shade and wove it into the haunting chorus that crested within her. A shroud of lavender flame slowly rolled up from her boot heels, twining around her legs and up her entire body, but it was unlike any conflagration she had conjured before It spun and coiled within her, offering its eldritch might rather than being commanded to do so. The Witch of Pioneer Vale tilted her head back slowly, soaking in the energy that flooded her, and then with a sudden scream to the heavens, the fires erupted into a rolling inferno that swirled around her, and her voice echoed throughout the grove with supernatural power.

"This place was once the site of a supernatural battle, but from this moment on, I claim it as my own. Forevermore, shall it be known as the Grove of the Widow's Stone." A pulse of flame radiated out around her, the wash of heat blew back Henna's cloak, and rustled the branches of the trees. Kitchi shielded his face with his arm as the firestorm engulfed the woman and shot fire high into the night sky.

* * *

"Anne-Marie, stop! That much power will end ye, girl," yelled Henna as she stumbled forward against the onslaught of force emanating from her student. Anne-Marie had become the core of the sun, blinding in radiance, floating on eddies of raw power. She held her palms above the stone and lavender flames siphoned energy from the black marble into the young woman.

Henna covered her eyes and dragged Kitchi behind a sparkling green shield of her own device when the hem of her own cloak began to smolder from the seething heat. Anne-Marie faced them as a living elemental of fire fueled by power beyond this world. Her hair floated around her head, the color of her eyes lost in the raging conflagration that burned within her. She held her hands outstretched to her sides, fires billowing through her frame.

"What is she trying to do," Kitchi screamed over the roaring flames. His words were lost in the tornadic roar of raw magic. He cowered behind Henna's shield as lavender flame licked around the wavering edges.

"Lass, let it go. Calling forth such power will end ye," Henna yelled. She tried to step toward her student, but couldn't push forward against the wall of energy that punched into her defenses. She tried to draw in the strength to close the flow of magic, but her protégé's command of the might they shared swatted away her own attempts.

Anne-Marie brought her hands together in a sharp clap that sent a shockwave through the grove. She clenched her fists, gritted her teeth, and the world *rippled* around her. The air shimmered, not from the blistering heat, but as if the gesture alone had allowed the younger Guardian to grasp the edges of the fabric of space itself. The magic exploded around her in a lavender conflagration like an erupting volcano. Henna redoubled her shield, wrapping it tightly around her and Kitchi. A sharp keening filled the grove, crying out even louder than torrential fires that consumed Anne-Marie. It was the Whisper of the Elder but it screamed throughout the ancient forest as if in triumph of breaking free from the constraint that generations of Guardians before her had placed upon it.

*　*　*

The space between Henna and Anne-Marie warped and bent as the woman settled her feet back to the ground and braced herself. The grove quaked and the forest shook all around her. She forcefully pulled her fists apart, but her arms trembled as something fought against her from beyond our world. Her grief, rage, and desperate love for her children became a living force, and she channeled the raw emotion in her heart into her magic. Blood trickled from her palms as her fingernails dug into her flesh and trickled through clenched fingers. Her head was crowned in fire, for surely she was in that moment a queen among the forces of nature. With one last fury induced scream, her magic pulsed outward. A soft slow ripping sound echoed through the clearing, and then all fell silent for a heartbeat.

An unearthly shattering like that of a thousand mirrors breaking all at once threw Henna and Kitchi to the ground and forced them to cover their ears. The old witch's mouth dropped open as she saw a fiery hole rip wide in the air in front of Anne-Marie. Beyond the swirling flames, the fields and buildings of Carmichael Farms stood but a few steps through the gateway. The air around her shivered and quaked as Anne-Marie held open the tear in reality and like a phoenix aflame stepped through, crossing the miles in a single stride.

"Go with Kitchi and see that his people are safe," the witch said. "Convince them that the folk of Pioneer Vale did not attack them. Shade and his servants will suffer for all of the innocent blood that they have spilled today. I will find you as soon as I have rescued my boys." Her words were like the thunder of a tempest, powerful and deafening. She bowed to Henna, just as the barn erupted in flames and two shrill screams of terror echoed in the night.

The rift slammed shut with boom and hiss, leaving Henna and Kitchi huddled together in the smoking grass. The young warrior rose first and walked over to where the fiery portal had stood but a moment before. The old woman crawled across the scorched ground and cradled Jeremiah's head, bending her head and offering a silent prayer for the man. Lightning flashed in the night sky and the rain began to fall harder.

"My dear girl. What have ye begun?"

* * *

Abel Harmon closed the doors of his tool shed when the hairs on the back of his neck stood up. His ears picked up the slight strains nearly lost beneath the rolling patter of the falling rain. He looked westward into the setting sun, to where the deep forest of the unexplored frontier loomed.

"Josiah," he called to his youngest son, who stacked firewood nearby. Abel glanced quickly at his child, still a boy really with the downy fuzz of manhood just starting to color his cheeks, and fearing that his son's childhood innocence was about to be stripped away. "Get the wagon hitched up, boy. Do it now. Throw in a few of those sacks of provisions, and grab your musket. Elias," he shouted to the barn. His oldest son stuck his head out around the door. Abel hobbled toward him as fast as his weary old legs would carry him.

"Paw, what's got you worked up?" the young man asked.

Abel grabbed his son's hands. "Throw a saddle on Clopper," he said as he jerked his thumb toward the old plow horse. "Ride as hard as she'll let you, son. You need to spread the word to all of the outlying farms. The Littleton's, the Carter's, any others that you can make your rounds to quickly. Tell them all to gather what they can and hurry themselves to town. Lives are at stake, boy, so don't delay. Warn all of those you can then get yourself behind that new wall they've been building. Don't let them keep you outside just because the sun's going down. We're leaving right along right behind you."

"But, Paw, this storm is coming on hard."

Abel grabbed his son by his shoulders and looked deeply into the young man's eyes. "There's an even bigger storm brewing, lad."

"Do as your father says, Elias," said a dulcet voice from behind. The men turned to see Nell Harmon, wiping her hands on the apron she had untied from around her waist and then tossed on a bench by the barn door. Her graying hair framed a face just beginning to show the lines of time, for she was several years younger than her husband. "Your father wouldn't send ye off in this without cause."

"I meant no offense, Paw. You can count on me." The young man gave his mother a quick peck on the cheek and dashed back into the barn amid the clatter of tack and harness.

"I've not seen the soldier come out in you for ages, Abel," said Nell. "What do you know?"

He forced a smile to his face but his wife scowled. "No fooling you, I suppose. I may just be jumping at shadows, but I want you and the boys to safety in case I'm wrong. When you get into town, go straight to Marcus Brenner. He'll know what to do, and how to get preparations started."

Nell crossed her arms over her chest. "And what'll you be off doing while we cower behind that pretty new palisade they're building?" He lowered his head and closed his eyes, reaching out to take her hands. He felt the calluses of her fingers, badges of honor for the hard work she did every single day, standing beside him. He knew every crease of her face, the lines of laughter, and of sorrow. The tracks of the life they had lived together.

"I'll do what I can to keep you all safe. Same as I ever have." She lifted his chin and kissed him.

"I'll save your seat for you at the Huntsman." She turned as Josiah and Elias reappeared from the barn, his oldest astride the plow horse, and the younger boy driving the cart. Abel helped Nell climb up beside their son in the driver's seat.

"Off with you, now. Don't waste any time." He smacked Clopper on the rump and the old nag trotted off. Josiah cracked the reins and their cart horse followed along. Nell spared a glance over her shoulder, blew a kiss to her husband, and then wrapped her arm around Josiah's shoulder. Abel thanked the falling rain for it hid the tears that streamed down his face.

As he watched his wife and children head down the road, Harmon heard the noise again, a subtle rumbling beneath the booming thunder that clapped through the sky. He shivered as a chill ran down his spine. The volume increased and he shook his head in silent acceptance of something that he hadn't heard since his earliest days on the shores of this new land. It seemed so much more disquieting now, shattering the years of their tranquil life to know what was coming.

The old farmer went inside the farmhouse and opened the trunk at the foot of his bed. He pulled out his old bronze medal and held it in the palm of his hand. With the crack of a smile, he wrapped it in his handkerchief and stuffed it into his shirt pocket. He opened the front door and grabbed his trusty musket, the powder horn, and a pouch of lead balls and slung all of it around his neck. He checked the long-bladed belt knife that he wore at all times, and with one last sigh, he marched toward the tree line at the edge of his land.

Somewhere ahead of him, he knew that the warriors of the Nipmuc tribe howled and danced, their faces painted with images of spirits and animals that they held sacred. Weapons were brandished, sharpened, and readied as they gathered the strength to face the dark times approaching. Meanwhile, the rhythmic thumping of the tom-toms, for that was what Abel's keen ears had heard, whipped the warriors' blood into a boiling frenzy.

They were the drums of war and they promised doom.

To Be Continued...

www.ingramcontent.com/pod-product-compliance
Lightning Source LLC
Chambersburg PA
CBHW071504110726
47908CB00003B/721